The Contract

S. Hawke Investigations - Book 1

William Coleman

THE CONTRACT

Dedicated to my lovely wife, Vicki, who has supported me every step of the way through each of my novels by allowing me the time to write, being my first beta reader as well as my main editor. By being my biggest fan and my sharpest critic, she has helped me produce final manuscripts for you to enjoy.

1

Sebastian Hawke sat disheveled in the center of a hard wood park bench, a half-eaten sandwich in one hand, a half-smoked cigarette in the other. He was staring blankly at the pigeons gathered at his feet, making him feel a bit like the Pied Piper. He knew they had not come for him. They had come to fight over any crumbs that might fall from his lunch. He considered throwing the remains of the sandwich to them, but that would be disrespectful to what some considered a work of art from the Uptown Deli on the corner of Third and Market.

He took a long drag from the cigarette and held the smoke in his lungs for a moment before letting it out slowly. As the cloud about his head dissipated, he bit into the perfect blend of bread, meat, cheese, vegetable and condiments. Despite the craftmanship of the deli's owner, Hawke glanced from sandwich to cigarette and concluded they tasted the same. It was a reflection of his life, everything dull and without flavor. His mind drifted to the circumstances that had brought him to this bench with its dedication placard digging into his back.

As a teen, he had been a troublemaker. Getting into fights, vandalism and destruction of property were at the top of his resume. It was during that time of his life that he tried his first cigarette, stealing one from the pack his father always had nearby. His father, a hard man working second shift as a firefighter, had not been there to discipline his son when it was needed. Instead, he handed down punishment after the fact in varying degrees.

It was after Hawke graduated from high school that he began to pursue more serious infractions. Shoplifting and joyriding became the regular activities of he and his friends. On his eighteenth birthday, he declared that as an adult, he could not be told what to do. A few short weeks later, just after his father had finished a grueling shift, the police showed up at their home with Hawke in tow. It was a courtesy to the fireman that his son was not in jail on charges of breaking and entering.

Hawke's father was furious and laid out options for his son. He could get a job and make his own way, or he could enlist and let the military teach him how to be the man he should be. Either way, he was no longer welcome in their home. After that, he bounced from job to job and from couch to couch. Ultimately, he found himself standing in a Naval recruiting office.

After four years regular active duty and another four years as a Seal, he returned home seamlessly, trading his fatigues for a police uniform and, instead of routing enemy combatants from partially destroyed buildings, he chased criminals on the streets. He spent four years in blue before he took the detectives' exam and started carrying a gold badge. He enjoyed being a detective and was good at it. His clearance rate was high, and he was drawing the right attention from the brass. Until one incident brought it all crashing down.

He was a man with three vices. One he held in his left hand, the second in his right. The third was challenging authority when he felt it was wrong. In the military he had seen good men killed while following bad or misinformed orders. There had been a couple of close calls of his own. While he did nothing at the time, after turning in his uniform he began questioning what so-called leaders said; a characteristic the captain of the homicide department did not appreciate. They butted heads often, leading to yelling on several occasions and a well-placed punch, once.

That was over six months ago. His fall from grace had been quick and painful. Because the one vice left him jobless, he focused his energy on the over-eating and chain-smoking. It was a slow road to suicide, but he felt it was worth a try. The problem with his plan was a dwindling supply of funds, which brought him to this damned bench.

Having drinks with a friend, the two discussed options for Hawke's next career path. The friend jokingly suggested Hawke become a private investigator. A suggestion that was shot down immediately, only to rear its head again after a few more drinks. The next thing Hawke knew, he was the moderately proud owner of a PI license and had signed a lease on a one-room office located above none other than Uptown Deli. After a month of thinking he had made a huge mistake, his phone finally rang with a possible job.

The call had been a lawyer who had asked to meet him somewhere other than their offices to discuss the work he needed. So here Hawke sat, appearing more like a homeless man than an investigator, on the designated bench in the designated park, wondering why they weren't meeting somewhere air-conditioned. The sun, high in a cloudless sky, baked the earth with extreme efficiency. It made the jacket Hawke wore to cover his weapon almost unbearable.

Hawke spotted the lawyer even before he stepped out of his flashy BMW in the parking area along-side the street. A bulky, yet surprisingly solid man, he was just shy of Hawke's six-foot-two stature. He was dressed in an expensive suit that found Hawke brushing subconsciously at the wrinkles in his slacks. He walked with a confident stride that told others to make way for an important man. The briefcase swinging at his side emphasized the point. Hawke took an immediate disliking to him.

"Sebastian Hawke?" the lawyer asked upon reaching the bench. The pigeons scattered. Apparently, they took a disliking to him as well. He glanced at the bench with a visibly crinkled nose.

Hawke nodded. "And you are?"

"Just call me Steve," the man said, still eying the bench as if deciding whether it was safe. Concluding it was, or perhaps that there was just no other choice, he turned and sat heavily next to Hawke, setting the briefcase on the ground between his feet. Making eye contact with the former detective, he continued. "This is a nice place. Honestly didn't know it was here."

They sat silently, sizing each other up. The lawyer's gaze dropped on occasion to take in Hawke's appearance, always returning to the eyes with an intense stare. Hawke, on the other hand, only focused on the lawyer's eyes, the left in particular, with a certain amount of disinterest.

"You have a job you want done?" he finally asked, getting bored with the rooster posturing.

"A man of few words," the lawyer grinned. "I like that."

Hawke only stared, confirming the man's description of him. He put the cigarette to his lips and inhaled, then blew the smoke over the other's head. The lawyer's grin faltered slightly. "Okay, listen. Mr. Hawke, er, Sebastian. May I call you Sebastian?"

"No. You may not."

The lawyer's grin faltered again. He seemed at a loss for words momentarily and Hawke found himself wondering if, as a trial lawyer, he was so easy to addle in front of a jury. The man shifted his bulk and gave up on the grin completely. "Mr. Hawke, I have a client, a wealthy client, who suspects his wife is cheating on him. He wants to end the marriage, like yesterday, but needs proof of this affair so he doesn't have to give the bitch half his assets. You know what I mean?"

The man stopped talking and held Hawke's gaze, apparently expecting Hawke to give him a thumbs-up or something equally absurd. Hawke contemplated whether he wanted to spend his time stalking a woman in an attempt to find evidence that would cut her out of the money she may very well deserve, but he knew if he didn't take the job someone else would and he needed the cash.

"Mr. Hawke," the lawyer was becoming impatient, which humored Hawke. "Do you understand the assignment?"

"You want pictures of this woman in a compromising position with someone other than her husband," the PI summarized. "Five-grand plus two-hundred a day for expenses."

"That's a bit steep," the lawyer protested.

"You told me your client is wealthy," Hawke reminded him. "I'm sure he stands to lose a lot more than that. If you want results, that's what it'll cost."

The lawyer let his mind run the numbers, wondering how it could cost two bills a day to sit in a car. In the end, he sighed heavily, "Fine. But how do I know you won't drag this out for weeks on end?"

"If she's cheating like the man says, it shouldn't take long to get a few pictures, now should it?" Hawke said. It dawned on him that he didn't own a camera. "I'm going to need half the five up front."

The lawyer opened his mouth to protest but closed it with a grunt. His hand slipped inside his jacket and withdrew his wallet. Thumbing through the bills inside, he pulled several out. He waved them at Hawke like a fan. "All I have on me is two thousand. That'll have to do."

"That'll work," Hawke dropped the spent cigarette butt to the dirt and ground it in with his toe. He took the money, considered lecturing the man on carrying so much cash but decided he didn't care. He folded the bills over and stuffed them deep in his pocket. "Now, who am I following?"

The man leaned forward, opened the top of the briefcase and reached inside. He leaned back again, pulling with him a manila envelope that he handed to Hawke. "Her name is Madeline Rochester. Information and photos are inside. Also, there is a list of days and times that the cheating may be occurring. Follow her at those times only. The client is adamant that she is not followed any time not on the list. Is that understood?"

"She can't cheat on him when he's with her," Hawke nodded. "I get it."

The lawyer stood, pulling his briefcase close to him. "I'll contact you in a few days to see how it's going."

"How do I reach you?"

"I'll contact you," the man said.

"And if she isn't cheating?" Hawke looked up at the man. The sun was just over his shoulder, so his face was in shadow. Regardless, Hawke was sure he saw a smirk on the man's lips.

"My client is sure about this," he said. "You just get the pictures."

The lawyer turned and walked away. Hawke sat on the bench, thumbing the stack of bills in his pocket and watched the lawyer's retreat until the BMW had driven from sight. Soon after the man walked away, the pigeons began gliding in on spread wings, gathering at Hawke's feet again. The birds were smarter than he thought.

2

Two hours after abandoning the park bench, Hawke sat wedged behind the wheel of his car, taking practice shots with his newly purchased camera. He drew more than a few glances from passersby as he photographed increasingly angry expressions and a couple of obscene gestures. He laid out half the money the lawyer had given him to buy the best camera and the longest lens he could get. He knew little about photography and the clerk directed him to an aim and shoot, digital camera with a high pixel count. The memory card would hold thousands of photos. All Hawke needed to do was find the woman, aim and press the button until he got the shots he needed.

As a cop, he had dealt with stalkers. The worst were the peeping toms. They were a sad bunch; too shy to approach women, too obsessed to stay away. And here he was getting ready to look through a woman's windows in hopes of taking pictures of her with her lover. It made his skin crawl. It didn't help that the voice in the back of his head was telling him there was something wrong with the whole scenario, causing him to have doubts about the job. In the end, his need to be paid won out and he set the camera on the passenger seat and opened the manila envelope for the third time.

The first item in the thin file was a portrait of a beautiful woman with bright green eyes, strawberry red hair and just the right number of freckles. Hawke had seen a lot of attractive women over the years, but simply put, Madeline Rochester was in a class by herself. It was not a professional photo. She was smiling at the photographer in a way that made Hawke wish it were him. Whoever was behind the camera had been someone Madeline cared about a great deal. If it were her husband, it was hard to believe she would be cheating on him. If it weren't then having the photo would suggest the lawyer might already know who she was cheating with.

The second item was the schedule he was to follow to surveil the woman. Each entry listed the location where Hawke could find her at the start of the timeframe and the length of time he would need to tail her. There were few of these blocks of time and none lasted more than half a day. Hawke almost felt guilty about the payment he demanded. There were huge gaps in the schedule that the lawyer said the husband was, how had he said it?, 'adamant that she is not followed any time not on the list'. Looking at the schedule, it was hard for him to believe the couple spent that much time together.

The third was a list of alarm codes for various properties she might go. They were supplied in case Hawke might want to enter for a better opportunity to get the required photos. For the life of him, he couldn't think of a single scenario where it made sense to give a complete stranger that much information. What was to prevent him from going straight to one of the properties and taking what he wanted? He had no intention of entering any of the locations indicated.

The next block of approved surveillance time was coming up in twenty. The schedule indicated the subject, Madeline Rochester, would be leaving the Woods and Irons Country Club at eleven. Hawke wondered if she played tennis or golf. He really hoped it was the former, he really liked the little skirts the women wore. From there, she had a half-hour to get to her yoga class, not enough time to sleep with anyone, but no address was given for the yoga, so Hawke would have to catch her at the club. He dropped the folder next to the camera and pulled into traffic.

The Woods and Irons Country Club was not the kind of place Hawke would frequent. Not because he didn't play golf or tennis, which he didn't. It was because his salary as a detective, when he was one, would not cover the annual membership dues. It was probably for the best. He would have a hard time holding his tongue surrounded by wealthy men talking about how bad things are for them because their stocks dropped in price by two percent. Or maybe they were going to have to find a new mistress because the last one wanted him to dump his wife and marry her.

He sat in his rust bucket of a car watching club members arrive and leave. He waited patiently for his mark to appear, wondering how long it would take security to come ask him to leave. The lines of luxury and sports cars were surely a temptation to the wrong elements of society.

A few minutes before eleven, a black SUV with tinted windows and gaudy, over-sized chrome rims parked a few spaces away, effectively blocking his view of the clubhouse exit. Hawke cursed under his breath, started his car and rolled forward to another space. Shortly after, Madeline Rochester pushed her way through the doorway chatting happily with three other women. Each, to Hawke's pleasure, wore the short-skirted outfits he had hoped for and carried bags with tennis rackets over their shoulders. They laughed as they walked, and Hawke was mesmerized by Madeline's aura. Hawke lifted the camera and clicked off a half dozen shots.

The four women, all in their late twenties or early thirties, slowly made their way to the parking lot, stopping often to delve more deeply into their conversation. A cute little brunette with a ponytail was the first to break ranks, excusing herself and bouncing to her car. Hawke watched the petite woman go, wondering how anyone who had just finished playing tennis could still have so much energy. He took a long drag from his cigarette and turned his attention back to the three remaining women.

To Hawke's relief, Madeline was next to say her goodbyes. She walked away, without the exuberance of her friend, but with a powerful stride and an air of confidence. She moved with a grace that made Hawke think of actresses on the red carpet or possibly even royalty. She didn't strike him as the type to be meeting men in cheap motels or sneaking a quickie in a restaurant bathroom. But he supposed even the rich cheated, they just did it with more class.

She lowered her eyes to her phone while she weaved between cars in the lot. Hawke lost track of her for a moment as she moved to where the gaudy SUV blocked his view. He panicked for just a second, worried he might not see which car she entered. He was about to put his car in gear and roll back to his original space when she reappeared, stopped to open the trunk of her car and dropped her tennis bag inside. From his angle Hawke could only see the royal blue of the open trunk lid. It was enough to know he could spot the vehicle when it left. Hawke flipped his cigarette butt through the window and backed out of his space and drove down the driveway to the street, where he pulled to the side of the road and waited.

There was no mistaking the woman as she left. The top was down on her Tesla convertible and her strawberry hair flew freely behind her. Hawke let her pass, waited a moment and pulled onto the street behind her. A horn blared and he checked his rearview mirror. That same black SUV was bearing down on him. Hawke cursed under his breath and applied more pressure to the accelerator to put some distance between them. Five minutes later, Hawke was parked across the street from a smoothie shop where Madeline had stopped.

Another cigarette burned between his fingers. A thin line of smoke drifted up and out of the car as he watched the door for her to exit. The idea of drinking a slurry of fruits and vegetables held no appeal for him. He was a coffee drinker, black, no sugar, the stronger the better. It was a taste he had acquired while in the service, along with the smoking.

Madeline stepped through the door, held open by a thin, college-aged boy with a book bag slung over his shoulder. With hair down to his shoulders, the boy reminded Hawke of his kid sister when she was that age. Madeline held a plastic cup filled with a green concoction that made Hawke cringe just a little.

Back on the road, Hawke followed about three cars back, even though he was sure she had no suspicions she was being followed. Arriving at the yoga studio fifteen minutes later, Madeline parked, jumped out of her car and opened the trunk again, this time to retrieve another shoulder bag complete with yoga mat. When he was sure she was inside, Hawke pulled back onto the street and drove to a nearby convenience store to hit the head and refill his coffee. He returned well ahead of the half-hour mark when she would be finishing her class. He parked so he could easily monitor the door and noticed the same SUV parked a few spaces down from him.

3

Either Madeline was being followed or Hawke was, of that he was sure. Had the husband hired two investigators? If he had, it was a complete waste of money. If he hadn't then the question became, who were they and why were they there? Hawke jotted down the tag number in a pocket notebook he carried for just such an occasion. If he were in his office, he could use his access as a PI to run the number and know who owned it in a matter of minutes. Now he had no option but to wait until he was done following his mark for the day, or call his old partner for help.

He was still trying to decide if he wanted to waste a favor when Madeline emerged from the studio. This time she wore tights, and her hair pulled back in a ponytail as her brunette friend had earlier. By the time she reached her car, she had pulled the ribbon to release her tresses. With the bag secured in the trunk, she was on her way.

It was the moment of truth. If she were planning a secret rendezvous with a lover today, it would have to be now. There was nothing on her schedule for an hour and a half when she had an appointment with a therapist. For the third time, Hawke fell into line behind the blue Tesla, this time watching his mirrors as the SUV joined them. Any remaining doubt was removed. They were definitely being followed.

Maddie changed lanes abruptly, gliding into the left and then the turn lane in quick succession. Hawke was blocked by another vehicle and unable to turn. He wondered if she had spotted the tail and was trying to shake him. Glancing in his rearview, he saw the SUV make the same lane changes and follow her around the corner. Hawke grumbled and slowed to shift in behind the car that had blocked him. From there he made an illegal U-turn and doubled back to the intersection where she had turned.

Rounding the corner, Hawke could not see the royal blue convertible, but there was no missing the SUV. He sped up to close the distance. A couple car lengths away he slowed down to fall in pace with the larger vehicle. Drifting to the left he spotted Maddie's car a short distance ahead of them. Hawke wondered if the driver of the SUV might be her lover. It was obvious now that they were following the woman and not him.

A few minutes later, the convertible turned into a restaurant called La Cruste. Maddie parked and half jogged to the door. The SUV slowed, continuing down the street before pulling to the curb. Hawke pulled into the parking lot and parked in the far corner. He considered going in to get eyes on whoever, if anyone, Madeline was there to meet. One glance at the row of cars, similar to those of the country club, told Hawke he wouldn't be able to afford to eat in La Cruste, even with the lawyer taking care of his expenses.

To do the job he was being paid to do, Hawke needed to put eyes on the woman and anyone she was with. He pushed the car door open and slid out. Reaching back for the camera, he thought better of it and left it on the seat. Trying to get a photo inside a busy, upscale restaurant without being noticed didn't seem too likely. He stood, stretching to his full height, twisting from side to side attempting to relieve the stiffness of his lower back. He strolled through the cars, trying not to peer inside the luxury interiors as he went. It wouldn't do to look suspicious and have the police called on him.

He stepped up onto the sidewalk that ran the length of the building and angled for the front door. Walking at a leisurely rate, Hawke tried to catch a couple of glances through the windows as he went. His vision was hampered by dark-tinted glass and his own reflection. He was going to have to go inside, a thought that made him more uncomfortable than it should.

He reached the corner of the building where the entrance was located and looked down the street to where the SUV was still parked. No one had left the vehicle that he could tell, the occupants seeming to be content with waiting. It was unlikely her lover would not join her inside, which made Hawke return to his original conclusion that the husband had hired two investigators to follow his wife. For a moment he considered returning to his car, because they may know something he didn't. But the cop in him refused to let him do a half-assed job. He turned back to the entrance as an elderly couple stepped through. He quickly grabbed the heavy wood door and held it open for them. The woman, in a large print floral dress, nodded and smiled. The man wore dark slacks and a baby blue jacket. He paused in the doorway, trying to pull a five-dollar bill out of his money clip.

"Keep it," Hawke held up his hand. "I'm not the doorman."

The man eyed Hawke, nodded and moved along. Their Mercedes, parked in a handicapped space, was not far away. The navy-blue car complimented the man's jacket, making Hawke wonder which of the couple selected his clothing. His money was on her.

A young couple stepped out of the restaurant before Hawke could enter, their heads bent down to their respective phones. The young man, no more than a teenager, walked straight into Hawke, his phone tumbling to the ground.

"Shit!" he said, stooping down to pick it up. He examined it quickly. "Damn it. It cracked the corner. Thanks a lot mister."

"Try looking where you're going," Hawke said, disappearing inside the building.

A man in a suit and tie half-bowed when he greeted Hawke, although the investigator could clearly see his eyes giving him the once over. "May I help you, sir?"

"I doubt it," Hawke muttered.

"Excuse me, sir?" the maître d' said.

"I said," Hawke said. "I hope so."

The maître d' tilted his head, clearly knowing that was not what Hawke had said. He made no move to help, nor to inquire more.

Hawke pulled his PI license from his jacket and flashed it quickly to the man. At a glance it appeared as much like a federal agent's ID as it did anything else. He pointed a thick finger toward the dining room. "I need to see one of your guests."

"Excuse me," the maître d' said. "I don't think this is appropriate."

It was Hawke's turn to tilt his head. "What the hell does that mean? What do you think I'm going to do?"

"A lot of very important people patron this establishment," the man said. "You can't just muscle your way in."

"I can muscle my way in," Hawke said. "But I'm trying to avoid that. Which is why I am talking to you instead of pushing you aside. I don't want to cause a scene. I just need to confirm that . . . that he's here."

No point in letting the man know details about his target. He just took suspicion off all the women, and Madeline along with them. The maître d' considered Hawke's request for a little too long.

"Or I can just barge in," Hawke offered.

"Fine," the maître d' said. "But don't draw attention to yourself. What is his name?"

"His name?" Hawke asked.

"The man you wish to see," the man said. "What is his name? I can tell you where he's sitting."

"I'm not giving you a name," Hawke said. "I'm not letting you mess up months of investigation by letting you warn him."

The man's face flushed, and Hawke took some satisfaction in that. Without waiting for him to say anything further, Hawke moved to the doorway that led into the dining room. He stood in a corner, half-hidden by a large potted plant, scanning the tables for Madeline. He finally spotted her, on the far side of the dining room deep in conversation with a blonde woman. Hawke recognized her as one of the tennis players from the county club. Hawke nodded and turned back to the entrance.

"Were you successful?" the maître d' asked.

"Nope," Hawke lied. "Not here. See that wasn't so painful."

The investigator used his bulk to push the door open and stepped back out into the sunshine. A quick glance before he returned to his own car confirmed the SUV had not moved. As he worked his way back into the driver's seat, he adjusted himself until he was as comfortable as he could expect to be.

He lifted the camera from the seat deciding he would take a few shots of them as they left, but unless Madeline was sleeping with her therapist, she wasn't cheating on her husband today.

Hawke flipped his notebook open to the SUV's tag number that he had written down earlier. He took out his phone and selected a name from the list of contacts. He put his cigarette between his lips and drummed the steering wheel while he waited. He was about to give up when the call connected.

"Hawke," the familiar voice said. "Been a while. What do you want?"

"Can't a guy call his former partner just to say hello?"

"A guy can," he said. "But we both know you ain't that kind of guy."

"Got me there, Rog," Hawke said. He had been teamed with Detective Roger Jackson the day they handed him his gold badge. They worked well together, and had become friends.

"Don't call me Rog," he said. "My name is Roger. Didn't like Rog when you were my partner. Don't like it now."

"Okay Roger," Hawke said. Maybe 'friends' was a little strong. "I need a favor."

"That's what I expected," Roger said. "Need a DUI to disappear? Cause I can't help you with that."

"Jesus," Hawke said. "How bad off do you think I am?"

"What's the favor, Hawke?"

"I need you to run a plate for me," Hawke said. "For a case I'm working on. I'd do it myself, but I'm not at the office."

"And you need it yesterday," Roger said. "What do you mean you're working a case? What kind of . . . oh, wait, I heard you crossed to the dark side. Went through with the PI thing, or something like that."

"Something like that," Hawke said. "Can you run the plate for me?"

"Give it to me," Roger said. "But I'm busy. It could be a while."

Truth was Roger had been Hawke's partner for over two years and they never really gelled. Hawke was pretty sure the detective was no busier now than he had been when Hawke carried a badge. He read off the tag number, twice. "Just call me when you get something."

"Sure thing," Roger said, just before disconnecting the call. Hawke was positive he heard sarcasm in his voice.

Hawke had to wait nearly an hour for Madeline and her lunch companion to emerge from the restaurant. He occupied that time by checking emails, surfing the internet and playing a frustrating game on his phone that required matching three or more tiles to eliminate them. He blamed the latter, more than anything, for how much he was smoking these days.

The two women walked close to one another, talking and laughing as they went. Hawke considered the thought that the blond was her secret lover. It would not be the first time someone 'came out' after they had already married. He watched how they leaned into one another when they laughed. A hand touching an arm from time to time. The hug they gave one another before parting for their separate cars. But there were no lingering looks, no attempts to steal a kiss. Nothing that would suggest anything more than a close friendship.

He took the pictures and tossed the camera back into the passenger seat. He would follow her to the therapist's office, but he was not supposed to follow her after, so he would leave once she was inside. Those sessions were private. There was no way he was going to get inside to see if she was dancing naked with him.

Hawke pulled in behind Madeline and tailed her onto the street. The SUV pulled in dutifully behind him, and the three of them drove down the street in a broken line. Traffic had picked up, making it easier for Hawke to blend in with the vehicles between the flashy blue convertible and the eyesore of an SUV. They only had a few minutes before her appointment, for which Hawke was relieved. He was ready to be done for the day. Money or no, he still felt like a stalker creep following the woman.

As expected, it didn't take long for them to arrive at the therapist's office. The parking lot was small making it too easy to be noticed. Hawke picked a parking spot on the street across from the small office building. To his surprise, the SUV pulled into the lot behind Madeline.

Hawke's phone rang and he pulled it out and saw Roger's name on the screen. He pressed the talk button and put the phone to his ear. "Well, that was fast."

"Where are you, Hawke?"

"I'm working a case," Hawke said. "I told you that."

"Is the SUV still there?" Roger asked.

"Yes. Why?"

"Where are you?" Roger asked again.

"A therapist's office," Hawke said, giving him the address. "What's going on?"

"That SUV was carjacked yesterday," Roger said. "I'm sending a car. Don't approach them."

"Why?" It was not lost on Hawke that his old partner didn't even try to make a crack about him being at a therapist.

"They killed the driver," Roger said. "Assume they're armed."

"Jesus," Hawke said, reaching for his glove box. "They've been following this woman all morning. And whatever they're planning, I think it's going down now."

4

Hawke disconnected the call and pulled his Glock from the glove compartment where it rested on top of his insurance papers. He checked the magazine and opened his door. Timing the space between passing cars, he jogged across the street toward the parking lot where Madeline was just getting out of her car.

The SUV rolled to a stop between Madeline and her destination. Hawke could see the woman slow, sensing something was wrong. A door slammed on the other side of the black vehicle and a man stepped around the rear. He wore a ski mask. Hawke began to run. Just as the masked man was coming into Madeline's view the back door of the SUV on her side opened and a second man wearing a similar mask emerged.

Madeline turned and screamed, ready to bolt to safety, but they moved too fast and were on her in seconds. Hawke was close, choosing to head them off before they could drag her to the SUV rather than a straight assault. To Madeline's credit she was putting up a hell of a fight, effectively slowing them down. Hawke moved in and slammed his pistol into the head of the first kidnapper with everything he had. The man went down hard but wasn't out. He was pulling himself to his feet even as Hawke was wrapping a meaty arm around the second attacker's neck, forcing him to let go of the woman and concentrate on saving his own life.

"Run!" Hawke yelled at Madeline. She didn't need any more encouragement than that. She sprinted down the street.

"Get in," a voice from inside the SUV called out.

The man Hawke had clocked fell into the backseat and they started to drive away. Hawke, realizing they were going after Madeline, released the man he was choking so he could go after her to stop them. As the man slipped from his arm, Hawke grabbed hold of the mask and yanked it up. The face Hawke saw was someone he knew, Richard Hendrix, a two-bit thief he had arrested a couple years back, one of the first cases he and Roger had worked together. There was no mistaking the snake tattoo on his neck or the scar over his left eye that gave the appearance that he had three eyebrows.

Hawke turned and ran the direction Madeline had gone. The SUV turned onto the street to follow and Hawke opened fire. Two hits to the windshield were all it took to turn them away. As they did, they slowed enough to pick up Hendrix before speeding away.

Hawke stopped running and bent over at the waist, coughing like the smoker he was. Sirens were approaching from two sides. Not wanting to be shot, Hawke lay his weapon on the sidewalk and took a step back with his arms raised. Two squad cars and an unmarked squealed to a stop in front of him. A second later, Roger stepped out of the unmarked and gave Hawke a long, hard stare.

"You look like shit," Roger said.

"Feel like it too," Hawke said.

"No wonder you need therapy."

There he was. Just like old times. "Separation issues. Lost my partner and all."

"Aw, now I'm going to need therapy," Roger said.

"You've always needed therapy," Hawke grinned.

"This case you're on somehow involves a carjacker," the detective said. "Want to explain?"

"Do I have a choice?"

Madeline stepped out of a nearby storefront and walked toward them. Even after what had just happened, she walked with an air of confidence and grace: head high, shoulders back, eye-contact.

Before she got too close, Hawke leaned into Roger. Lowering his voice he said, "She's the subject of my case. I'll give you details later. For now, I have to lie."

Roger shook his head, but before he could respond the redheaded woman was there. Hawke took the reins and explained how he just happened to be in the right place at the right time to thwart the kidnappers. For Madeline's part she gave him everything she knew. She arrived for her appointment, these men attacked her, and Hawke came to her rescue, her knight in shining armor, per se. Although Hawke's armor was an old wrinkled suit.

One of the officers took Madeline's statement in full while Hawke and Roger moved off so the PI could fill in the details of the morning leading up to the attempted kidnapping. He told him everything from the lawyer hiring him to the moment the detective arrived.

"What I don't get," Hawke said. "They were following us half the day. Hendrix had to have seen me. Why didn't he warn the others and call it off?"

"Greed," Roger said. "Probably thought as long as they had the masks you wouldn't be able to ID him. We'll round him up later and question him."

"Let me know what he says," Hawke said.

"What about her?" Roger said. "You still going to tail her?"

"It's what I'm getting paid for, although my cover is blown," Hawke said. "But I wouldn't mind hanging around to be sure they don't try again."

Roger glanced over to where Maddie was talking to the officer taking her statement. "She's way out of your league, man."

"God, Rog," Hawke said, "uh, Roger. I'm following her, not asking her out on a date. Besides, she's married."

"Yeah," Roger said, "because that would be crossing a line."

"What the hell does that mean?"

"Forget it," Roger said. "Come to think of it, Linda was out of your league too."

"Don't you have some paperwork to file?" Hawke said. Linda was his ex-wife. Their marriage had ended about two years before the punching incident.

Roger handed him his Glock and walked to where one of the department photographers worked diligently to record anything and everything that might have to do with the incident. Hawke tucked the weapon into his belt at the small of his back. He needed a cigarette but had left the pack on the passenger seat next to the camera. He walked in the direction of his car. Only a few steps into the journey, a voice stopped him.

"Excuse me," it said. "Sir."

Hawke cringed. He wasn't very fond of being called sir, but worse, he was pretty sure he knew who was trying to get his attention. He considered moving on as if he hadn't heard but knew that wasn't an option. He turned and saw Madeline walking toward him and waited in silence for her to close the distance.

"I wanted to thank you," Madeline said when she was close enough not to need to yell. "For what you did."

"No thanks necessary," Hawke said. "Just did what anyone would have."

"No," she said. "That's not true. Most people would have watched, horrified or disinterested, while those men took me. You saved me, Mr. . . ."

"Hawke," Hawke said. "Sebastian Hawke."

"My name's Maddie," she said, offering her hand. "Maddie Rochester."

Hawke shook her hand. "I'm glad you're okay. Really. But I need to be somewhere. So, I'm going to go now."

"Of course," Maddie said and without warning, she stepped forward and threw her arms around his neck. "Thank you."

She backed away again, and Hawke found himself at a loss for words, his jaw a little slack. She smiled at him and he raised the corner of one side of his lips. She glanced at the building housing her therapist, "I have an appointment anyway."

Hawke's eyes shifted toward his car and then back to the woman. He wanted to walk away and disappear. He also felt it would be rude to be the first to move. He held her gaze for a moment and saw in her eyes a woman a little less content, a little less confident than the woman he had seen before. Or maybe he was seeing past her normal facade. After all, she was here to meet with her therapist. He said, "I'm glad I was here to help."

"I should let you go," she said. She took a few steps backward before turning and walking to the building, where she passed through the doors. Hawke watched her every step of the way.

He returned to his car and settled in. He started the engine, but rather than drive away as he planned, he moved to a less conspicuous spot to observe the door to the office building Maddie had entered. He sat there watching every vehicle that pulled into the parking lot or even slowed in front of the building until Maddie emerged over a half-hour later. She walked to her car, her eyes darting from side to side as she went. She raised the convertible top before driving away.

5

The schedule provided indicated no more time slots for Hawke to follow Maddie for the rest of the day. He considered continuing anyway, just to be sure she was safe, but in the end, his instinct to protect lost out to his hunger. He would have to assume she would be safe wherever she was going, and he would be able to catch her first thing in the morning. Although what little enthusiasm he had for catching her with a lover had vanished completely.

He turned north in search of food. Somewhere out there was a greasy burger with even greasier fries awaiting his arrival and he did not want to disappoint. Searching the streets for a place to get his dinner, his mind drifted to Hendrix. When Hawke and Roger busted him, the worst thing he had ever done was break into some apartments and steal whatever he could carry and pawn. It was a huge leap to kidnapping. From what Hawke remembered of the man, he wouldn't have the smarts to plan anything like this.

Hawke tried to remember where Hendrix lived, but drew a blank. It had been two years and a lot had happened since then. He could ask Roger for the address but was sure his former partner would not be forthcoming. It was a police matter, and Hawke wasn't a detective anymore. He really wanted to know what the plan was after they took the woman. Ransom? Something worse? How far had Hendrix fallen?

He spotted a diner and pulled in. He hated fast-food chains. Any chain restaurant really, where they formulated the flavor out of everything in the name of saving pennies. Give him a mom and pop local joint any day. He scooped up the file on Maddie and his camera before entering. Inside, he found a corner booth and started reading over the menu. A waitress appeared out of nowhere with an order pad and pen.

"What can I get ya' hon'?" Her blonde hair was a little too blonde to be natural, her lipstick and nail polish, a little too red.

"Coffee," Hawke said. "Black. I'll need a minute for the rest."

"Be right back," she smiled. It was a forced smile, making Hawke wonder how many hours she had been on her feet.

Hawke opened the file and started reading the information provided to him with renewed interest. Men had tried in broad daylight to abduct the woman. Usually kidnappings for ransom were done quietly. They don't want the police involved. It decreased their likelihood of succeeding in collecting the money they craved.

Kidnappings for more sinister reasons were known to happen in more public settings, but they were usually chance meetings between a victim and a pervert looking for an opportunity. And they were rarely more than a single man looking for a woman.

Maddie was attacked by two men and a driver after they followed her half the day. They made no attempt to be discreet and they did not wait for the perfect opportunity. At least Hendrix had to know Hawke would try to stop them.

The waitress set a cup on the table and expertly poured coffee from a glass pot. When it was full, she slid it a little closer to her customer. "Ready yet?"

"Cheeseburger, medium-rare," Hawke said. "Put the works on it. And a side of fries."

"Got it," she said. She glanced down at the photo of Maddie in the file. "Pretty girl."

"She is," Hawke nodded.

The waitress smiled and went to put in his order. Hawke studied the photo with Maddie's piercing eyes staring through the lens to the photographer, and her inviting smile. Was that all this had been? A group of scumbags see a beautiful woman and follow her waiting for an opportunity to snag her? No. It couldn't be. The SUV showed up at the country club while she was still inside, and the men brought masks. This was planned.

The question was, did they plan to grab Maddie or would any woman do?

According to the lawyer who hired him for the job, the husband was wealthy. There were different levels of wealth. Level one was composed of those who lived well, held high paying jobs and managed their money. They drove nice cars, lived in large homes in manicured neighborhoods. They took vacations in exotic locations and never worried about how they were going to pay for anything.

Level two lived in gated communities and owned businesses, usually more than one. They hired level ones to run their companies and manage their money. They didn't take vacations, they traveled. They bought things like art, collectors' items and stocks. When opportunities knocked, they wrote checks. They donated money to worthy causes either because they believed in doing good, or to pay penance for what they did to get to where they were. Flashy cars, yachts and personal planes were just a way of life. And if needed, they had lawyers on retainer.

Then there was level three. These people did not work. They owned more companies than they could track on their own. They had drivers and bodyguards and lawyers on staff. They collected cars, art, jewelry. Their company jet was always fueled and ready. A vacation just meant they were going to live in one of their other properties for a while. Some of them donated to charities, others started them. Everyone wanted a piece of their fortunes and they were usually surrounded by friends or family who worried more about what they were going to get than what they might have to give.

Which level Mr. Rochester was made a difference in how he might be able to pay any ransom asked of him. Level three could write a check and be done. Level two could move some money to pay. Level one would have to liquidate something because, although they had money to burn, they didn't have that much that wasn't tied to something.

The waitress delivered his burger and fries and he let his thoughts drift from the case. Clearing his mind while he ate was something his ex-wife had taught him. The way she explained it was, if you eat with all those toxic images and thoughts, you swallowed the evil and it rotted away at your soul, not to mention your stomach. Hawke didn't buy into any of that nonsense, but he did find he could enjoy his meal more if he wasn't thinking of dead bodies and violent crime scenes. Four years later, the mind-clearing technique was all he kept of the marriage.

His family, friends and Roger all believed that Linda had been the best thing in Hawke's life and losing her was a devastation that he would mourn for years to come. What they didn't know was swallowing evil, and a few other idiosyncrasies they knew, were just the tip of the iceberg in the crazy that was Linda. She wasn't a horrible woman, in fact Hawke adored her. If he had a normal job, one that didn't have him receiving calls at all hours, which ultimately resulted in her insisting to know "her name", he may have had the will to fight for her and get her the help she needed. But as a detective he saw far too much irrational behavior at work. He couldn't handle it at home.

He had now been divorced as long as he had been married and thought of her less and less. He hadn't visited his family in over a year because they seemed more concerned with her wellbeing than his and he was tired of avoiding their questions. There was no benefit to come from tearing Linda down in their memories. Sure, they might finally understand why everything had come apart at the seams so quickly, but it wouldn't really change anything.

The burger was cooked the way he liked, the meat charred on the outside, red and moist on the inside. Each bite was a blissful journey of flavors. The fries were dark and crisp, seasoned perfectly. He would have to remember this place for the future. The waitress checked on him a couple of times, refilling his coffee with each visit. She made no further comments about the photo of Maddie that lay on the table watching him eat.

He finished his meal and pushed the plate across the table. Picking up the camera he fumbled with the buttons on the back until he figured out how to review the pictures he had taken. Flipping through the images, he ignored the main subject of each and concentrated on anyone standing in the background looking Maddie's way. Each was a possible look-out. Each a suspect. He knew most would just be men whose attention was captured by the beautiful woman crossing their paths.

He saved the photos of the SUV for last. He had only taken a few shots of the vehicle. There weren't a lot of ways to show it that would tell anything more than what a single shot would. He scanned them anyway, hoping to see something he had missed while he was framing the shots. When nothing presented itself, Hawke set the camera aside. He spent another half hour sipping his coffee and watching the waitress juggle her customers, her coworkers and trays of food. He marveled at the woman's ability to keep everything straight and remain composed.

He paid his bill, leaving a healthy tip, closed the case file and slung the camera strap over his shoulder. It was still early, but he wanted to get home and catch some shut-eye. Maddie was scheduled to work in the morning and Hawke wanted to be parked in front of her home well in advance of her departure time. The information the lawyer had supplied was intentionally vague. Obviously, they knew where she worked, but the address was not supplied. Any chance he might miss her was one he couldn't take. Nothing says change your routine like a near abduction. The waitress yelled a thank you to him as he pushed his way into the sunlight. It was still hours before dark. He wondered where Maddie was and whether she was safe.

Hawke had, years ago, invested in black-out curtains for his bedroom. Working all hours was easier when he could sleep at all hours. The military had trained him to catch z's on a moment's notice. Being in a near black room made it all that much easier. He settled in and set his alarm for five. That would give him time to stop for food and coffee on the way.

Hawke was dead asleep when his phone woke him. He didn't feel as rested as he should and considered changing the alarm to five-thirty. The realization that he was hearing his ringtone, not the alarm, brought him to full alertness. He squinted at the screen, and seeing Roger's name there, answered.

"What the hell, Rog?" Hawke yawned. "What time is it?"

"It's two in the morning," Roger said. "You already in bed? How old are you?"

"Very funny," Hawke said. "What do you want?"

"Thought you might want to know we went to Hendrix's place," Roger said.

Hawke sat up. "What did he have to say for himself?"

"Nothing," Roger said. "He wasn't here."

"You're still there?"

"Yep," Roger confirmed. "Searching the place."

"And you called me," Hawke said. "What? You were jealous I might get some sleep?"

"I don't think he left on his own," Roger said.

"Why do you think that?"

"Microwave dinner," Roger said. "Half-eaten. Still on the table."

"That doesn't mean anything," Hawke said. "I don't finish those things sometimes."

"A beer," Roger said. "Opened but not consumed."

"Okay," Hawke said. "That sounds like he left in a hurry."

"Thought you might want to know," Roger said.

"Thanks," Hawke said. "You think this might have something to do with the abduction attempt?"

"Don't complicate this, Hawke," Roger said. "Until we can get our hands on Hendrix or one of the other two men in that SUV, we aren't going to draw any conclusions."

"Whatever, Rog," Hawke said. "I've gotta go."

Hawke disconnected the call. Roger always was a little shortsighted in his investigations. He followed the clues with tunnel vision until he had a reason to veer in another direction. In most cases, that method worked just fine. But there were always exceptions. Hawke had a feeling this was one of those cases. They started with a carjacking where they killed the owner. They tried to abduct Maddie in daylight, in a public place. They weren't operating under the radar. They were front and center. They were in a hurry, on a deadline, desperate. With Hendrix missing, they were either keeping him out of sight, or they were already working on a new plan. The question was, would they try to go after Maddie again or find another target?

There was no going back to sleep. Hawke rolled out of bed and headed for the shower. He would definitely have time for breakfast and coffee.

6

By the time Maddie's royal blue Tesla backed out of the garage, Hawke had been sitting across from her home for over an hour. He was violating his client's orders, watching the woman outside the scheduled surveillance times. While he waited for her to emerge, he had noted two women and one man walking dogs, two joggers and one cyclist. A dozen cars passed but none more than once and the only one that slowed threw a newspaper into the driveway.

Maddie backed the length of the driveway, stopping to snatch up the paper before pulling onto the street. It was seven-fifteen. If she started work at eight, she had forty-five minutes to get there. He was curious where she spent her days other than the country club, restaurants and her therapist. He gave her a few seconds before pulling out to follow.

Shortly after leaving her neighborhood, Maddie pulled into a coffee shop. She stepped out of her car wearing a dark suit that screamed executive. She walked briskly inside and emerged moments later carrying a paper cup. Hawke envied her as he had emptied his own cup about a half-hour before.

The next stop was just under a half-hour away. A five-story free-standing building with clean lines, a mixture of metal and glass. The sign next to the street said, Rochester-Kinsley Incorporated. She worked for the family business. Hawke wondered if that was how she met her husband, working for him first. He also wondered where the husband was. He had not left the house before Maddie. If there was indeed a strain in the marriage, it would make sense that they wouldn't share a ride.

Hawke just found it odd that the husband who suspects his wife of cheating wouldn't want to arrive close to the same time, just in case her lover works for them.

Once she was inside, Hawke returned to the main drive and found a restroom and another cup of java. He had no way of knowing if she might have off-site meetings or if she would leave for lunch. He raced back to the office building and found an observation point where he could watch her car and wait all day if needed.

For the next half-hour, he watched cars arrive and park in the lot. Each time a man walked up to the building, Hawke wondered if he was Maddie's husband or possibly her lover. When the cars stopped arriving he settled in to play the waiting game.

The combination of the sun turning his car into an oven and lack of sleep, Hawke caught himself dozing off a couple of times. Both times he promptly checked that her car was still in its parking space and hoped she hadn't left with anyone else. He started the car and ran the air to cool off.

At eleven-thirty, Maddie exited the building with another smartly dressed woman. The two of them carried briefcases and talked as they walked. They went to Maddie's car and the two of them left together. Hawke took his place behind them, scanning for possible tails as they went. If the kidnappers were trying again, they were being much more cautious. He didn't spot anyone following them. He hoped that meant they had lost the stomach for it.

Maddie drove just under the speed limit, forcing Hawke to slow down in order to match her speed. He wondered if she had spotted him and was trying to get him to pass. If he was blown, the whole day would be a bust. He would have to get another car and try again later. If she hadn't seen him, it would be pointless to pass and lose the advantage of following. He stayed about three car lengths behind.

A twenty-minute drive landed them at a restaurant chain that even Hawke could afford. He was relieved. He wasn't fond of chain restaurants, but he was even less fond of starving. He would give her ample time to get seated then enter, making sure he kept out of her sight. He would order something quickly so he wasn't still waiting for his food when she left.

The two women walked in carrying the same cases they had with them when they left their office building. A working lunch. Hawke waited about two minutes before pulling himself from his car and trekking across the parking lot to the entrance. He kept his head down in case Maddie happened to be looking out the windows. Although she had spoken to him just the evening before, he knew by experience she would most likely not recognize him, but he wasn't taking chances.

Inside, he stepped up to the hostess desk while scanning the dining area for the women. He spotted them in the corner, sitting at a large round table. They were expecting others. Hawke was relieved that Maddie was seated facing the wall. Hawke then noted the location of the restrooms and the path from there to the women's table.

"How many in your party?" an overly friendly blonde with an oversized smile greeted him.

"Just me," Hawke said.

"Follow me," she tilted her head in a way that combined pity for his dining situation and an indication of the direction they would go.

"Can I have a booth in this area?" Hawke pointed at a table that would give him a clear view of his subject without leaving him overly exposed.

The girl's smile faltered a little. "But that's a four-top," she said without really speaking to him.

"I promise to be fast," Hawke lied. "Be out before it gets too busy."

Realizing she had spoken out loud, her smile returned to its original brightness and she changed direction, leading him to the booth he had indicated. He slid onto the bench seat facing Maddie and her companion. The hostess handed him a menu and bounced away to seat other guests. Hawke gave the menu a cursory once over and set it aside. He pulled out his notebook and wrote notes about where Maddie was, who she was with, co-worker, and what time they arrived. When he raised his head a woman in her forties wearing a waitstaff uniform stood next to him.

"What can I get you to drink?" she asked, pen poised over her own notepad.

"Gin and tonic," Hawke said.

"We don't serve alcohol, sir," the waitress said.

"I know," Hawke sighed. "How about iced tea?"

"That we have," she said, scribbling on the pad. "Sweetened or plain?"

"Plain."

"Be right back," she turned on her heels and stopped at another table for their drink order.

Hawke pulled out the schedule the lawyer had given him and reviewed the upcoming activities. It was a simple day. Work was listed from 8:00 am to 5:00 pm. Then there was a two-hour block with nothing scheduled, prime time for following her. Then 7:00 through the rest of the day was blacked out. There wasn't much for Hawke to do. After the lunch meeting, he expected she would return to the office where he would get to sit in his car for four or five hours waiting for her to leave for the day. The two hours between work and the blackout time was his opportunity to catch her, get his photos and be finished with the whole creepy stalker thing.

The waitress returned with his drink and asked him for his order. He wanted the burger and fries, just like the night before, but ordered grilled chicken and steamed vegetables. At his last visit, his doctor had the audacity to tell him he needed to lose some of the weight he had gained since leaving the department. In truth, the doctor told him to lose all the weight gain and about ten more pounds on top of that. Hawke felt he was paying the man to tell him he was fat, sprinkled with phrases like 'men your age' and 'your body type'. In the spirit of trying, Hawke occasionally ordered the healthy option. Unfortunately, he also occasionally ate the healthy option and chased it down with a burger and fries. Not quite the doctor's plan.

Maddie's table slowly filled with business suits. One man brought Maddie to her feet. Hawke wished he had his camera. He studied their mannerisms wondering if this was the husband or possibly the lover. They clasped hands in a motionless handshake and talked briefly, eyes locked and casual smiles.

When they parted, the man took a seat three chairs away from Maddie. Not the husband.

Hawke started taking notes on the man's appearance, tall and muscular, graying hair with a high-dollar cut and style, angular face with a full beard. Hawke would have to be at his car with camera in hand to catch some shots of the man as he left. The waitress for the business meeting brought them drinks and breads and began taking their orders. Once she completed her task, the young woman sought out a free terminal to punch in their requests. Those at the table began pulling out folders and notepads. The woman who had ridden with Maddie set a recorder in the center of the table.

The meeting was well underway when Hawke's waitress set his meal in front of him. He eyed the grill-marked bird and brightly colored vegetables with skepticism. He reached for the salt, stopping short as his doctor's warnings about the granulated killer came back to him. Dismissing the warning, he snatched up the shaker and vigorously applied instant flavor to his plate.

The meeting table became a flurry as the participants shifted papers and other articles to make room for plates. They continued talking while they ate, at times using forks like pointers. Hawke ate slowly as he watched the group, concentrating primarily on the man Maddie had stood to greet. The two of them did most of the speaking, often ignoring the others while they conversed. Everyone else at the table took notes, smiled and nodded in unison as if cued. Maddie and the man were the alphas. This was their meeting. The others were there to support or learn, possibly both.

Hawke finished his food and pushed the plate to the far side of the table. The waitress refilled his tea and carried the dish away. She reappeared a moment later and dropped a ticket on the table, thanking him for his patronage. He grinned before she left then lifted the paper and checked the total. In his notebook he wrote down the restaurant name and the total along with a notation on the paper's edge to indicate the entry as an expense.

Hawke had paid and was almost finished with his tea when one of the suits at the business meeting rose, packed up his things and headed for the exit. The meeting was coming to a close. Time for Hawke to get to his car. He stood, stretched his back and made his way to the restroom. One cup of coffee and two glasses of iced tea demanded he stop in. As he stepped to the sink to wash up the door opened and one of the men from the meeting walked in. Average height and lean, he wore his dark hair close-cropped, almost boyish. It didn't help that he sported no facial hair, adding to his youthful appearance. The man looked the part of businessman but his mannerisms suggested he would more comfortable in blue jeans. Hawke continued with his menial task while watching the man in the mirror.

Instead of heading to a stall, the man pulled out his phone and made a call. Hawke made a point of washing every inch of his hands and forearms.

"It's me," the man said. "Yeah. I'm here now."

He listened for a time as Hawke worked at trying to free several paper towels from their prison on the wall. He didn't have to act like it was difficult, the roller was stuck.

"I know what I said," the man spoke in a whisper that did nothing to prevent Hawke from hearing. "Things aren't going as planned. She's not budging. She doesn't want to sell."

Hawke slapped the side of the paper towel dispenser and twisted on the manual roller. A partial piece of paper fed out. He grabbed the corners and pulled. The paper tore off, giving him a half sheet to dry his hands with.

"After we wrap things up here," the man said, "I'll be there like I said."

He disconnected the call and dropped the phone into his pocket. Without even a glance in Hawke's direction he left the room. The PI dried his hands on his shirt as best he could and followed. The meeting at the round table was breaking up. The man was standing next to Maddie again. They spoke with large smiles and laughter. Their body language was friendly. It seemed to Hawke that everything was good between them. Although he couldn't help but wonder, if the man was Maddie's husband, who he had to sneak to the restroom to make plans to meet. Was he having an affair of his own? Was that why he wanted incriminating pictures? To initiate a divorce so he could move on to a new conquest?

Hawke left the building and made his way back to his car where he readied his camera waiting for the men to emerge. He took a number of shots of the other participants as they left, but took a dozen or more of the two men of note, the man Maddie was so friendly toward and the man in the restroom.

Hawke followed the women back to their office and parked. He settled in for what he suspected to be a long wait.

7

Just before five, Maddie exited the office building and walked to her car. Hawke waited for her to close her door before starting his engine. In the next two hours, he would hopefully have what he needed to complete the job at hand and move on. She pulled out of the parking lot and he fell in behind her far enough back to not cause her suspicion. Staying close enough not to lose her, he still almost did just that twice; once when a light changed just as she went through, forcing him to risk running a red to keep up and again when a carpet cleaning van pulled out in front of him, blocking his view. He passed on the left and almost missed the right-hand turn Maddie made.

After that, Hawke closed the distance between them to keep from having to draw attention to himself in his attempts to stay with her. He eased back when he felt he could but remained close overall. When she finally turned off the road, it was into the parking area for a local park, complete with a walking trail. Tennis, yoga and now this. She was clearly into fitness, the polar opposite of Hawke. He hoped she was just there to enjoy the fresh air and not to walk, or worse, run. Following someone in this type of setting was more difficult because it was harder to blend in. And if she ran, there was a matter of him being able to keep up.

She parked in front of a picnic table giving him hope that she was planning to sit in the sunlight, possibly meeting up with her lover for a photo-op. He parked a short distance away where he could observe, with camera ready. She walked up to the table and sat, bending over to change her shoes. She wasn't planning to stay seated.

Trying to decide what he was going to do, Hawke followed the trail with his eyes to identify what blind spots he would have to deal with. In doing so, his eyes fell on the carpet cleaning van that had cut him off earlier. While he calculated the odds the van's driver just happened to be headed to the same park as Maddie, it started to roll forward. Hawke glanced to Maddie and saw that she was approaching her car with her non-athletic shoes in her hand.

Hawke weighed his options. He could cut the van off. But if it was just a coincidence and they were only carpet cleaners, he would blow his cover for no reason. He could wait, but if they were there for Maddie, they may have learned from their mistakes and grab her faster and be gone before Hawke could interfere. He stared at the driver as the van approached. The man's head was turned toward the park, but not necessarily at Maddie. Hawke started his car and put it in gear.

The van stopped suddenly when it was even with Maddie and Hawke released the brake and stepped down hard on the gas. He lost visual on Maddie, but he heard her scream. It was all the confirmation Hawke needed. He did not slow, ramming the back of the van with his car, sending it rolling two car lengths forward and into a parked pickup. Hawke was out of his car, gun in hand, before the van came to a complete stop. Maddie was struggling with a man who had her around the waist, trying to drag her to the now moved van.

The driver's door of the van opened and the man inside rolled out, holding a military-style weapon. He turned on Hawke and the PI opened fire, placing two shots in the man's torso. The man fell back, his finger clasping the trigger and spraying the sky with bullets as he fell. The park filled with screams of panic and people running in all directions away from the gunfire. Satisfied the driver was down, Hawke turned his attention to the other man who had already released Maddie and was reaching for a pistol tucked into his belt. Hawke held his pistol aimed at the man's face.

"Don't," Hawke yelled.

For a second, the man froze, but Hawke saw the look in his eyes that told him surrender was not an option. The would-be kidnapper pulled the gun up and out, but rather than pointing it at Hawke, he swung his arm wide and toward Maddie. Hawke pulled the trigger twice and the man crumpled to the ground. The PI ran up and kicked the gun out of the dead man's hand, glancing toward the van to be sure the other man was still down and no one else was coming, before turning to Maddie.

"You okay?"

"You?" Maddie said. "But how? Why? Who are you?"

Hawke tilted his head and half shrugged as he pulled his phone out and called 911. Before the call connected the wail of sirens filled the air. He spoke to the dispatcher and lay his pistol on the hood of Maddie's car. He examined the crumpled front end of his own car. There was no way it was going to run again.

8

Police arrived and swarmed Hawke slamming him into the car and handcuffing him. An ambulance followed and paramedics raced to the two men. They were both gone. Maddie stared at him from the other side of her car, tears rolling down her lovely cheeks. Hawke gave his name and asked to speak to Roger. They ignored him at first, but one of them must have made a call because they soon started acting a little more cordial and told him Roger was on his way.

When his former partner arrived, the officers had rounded up potential witnesses and were questioning them for details. A female officer stood with Maddie, writing down everything she said. Another officer held Hawke by his elbow and stood at attention until the detective joined them.

"Remove the cuffs, officer," Roger said. "I'll take him from here."

The officer gave him a concerning glance, matched by a 'do as I say' look from Roger. Seconds later, Hawke rubbed his wrists and thanked him.

"Don't thank me," Roger said. "Tell me what happened. And make it good or I'll put the cuffs back on you myself."

"I was watching the vic," Hawke said. "trying to get the photos I need when I noticed the same van I had seen earlier."

"The cleaning van?" Roger pointed.

"That's the one," Hawke nodded. "I had seen it earlier and when I saw it here, I got concerned for Maddie, er, Mrs. Rochester. When it became apparent they were attempting to kidnap her again, I took action."

"You rammed their van and shot them," Roger said.

"I did," Hawke confirmed. "To protect Mrs. Rochester."

"And when did you call 911?" Roger asked.

"After it was over," Hawke said.

"Not before?"

"Didn't have time," Hawke said. "Had I waited, I would be giving you a description of the van so you could search for Mrs. Rochester. I chose to stop it from happening."

"This is twice, Hawke," Roger said.

"That's right," Hawke said. "I was there both times."

"My point exactly," Roger said. "By the way, I think your cover is blown."

"You think?" Hawke said, glancing to where Maddie stood talking to the female officer. Maddie was not looking at the woman. She was staring at him.

"We're going to have to keep your gun," Roger said.

"I know," Hawke said. "I have another."

"Great," Roger said with just enough sarcasm. "The idea is for you to stop shooting people."

"There's nothing I would like more," Hawke said. "I think you need to find Hendrix for questioning. He wasn't here this time, but he knows why this is happening."

"There's a problem with that one," Roger said.

"You think he ran?" Hawke asked.

"Don't know," Roger said. "We've had a car watching his place all night and he hasn't returned."

Movement caught Hawke's eye. Maddie was walking their way.

"This should be good," Roger said, taking a step back to watch the show.

Hawke sneered at the detective before turning back to Maddie with what he hoped wasn't too much of a smile.

"You're following me," Maddie said. Not a question. "I want to know why. And I want to know who you are."

His cover was blown. The case was no longer about a woman cheating on her husband. It was about a potential kidnapping victim. Add to that, the fact Hawke didn't like the lawyer who hired him, and he was okay with unloading.

"Name's Hawke," he said. "I was hired by your husband."

"My husband?" Maddie was taken aback. "To protect me?"

"Not exactly," Hawke said.

"Then what?"

"Apparently, your husband thinks you're cheating on him," Hawke said. "He hired me to follow you and get some incriminating pictures. You know, to null the prenup."

"That bastard," Maddie said. "I'm not cheating on him. If anything, he's cheating on me. What about them?" Maddie pointed at the sheet-covered bodies.

"Don't know anything more about them than you do," Hawke said. "I'm just glad I was here to stop them."

"When you met with my husband," Maddie said, "did he mention who I was cheating on him with?"

"I didn't actually meet with him," Hawke said.

"Then how did he hire you?" Maddie said. "And how did he pay?"

"I met with a lawyer who arranged everything," Hawke said. "Lawyer said his client was wealthy and gave me cash."

"Wealthy?" Maddie's eyes narrowed. "He's not wealthy. I'm wealthy. He's an unemployed talentless artist."

"If you're wealthy, doesn't that kind of make him wealthy?" Hawke asked.

"In most marriages, maybe," Maddie said. "But, Mr. Hawke, my marriage isn't like most. I had money when we married and have grown it into much more. My husband spends like it grows on trees. I give him an allowance, but he has no access to the accounts. I learned that within the first year."

"He must be hoping to change that," Hawke said.

Maddie stared at Hawke for a long moment. Then she said, "How would you like to work for me?"

"For you?" Hawke said. "Doing what, exactly?"

"Same thing you're doing now, basically," Maddie said. "Follow my husband. Get proof he's cheating on me."

"How am I supposed to follow him and protect you at the same time?" Hawke asked.

"Protect me?" Maddie said. "Protect me from who? You killed them."

Hawke remained quiet. He glanced at Roger then back to the woman. She studied him for a moment.

"You don't think it's over," she said.

"I didn't say that," Hawke said.

"You didn't have to," she said. "I see it in your eyes. You think someone else is behind this."

"Possibly," Hawke said. "But I don't know for sure."

"But if you're right," Maddie said, "the only way to know is for someone else to try to kidnap me."

"That's one way," Hawke nodded.

"You have to protect me," Maddie said.

"Which is why I can't follow your husband," Hawke said.

"I'll double what my husband promised you if you do both," she said.

"I can't be your bodyguard and follow your husband," Hawke said.

"There has to be a way," Maddie said.

"I'll follow your husband," Hawke said, "and you hire a bodyguard."

"I want you," she shook her head. "You've already saved me twice. I trust you."

"You trust the guy who was spying on you?" Roger said.

Hawke gave him a side glance. "Then hire someone else to follow your husband. I can't do both."

"You can if I'm with you," Maddie said.

"What?" Hawke and Roger both said.

"We spy on my husband," Maddie said. "Then you can protect me."

"Out of the question," Hawke put a hand up like a cop stopping traffic. "I work alone."

"I'll triple what he was paying you," Maddie said.

Hawke looked at her, thinking through the numbers. He turned to Roger who shook his head.

"If we do this," Hawke said, "there will be ground rules."

"Jesus, Hawke," Roger said.

"Keep out of this, Rog," Hawke said.

"We've got two kidnapping attempts and two bodies," Roger said. "We're not keeping out of anything."

"I can follow rules," Maddie said. "Sometimes."

"You will follow them," Hawke said. "Or you don't tag along."

"I'm riding with you," Maddie said, "You can protect me."

Hawke pointed at his car. "No one's riding with me in that."

"We can use my car," Maddie said.

"To follow your husband?" Hawke said. "Don't you think he might recognize it?"

"Then we'll get another car," she said. "One he wouldn't know."

"I'll see what I can come up with," Hawke said.

"This is a bad idea, Hawke," Roger said.

Maddie said, "I'll get us a car."

9

"You can't do a stakeout in that," Hawke said.

"Why not?" Maddie asked.

"It's a hundred-thousand-dollar car," he said, spreading his arms to take in the Porsche Panamera Turbo. "Everyone will look at it."

"It's only ninety-five-thousand," Maddie corrected. "And of course people will look at it. It's a beautiful car."

"The key to following someone," Hawke explained, "when you're trying to catch them doing something they aren't supposed to, is to not be noticed yourself."

"Then what would you suggest?" Maddie asked.

"A Ford or Chevy," Hawke said. "Maybe a Honda."

"You're talking about a family car," Maddie said. "You want a mini-van?"

"I didn't say mini-van," Hawke said. "A sedan or SUV would be good. Something roomy, comfortable."

"Have you ever sat in a Panamera?"

"No."

"Then you don't know what comfortable is," Maddie said.

"I'm not doing a stakeout in a Porsche," Hawke said, a little louder than he meant to. Several customers and salesmen turned toward the two of them. Hawke tried a reassuring grin that faded quickly. "Just mind your own business."

"I thought detectives liked flashy sports cars," Maddie said. "You know, like Ferraris"

"Magnum PI?" Hawke said. "You think I'm some kind of tv detective?"

"Well, no," Maddie said. "But . . ."

Pete, the salesman who showed them the Panamera, swooped in from nowhere, "Is there a problem?"

"No problem," Hawke said.

"He doesn't like the Porsche," Maddie said with an accusatory tone.

"Sir?" the salesman's face scrunched. "You don't like the Panamera?"

"I like it, okay," Hawke defended. "It just isn't practical."

"Practical?" the salesman said. Hawke could see the wheels spinning. "Perhaps I could show you . . ."

"No." Hawke turned to Maddie. "We're leaving."

"What?" Maddie said, hurrying after Hawke. "Why? I thought we needed a car."

"We don't need a car," Hawke turned back on her, causing her to stop abruptly. "I need a car. You have a car. If you want the Porsche, get the Porsche. I'm going to go find something useful that I can afford."

"But . . ."

"But what?" Hawke said.

"But I was going to buy you a car," Maddie said.

"What?" Hawke said. "Why? Why would you do that?"

"Because you saved my life," she said. "Twice. That's how you wrecked your car."

Hawke looked at her. There was a sadness in her eyes, a fear. "You don't have to do that."

"I want to," she said. "I need to."

Hawke scanned the showroom floor at all the people staring back at him. "Fine. You can buy me a car."

"Thank you," she hugged him. He was taken aback and stepped away. "Oh, sorry. So, the Porsche?"

"Not the Porsche," he snapped. "I need something I can use in my work. Not to mention something I can afford the insurance for."

He turned away and pushed his way through the doors into the harsh sunlight beyond. Maddie was directly behind him. As they approached her car, she said, "What then?"

Hawke put his elbows on the roof of the Tesla to answer, but his focus did not land on her but rather the car lot behind her.

She turned to follow his line of sight. She turned back to him to find he was still looking past her.

"Really?"

"What?" he said.

"That's what you want?"

"That? No," Hawke said. "I mean, yes. But, no."

"It's not a sedan," Maddie pointed out.

"That's why I said, no," Hawke said.

"But you like it," Maddie said.

"Of course," Hawke said, "but that's not what matters."

"But it should," she said.

"But it doesn't," he said.

"But it should," she insisted. "Let's take a look at it."

Before he could argue she turned on her heels and walked to the vehicle in question, a completely restored, charcoal grey 1950 Chevy pickup with custom rims. He had always been a fan of the classic and was impressed with the level of detail on this one. As he walked around the truck, Maddie leaned against the cab and glanced inside.

"This is what you like?" she asked. "That seat doesn't look comfy at all."

Hawke ran his hand along the front fender. "It's comfortable enough."

"She's a beaut' isn't she?" a voice drew their attention. They turned to the man approaching them. "Owner traded her in for a Porsche. Big mistake if you ask me."

"Didn't ask," Hawke muttered. He glanced at Maddie who had moved to the far side of the truck. "Let's go."

"Don't you want to take it on a test-drive?" Her face scrunched into a pout. From the reaction, Hawke gathered that she was not going to take no for an answer.

"Fine," he said. "We drive it. Then we go."

Her lips curled into a smile that made the hair on Hawke's arms stand up. He had been married, twice. No woman had ever smiled at him like that. He closed his eyes a moment, wondering what he had gotten himself into.

"I'll get the keys and a tag," the salesman smiled too. His was creepier, more wolfish. A completely different feeling hit Hawke but resulted in the same thought.

Tagged and ready to go, Hawke slid into the driver's seat while Maddie climbed into the passenger side. The salesman handed him the keys and Hawke inserted the ignition key and turned it. The engine roared to life. Hawke's brow furrowed and he looked the salesman in the eyes, something he had managed not to do up to that point.

"I should have told you," the salesman said, "the restoration isn't a hundred percent to factory specs."

"Meaning what exactly?"

"Meaning the factory original 216 was replaced with a 454," he said. "This baby has 450 horsepower."

Hawke turned to Maddie, "You buckled in?"

"Yes, but," Maddie started. Her thought, like her sentence, was cut short as she was jerked forward when Hawke suddenly backed out of its parking space. Just as she was about to protest, she was thrown back into the seat as they were propelled toward the lot's exit. Unable to speak, a small scream escaped her lips.

Hawke shifted smoothly through the gears, accelerating down the service road leading to the on-ramp for the highway. The steering was firm and reacted similar to a sports car. Hawke maneuvered the traffic with a grin on his face. Maddie sank the fingers of her right hand into the armrest built into the truck's door and used her left hand to grasp the front edge of the seat. She watched Hawke's face and smiled.

"You're enjoying this," she said, finally feeling comfortable.

"What's not to enjoy?" he said.

"We're totally getting this," she said.

"No," he said. "We're not."

"Why?"

"Not practical," Hawke said pulling the wheel just in time to miss the slow, generic sedan in their lane. After flying past them, he cut back into the lane.

"No bad guy could get away if you're driving this," she said.

"I'm a private investigator," Hawke said. "I follow people. I don't chase them."

"You sit in your car all day," Maddie said. "You can sit in this."

"I have nowhere to secure my equipment," Hawke said. "No back seat. No trunk. The truck bed is exposed to thieves and the elements."

"They make those," Maddie gestured something that Hawke couldn't begin to understand. "What are they called?"

"I have no idea what you mean," Hawke said. He steered onto the ramp leading up to the highway, shifted gears and stepped down on the accelerator. The sensation of being hugged by the truck's seating was comforting.

"Those metal box things that go in the back of pickups for storing things," Maddie said.

"You mean a truck box?"

"Really?" Maddie turned to Hawke with her brow knotted. "That's what it's called? Men have no imagination."

Hawke started to say something, thought better of it and returned his attention to the highway. He slowly increased the gas and watched the speedometer climb.

"Then get a truck box and put your things in it," Maddie shouted over the roar of the engine.

Hawke was going to tell her the reasons that wouldn't work but couldn't think of a proper argument. Instead, he slowed and took the next off-ramp. A few seconds later he was on the highway again going back the way he came. Returning to the dealership, Hawke drove the posted speeds and took the corners slow enough Maddie didn't have to hold on.

Parking in the same space the truck had been when he first saw it, Hawke opened the door and slid from the seat to the ground a little less gracefully than he would have liked. The salesman was on them like a mosquito. Hawke tossed him the keys and started walking toward Maddie's car.

"What did you think?" the salesman asked, trying to match Hawke's pace.

Maddie lingered behind, looking the truck over one last time. She then strolled after the two men with no urgency at all. She knew her car was locked, and Hawke would be trapped. She watched as the PI tried the door, smiling at him when he made eye contact, pleading for her to let him in.

"Don't you at least want to hear the details?" she said when she reached the car.

"What details?" Hawke asked. "I don't need details. I need a car."

"That's why we're here," Maddie said.

"Here?" Hawke said waving his arm around to take in the entire dealership. "Here is not where people like me buy cars. People like me go to shady used car dealers and hope we aren't getting screwed."

"But, Hawke," Maddie said.

"But what?"

Maddie turned to the salesman. "How much is the truck?"

"Thirty-two," he said.

"Thirty-two?" Hawke's eyes widened. "I know you don't mean hundred. But you can't mean thousand."

"Thirty-two thousand," the salesman said. "Yes."

"Mrs. Rochester, please unlock the door," Hawke said. "Or I'll call a cab."

He hesitated a second before walking toward the street with his phone in hand. On the small screen, he started searching for the number of a taxi service.

"Hawke," Maddie called after him. "I'm buying you the truck."

He stopped and spun around. "You can't do that. Why would you?"

"I told you," she said. "You saved my life. You wrecked your car saving my life. I owe you."

"You don't owe me."

"Let me do this," Maddie pleaded.

"It's thirty-two thousand dollars," Hawke said.

"I think my life is worth thirty-two thousand," Maddie said. "Are you saying it's not?"

"The truck isn't," Hawke said.

"Then how much is it worth?"

"Fully restored?" Hawke said. "But with a non-original engine? I would say twenty-four tops."

Maddie turned to the salesman. "You heard the man. I'll give you twenty-four thousand cash."

"I can't authorize that," the man said.

"Then who can?" Maddie insisted. "Go tell your boss there is a cash offer. But it won't last long."

The salesman looked from Maddie to Hawke trying to determine if he was being played. Making up his mind, the man retreated to the office, presumably to discuss the offer with the sales manager. A few minutes later, he stepped out again and waved them toward him. They glanced at one another and walked side by side to the building.

Inside was a small showroom with a half-dozen cars Hawke could never afford. The perky receptionist greeted them with a smile when they passed. No one else in the space acknowledged them at all. Hawke leaned closer to Maddie and whispered, "You don't have to do this."

Maddie ignored him and followed the salesman into an office. He sat behind the desk and directed them to the two chairs facing his. They both sat; Maddie scooting her chair forward and Hawke sliding his back.

"I talked to the manager," the salesman said. "And he said he couldn't do twenty-four. But he will do twenty-nine-five."

The salesman gave his best smile to assure them he was giving them a great counteroffer. Hawke was thinking of wiping the smile from his face when Maddie surprised him. She stood and left the room. Hawke's eyes followed her back as she disappeared then turned to the salesman who had the same slack jaw he did.

Hawke stood and shuffled after the woman. He stepped through the doorway just in time to catch her entering another office. Hawke closed the distance and walked in behind her.

"Am I clear?" Maddie was saying as Hawke reached her.

The man behind the desk appeared smaller than he was. The nameplate on his desk introduced him as Cal Richardson, Sales Manager. "Yes, ma'am. I'll get the paperwork drawn up. Can I get you something to drink while you wait?"

"No thank you," Maddie said.

Cal glanced at Hawke, furrowed his brow then pushed himself up from his chair. As he rounded his desk to leave the room, he said, "I'll be right back."

With the manager out of the office, Hawke turned his focus to Maddie. "What just happened?"

"I bought you your truck," Maddie said, matter-of-factly.

"For?"

"Twenty-four," Maddie said. "As we agreed."

"But how did you get him to agree?" Hawke asked. "And so quickly."

"I reminded him how many cars my company has purchased from him over the years," Maddie said. "The fifty-five hundred he was trying to hold on to is just a drop in the bucket."

"Exactly how many cars have you purchased?"

"I don't really know," Maddie shrugged. "Evidently, enough."

The manager returned with paperwork to fill out. Maddie had everything put in Hawke's name, signed and wrote a check which Cal paper-clipped to his copy of the documents. The manager signed everything and handed the customer copies and the keys to Maddie, who promptly slid them to Hawke. Hawke stood awkwardly, unsure how he felt about the whole transaction. Cal eyed him again and Hawke got the impression the man thought something was going on between the two of them. Hawke suspected the man was trying to figure out why Maddie would be interested in him.

"Anything else we can do for you, Mrs. Rochester?" the manager asked.

"That's it for now," Maddie said. She draped her purse from her shoulder and stood.

Reluctantly, Hawke gathered the papers and folded them. He placed the keys in his pocket and wondered where he was going to put everything until he found a truck box that would fit the old Chevy. Then he realized his car was towed after he crashed it into the van and he had no idea where his things were. Walking out of the office, he pulled out his phone and scrolled through his contact list.

"Where shall we meet?" Maddie said, behind him.

"What?" Hawke said, his finger hovering over Roger's name.

"To stake out my husband?" she said. "Where are we going to meet? Since we can't follow him in my car, we'll have to leave it somewhere."

10

It was late when they left the dealership and Hawke was able to convince Maddie to go home with the promise they would start the surveillance of her husband the next morning. He followed her to her neighborhood just to be sure she was safe, then drove to his apartment to get some rest.

He had just sat down with a sad-looking microwave dinner when his cellphone rang. He thought about ignoring it until he saw Roger's name on the screen. He had called about his car and had to leave a message.

"Hey, Rog," he answered. "Thanks for calling me back. I . . .
"

"I think you should come down here," Roger said. The no-nonsense tone of his voice told Hawke he was working a case.

No longer on the force, it was unusual to be asked to a crime scene. And Roger wouldn't ask him to the department unless, well, unless he was a suspect.

"What's up?" he asked.

"Pier six," Roger said. "Just follow the lights."

Hawke was going to ask a follow-up question when he realized his old partner had hung up on him. He examined the unidentifiable piece of meat floating in gravy and the white substance that was supposed to pass for potatoes. Scooping it up, he tossed it in the trash, grabbed his jacket and walked out, hitting the light on his way out.

Finding Roger was as easy as the detective had suggested. The surrounding buildings were awash with blue and red flashing lights. Hawke parked his truck where it would be out of the way, but still in view. No point taking chances.

He had not been to a crime scene since he was a cop and wasn't sure he wanted to be at one now. Glancing at the faces of his former colleagues it was obvious they weren't sure he should be there either. There was also a hint of admiration. Hawke wasn't the first to want to punch the captain, he was just the first to do it.

He spotted Roger, with two uniformed officers, standing next to a sheet-covered body. Hawke had really hoped it wouldn't be that kind of crime scene, knowing with all the police presence it wouldn't be any other kind. Roger saw him and waved him over.

"What's the deal, Roger?" Hawke said. "Why am I here?"

In response, Roger didn't speak, he only nodded at the sheet.

"What?" Hawke's eyes fell to the sheet on the ground just a few feet away. "Someone I know?"

For a brief moment the image of Maddie crossed his mind. There had been two attempts to abduct her. Could they have been waiting for her at her house? But he quickly noticed the man's shoe sticking out from one edge of the covering.

"Take a look," Roger said.

"I'm not a cop anymore," Hawke pointed out the obvious. "I'm not contaminating a scene."

"For Christ's sake, you've changed," Roger said. He turned to the officer nearest the body. "Show him."

The officer kneeled and pulled back one corner of the sheet exposing the upper body of the victim. Richard Hendrix stared at nothing. Hawke noted the bullet wounds; two in the chest, one in the forehead. The killer wanted to be sure he was dead. Hawke nodded at the officer who let the sheet fall back into place.

"What do you make of that?" Roger asked him.

"You don't think I did this?" Hawke stared at the detective.

"No," Roger said. "I don't think you did it. Although, to cross the t's, you should probably give a statement of where you were this evening. But for now, I really want your take on why we find Hendrix dead hours after you saw him trying to abduct a woman."

"My take?" Hawke said. "I would say he's dead because I saw him try to abduct the woman. He opened his mouth and told his partners that I saw him and who I was. They knew it was just a matter of time before you guys swept him up and he started giving names to save his own ass. They put him down to protect themselves."

"That's pretty much what I was thinking," Roger nodded.

"You didn't need me down here for this," Hawke said. "Why am I here?"

"Come with me," Roger took his arm and turned him toward an old Acura covered with rust and primer. There was crime scene tape around the car. Its doors and rear hatch were all open. To Hawke it appeared to be another dead body. They stopped at the tape. "Recognize it?"

"No," Hawke said.

"You're kidding?" Roger said. "First time we busted Hendrix he was driving this car."

Hawke thought back about two years. The car had only been a few years old then and in good condition. Now, with the dents and dings and what little paint it had peeling, it looked like an entirely different machine. "It's in as bad a shape as its owner."

"Almost worse," Roger grinned. "Anyway, I saw it and remembered it was his. So we searched it for clues as to who may have had it out for him."

"Find anything?" Hawke asked, knowing the answer. Roger wouldn't be showing it to him otherwise.

"Just this," Roger held up a yellow folder with one gloved hand and a pair of gloves for Hawke in the other.

Hawke took the offering and slipped his hands into the latex. With that done, Roger handed him the folder. The PI opened it and skimmed the contents. It was a target package. There were schedules, dates, places. Detailed information on the target and a half-dozen photos. Four of the photos were of Maddie Rochester. The other two were of Hawke.

"He knew I would be there?" Hawke thought aloud. "I didn't even know I'd be there."

"You thought it was an abduction for ransom," Roger said. "But toward the back there are suggestions on how to kill her and where to dump her body."

"So, it was a hit?" Hawke said. "Why not just shoot her on the street?"

"Maybe whoever hired him wanted to be there," Roger suggested. "Wanted to watch."

"Or wanted something from her," Hawke said. He flipped back through the pages again stopping on the schedule. He concentrated on the blocks of time that were marked out, the times to stay away from Maddie. The schedule was almost identical to the one given to Hawke by the lawyer who hired him to follow her. He closed the folder and handed it back to Roger. "Hey. I just remembered I need to be somewhere."

"Hawke," Roger said. "I know that look, Hawke. I didn't ask you down here so you can go rogue. If you have information, you need to give it to me. Now, Hawke."

Hawke was already halfway to his truck by the time Roger gave up trying to stop him. He could hear his old partner cursing. He also heard Roger tell two officers to follow him. That made Hawke chuckle. He got into the Chevy and shut the door. Buckled in, he turned to the two officers as they were still walking to their cruiser. Hawke waved at them as he turned the key and the engine roared to life. Seconds later he was two blocks away, the cruiser just a dot in his rearview. He really liked the truck.

The first thing Hawke did was return to his apartment, parking in the back alley just in case Roger sent the officers to his place to find him. He maneuvered his furnishings in the dark, knowing exactly where everything was. He quickly gathered things he would need for a stakeout: camera, binoculars, insulated mug, some snack foods. In his closet, he changed clothes wanting to start as fresh as he could. From a safe on the closet floor he retrieved his backup weapon, shoulder holster and several clips of ammo.

Slipping out the back door, he loaded everything but the gun onto the passenger side. He needed that truck box. He also needed some things from his car and cursed himself for not getting its location out of Roger. He would have to call the department like everyone else. He put on the holster which fit too snugly, highlighting how long it had been since he had worn it and forcing him to loosen it a bit. With the gun secure, he covered it with a black leather jacket.

Twenty minutes later he was parked on the side of the street across from Maddie's home. He sat quietly, watching the house. He stayed awake as long as he could, but somewhere around 2:00 am his chin fell to his chest and he slept.

11

A knock on the driver's side window brought Hawke awake with a start. Maddie was standing in the street with a cup of coffee in her hand. Hawke gripped the handle and rolled down the window until it was lowered enough for the cup to pass through.

"Thought you could use this," Maddie said, offering the hot black liquid. "You been out here all night?"

"A while," Hawke said, pulling the cup to his lips. He blew on the surface and took a sip. It warmed his insides, but it was the flavor that struck him. "This must be expensive."

"Not cheap," she admitted. "I can get you a bag if you want."

"No," Hawke shook his head. "Thanks for this, but I don't need any more."

"Suit yourself," she said. "Why are you sleeping out here, by the way?"

"I wasn't sleeping," he said.

"I saw you," Maddie said. "You were definitely sleeping."

"Originally, I wasn't," Hawke said. "I was watching the house. Obviously, I dozed off."

"Obviously," she smiled. "Listen, I'm almost ready. Thought we could leave my car at the office while we follow Ricky."

"Ricky?" Hawke said. "You married a guy named Ricky?"

"Don't judge me," she said. "I was seduced by his charm. And his body."

"And you don't want me to judge you?" Hawke said.

"You've got me there," she said.

"Wait," Hawke cocked his head. "Your husband's name is Ricky Rochester?"

"Lord no," Maddie said. "I kept my maiden name. He's Ricky Gillihan."

"Good choice," he said. "Keeping your name."

"I'll be right back."

"What about the mug?" Hawke held up the coffee.

"I'll get it back later," she said. "When you pick me up at the office."

Hawke watched Maddie retreat to the house. He scanned the windows for a sign that her husband Ricky might be watching them but all the curtains were pulled together. Still, if they were going to use the truck to follow the man, it would be best not to be seen in front of the man's house. Hawke started the engine and coasted two houses down before stopping again. He watched Maddie's driveway in the rearview mirror and drank the coffee she had given him. He was finished minutes before the Tesla pulled into the street.

When she passed, she waved at him. He fell in behind her and followed the same path they had taken the day before to Rochester-Kinsley Incorporated. Maddie pulled into the same parking space she had a day earlier. Hawke rolled to a stop behind her and she approached the passenger side. When she opened the door, Hawke held out the empty coffee cup. She looked at the mug, then him. He did not move. Taking the mug, she pushed a button on her remote and the trunk of her car opened. She placed the mug inside and slammed the trunk closed.

She turned back to the truck and climbed in next to the PI. He drove away and steered back onto the street in the direction of Maddie's house.

"What time does he usually leave the house?" he asked.

"I don't know," she said. "I'm always at the office before he gets up."

"Where does he go?" Hawke asked. "What does he do with his time?"

"I can tell you what he doesn't do," she said. "He doesn't paint. That's what he's supposed to be doing with his time. Not that it would do any good if he did. His art is crap."

"You harboring some anger there?" Hawke asked.

"Not harboring it," she said. "I share it with anyone who will listen. He thinks he's the next Rembrandt but he never paints anything anyone would want to see."

"Did you share your views with him?" Hawke asked.

"Of course I have," she said. "We've been together for eight years. He hasn't worked a day. And no one will pay a cent for his so-called art."

"So you're resentful?"

"I guess," Maddie said. "What's with the third degree? You're treating me like I'm the bad guy here."

"Sorry," Hawke said. "Interrogation comes naturally to me."

"I understand," she said.

"It's just that last night they found the third kidnapper," Hawke said. "From the first attempt."

"That's great," Maddie smiled. "So it's over. I'm safe."

"Not sure about that," Hawke said.

"What did he say?" she asked. "Did he say why they were trying to kidnap me?"

"He didn't say anything," Hawke said. "Seems having his mask pulled off convinced his friends that he was a liability. They killed him."

"My God," she said. "But still. That means they're all dead. Why wouldn't I be safe?"

"They recovered a folder from the scene," Hawke said. "They may have been hired to kidnap you. And possibly more."

"More?" Maddie said. "What more?"

"They may have been planning to kill you," Hawke said.

"What?" her voice cracked. "Kill me? They were going to kill me?"

"Possibly," Hawke said. "We're not sure."

"But why?" she said. "Why would someone want me dead?"

"That's what we need to find out," Hawke said. "And there's something you should know."

"What?" she asked. "You mean there's more?"

"I told you I was hired by a lawyer," he said. "He gave me a packet on you. Part of the packet included a schedule with specific times I was supposed to follow you."

"I don't understand," she said.

"At the time, I thought it was because you couldn't be cheating on your husband while you're at work or with him," Hawke said. "But when Hendrix was killed, they found a packet on you just like the one the lawyer gave me. With the same times specifying when the kidnapping should occur."

"You think the lawyer arranged for my kidnapping?" Maddie said. "Why would he do that? And why would he arrange to have me followed at the same time?"

"I think I was supposed to be a reliable witness to say your husband wasn't responsible for your disappearance."

"But you saved me," she said.

"I'm guessing they didn't count on that."

"And you think my husband is behind this?"

"It seems like a good possibility," Hawke said.

"That son-of-a-bitch," Maddie cursed. "I'll kill him."

"Whoa," Hawke said. "We need proof first. So, we're going to follow him as planned. But we're not just looking for who he might be cheating with. We're looking for who he might be meeting with. Particularly if he meets with this lawyer."

"And if he does?"

"Then we call the police," Hawke said.

"I think I'd rather kill him," Maddie said.

12

Because Maddie told him that her husband did not get up early, Hawke decided to stop for coffee on the way back to the Rochester home. When they parked half a block from the house it was shortly after 7:00 am. They sat back, drank their coffee and waited.

Within fifteen minutes Maddie started tapping her fingers on her legs. She readjusted herself several times and started humming. Halfway through the tune she looked over to see Hawke staring at her.

"What?" she said.

"Your humming," Hawke said.

"Yeah," she said. "So?"

"I'd rather you didn't," he said.

Maddie sat in silence, still tapping her fingers. The almost quiet lasted about ten minutes.

"This is what you do?" she said. "Sit and watch?"

"If that's what it takes," Hawke said. "Not as glamorous as TV detectives, huh?"

"Not even close," she said. "How did you get started in PI work anyway?"

Hawke turned away and tried to drink from his coffee but found it was empty.

"Really?" Maddie said. "You can't tell me why you became a PI?"

He sighed heavily. "I was a detective."

"You are a detective," she said. "But why did you become one?"

"No," Hawke said. "I was a homicide detective."

"A homicide detective?" Maddie said. "With the police?"

Hawke nodded.

"And now you're a PI?"

He nodded again.

"Why?" Maddie asked.

"Let's just say I have issues with authority," he said.

"What did you do?"

"I struck my captain," Hawke said.

"You're kidding?" she said.

"Nope," he said. "No joke."

"Did he deserve it?"

"I think so," Hawke said. "But they didn't take that into account when they fired me."

"I guess they wouldn't," Maddie said. "So that's why you're a PI now?"

"It is," Hawke said.

They fell into an uncomfortable silence. No finger tapping. No humming. They sat, watched and waited. Hawke reached into his pocket and withdrew a pack of cigarettes.

"What are you doing?" Maddie said.

"What does it look like?"

"It looks like you're going to smoke," she said.

"That's right," Hawke said.

"With me in the car?"

" It's not a car," he said. "It's a truck. But if you insist, I can roll down the window."

"That doesn't help," Maddie said.

"It's the best I can do," Hawke said.

"You could quit," she said.

"Excuse me?"

"You know smoking will kill you," she said. "You could quit."

"Everything I enjoy is going to kill me," Hawke said. "I'm not quitting."

He stepped out of the truck, lit the cigarette and leaned against the fender while he smoked. She sat inside drumming her fingers until he was finished. He ground the butt out with his shoe then slid back into his seat. Neither of them mentioned it.

When the clock on the dash read 10:00 Hawke was beginning to doubt his decision to stop for drinks, worried the man had left during that time. Another twenty minutes ticked away before there was any sign of Ricky. The man stepped out on the front porch wearing pajama pants and a robe. He stretched and sat on a rocking chair with a coffee cup. Hawke looked at Maddie who shrugged.

"I told you," she said. "He's not a morning person."

"Which begs the question," Hawke said. "How did you end up with him? You don't seem like the starving artist type."

"I'm really not, am I?" she said.

"I don't think so," Hawke said.

"How did we end up together?" she mused. "You've probably heard stories of girls who fall for the first guy they date and marry too young to know better."

"You?" Hawke said. "I would have never guessed you were that stupid."

"Not me," she said. "God, I deplored the idea of marriage when I was young."

"Then why are you talking about it?"

"It wasn't me," she repeated. "It was my best friend, Penelope. She married her high school sweetheart. Derek was a loser who couldn't hold down a job. He liked to gamble but wasn't very good at it. He liked to cheat on Penelope and didn't try to hide it. And he liked to party, a lot. When he partied, he drank. And when he drank, he was not fun to be around. So, when he threw his parties, Penelope would invite me, because I wouldn't take his shit."

"So under all this," Hawke waved his hand, "you're a badass?"

"At one of these parties," Maddie ignored him, "Derek's cousin showed up. He was quiet. Sweet. Handsome. Charming. Nothing like Derek. Oh, and he was a painter."

"Ricky."

"I was mesmerized by the tortured artist persona," she said. "I thought I would be his muse. Mostly because he told me I would be. So I married him. Turned out it didn't really matter if I was his muse or not. What he called art, everyone else calls landfill."

"That's harsh," Hawke said.

"Don't look at me," she said. "That was an actual review of his last show. If you could call it that."

"And yet he keeps trying," he said.

"He paints nudes," Maddie said. "You can't tell that from his paintings, but that's what they are. So he has young women undress and pose for him. Now why would he want to stop? Not to mention, I'm pretty sure he sleeps with some of them."

"You wouldn't take shit from your friend's husband," Hawke observed. "Why do you take it from yours?"

"I've asked myself that many times over the years," she said. "Best I could come up with is that I hate to fail. Throughout my life, I have succeeded at everything I've done, with the exception of my marriage. And If I call it quits, I would be giving up."

"And you're no quitter," Hawke said.

"Exactly," she nodded.

Hawke searched her eyes for a moment then said, "A wise man once told me, 'sometimes the only way to win is to walk away'."

"That's strange advice," Maddie said. "Who said it?"

"It was a buddy of mine," Hawke said. "After we left the military he became an alcoholic. He said it in a bar the night he quit drinking for good. Five years sober."

"That's not the same thing."

"No. But it still applies," Hawke said. "He couldn't win drinking. The only way to win was to stop. If your marriage is as bad as it sounds, you can't win at it. You can only win by letting it go. Start a new chapter."

"Who are you?" Maddie said. "Dr. Phil?"

"You watch a lot of TV don't you?"

"I used to," she admitted. "No time anymore. Which is probably for the best."

The garage door to Maddie's house opened and a bright red Camaro backed out and down the driveway. He didn't slow until he was on the street. Ricky changed gears and drove away.

"Damn it," Maddie said. "He never closes the garage."

Hawke chuckled. He started the truck and followed their subject at a distance that would hopefully keep them off the man's radar. The task was made more difficult by Ricky's erratic driving. He made sudden lane changes, cutting off other drivers who rewarded him with blaring horns. On open stretches he accelerated well above the speed limit, displaying the power of the sports car. Hawke did his best to keep a visual on the car without drawing attention to his own. All while safely maneuvering traffic.

For Maddie's part, she did a good job of not panicking or giving driving advice. About twenty minutes from the house, Ricky steered the Camaro into a coffee shop and parked. Hawke found a space on the edge of the lot and backed in so he could observe what the man was doing. Beside him, Maddie slid down in her seat as if to hide from her husband.

"I don't think he's looking for you," Hawke said.

'I just don't want to take a chance," she said. "Why do you think he's here?"

"Coffee maybe?" Hawke suggested.

"He just had coffee at home."

"True," Hawke said. "Maybe he's meeting someone. Perhaps the lawyer."

"Or a lover," Maddie sneered.

The sun was hitting the glass front of the shop in such a way that they could not see inside. Hawke considered going inside to put eyes on Ricky and anyone he might be meeting with hen he reappeared in the doorway followed by another man. Where Ricky looked like a model or actor, the other man was rounded and tousled. He looked like a smaller version of Hawke on a really bad day, of which he had had many recently.

"Not the lawyer," he said.

"No," Maddie said. "That's Derek."

"As in Penelope's husband?"

"That's the one," she said.

The two men walked to the Camaro talking and laughing. Derek climbed into the passenger seat and they were on their way. Hawke followed, closer this time since they were obviously preoccupied with their conversation and less likely to notice a tail.

"What are they up to?" Maddie thought aloud.

"This is a wait-and-see kind of thing," Hawke said. "We'll know soon enough. No point in speculating."

Maddie sighed and folded her arms across her chest. Waiting was not one of her top skills. They followed for another ten minutes until they pulled into the driveway of a home in a modest middle-class neighborhood. They exited the car and entered the house.

"You know this place?" Hawke asked.

"Penelope's," she said. "Ricky brought him home."

Hawke parked down the street and the two of them adjusted themselves to watch and wait yet again. Hawke stepped out of the truck and smoked a cigarette while Maddie hid inside. Returning to the truck he sat back to observe. It was only a few minutes before Maddie broke the silence.

"Your job is really boring," she said.

"Why do you think our rates are so high?" Hawke replied.

"Seriously," Maddie said. "It's like waiting for a toaster to pop. Only worse because a toaster does pop eventually."

"He'll come out eventually," Hawke said.

"That's not my point," she said.

"I know what your point is," he said. "And it's true. I used to do stakeouts to catch criminals doing crimes, to gather evidence. It took time, sometimes days. But in the end I knew I was going to put some piece of trash for a human being behind bars. This, I don't know what I'm going to get, if anything."

"Boring," Maddie reiterated.

"And what do you do?" Hawke asked. "What makes your job less boring?"

"I co-founded and run a company that develops software, apps and designs websites for clients worldwide," she said. "Last year our sales reached thirty million."

"Jesus," Hawke whistled. "That is a bit more than what I do. It must be very fulfilling to have accomplished so much."

"It is," she said. "At least it was."

"Was?" Hawke turned to her. "You bored with that too?"

"Don't get me wrong," she said. "I love my job, my company. But some days I think I might like to do something new."

"Like what?" Hawke asked.

"That's the million-dollar question," she said.

"What would you do with the company?"

"We had an offer," she said. "But it wasn't right. I'm sure we could find another if I decided to sell."

"You said co-founder," Hawke said. "Wouldn't the other founder have a say?"

"If he didn't want to sell," she said. "I could just sell my interest. It would almost be better that way. I would want to be sure the buyer wants the company as it is, with the people. I don't want anyone losing their livelihood. He would protect them."

The rest of the day was filled with small talk as they sat watching Maddie's best friend's house. It was nearing 6:00 pm when Ricky finally exited and the two of them followed him back to the Rochester home.

"God that was awful," Maddie said.

"And better yet," Hawke smiled. "We get to do it all over again tomorrow. That is, if you're still going to tag along."

"I am," she said. "What now?"

"Now we're done for the day," Hawke said. "I'll take you to get your car so you can go home and get some rest."

"I'm not going home," she said. "If that man hired someone to kill me, I'm not sleeping under the same roof. I'll get a hotel room."

"Won't he wonder where you are?"

"I'll call him and tell him I have to work late," she said. "I stay at the office a lot when we have deadlines."

"Fine," Hawke said. "I'll follow and make sure you get checked in."

13

With Maddie in the hotel, Hawke decided to take advantage of the alone time to recover his things from his car. He sat in his truck in the hotel parking lot and dug in his pocket for his phone. He found Roger's name and pressed call. His old partner answered on the third ring.

"What do you want?" Roger said.

"Geez," Hawke said. "You really know how to make a guy feel welcome."

"I don't have time for your shit," Roger said. "Do you need something? Or should I hang up?"

"I'm trying to find my car," Hawke said. "I need to clean it out."

"Call the impound number," Roger said.

"You know what a pain that is," Hawke said. "You can find it a lot faster than I can."

There was a sigh followed by the sound of typing. "Lot B."

"Is that the one on Parker?" Hawke asked.

"Look it up," Roger said. The call went dead.

Hawke looked at his phone to be sure the detective had indeed hung up on him. He chuckled to himself and started searching for impound lot B. He had been right. It was on Parker. Shoving the phone back in his pocket, he started the truck and pulled out of the hotel parking lot headed north. Fifteen minutes later he rolled up to the fence, searching the lot for his car. He spotted it among a line of wrecks.

"I'm here to clean out my car," Hawke said when he got to the counter.

"Name, make, model and color of the car," the uninterested woman said.

"Sebastian Hawke," he said. "Brown Ford Taurus. Was brought in yesterday."

"The front-end damage," she said. "We've got it."

"I know," Hawke said. "I saw it on my way in."

"Need to see identification," she said.

Hawke pulled his wallet and showed her his license. She held the corner to steady it and looked from him to it and back again.

"You've put on a few pounds," she observed.

"Thanks for noticing," he said. "Can I clean it out or what?"

"Sure," she said. "Right through that door. It'll be unlocked."

Hawke started to push through the door but turned back. "Do you have a box?"

She looked at him without expression.

"Okay, then. Thanks," Hawke said. He stepped through the door and into the yard. At the car he started sorting through the contents. He made two piles; one of things to keep and the other of things to leave behind. A box wasn't needed after all.

He pulled the trunk release and stepped to the back of the car. Inside were two cases containing the various tools of the trade he had selected based on his years in law enforcement. It humored him that with the number of items he had gathered, a camera had not made the list. As a detective, the department sent a photographer to document crime scenes.

Hawke took the cases out of the trunk and shut the lid again. He started to walk back to the office when he remembered the file on Maddie. He returned to the car and searched the front seat and floorboard. There was no file. It seemed to be the only thing missing. He would have to remember later to ask Roger if it had been taken for evidence.

He loaded the cases into the back of the truck and turned his attention to dinner. Lighting a cigarette he drove toward the business district in search of a restaurant. He chose a national chain geared more toward families. They made a good burger and that was what he was in the mood for. He sat in the parking lot watching patrons come and go while he finished his smoke.

Inside he was greeted by the odor of grilling meats and a hostess that was a little too perky for his taste. He followed her through the dining room to a small booth. He shook his head and pointed to a full-sized booth in the corner. She hesitated, and while she was deciding what to do he walked the extra steps and sat himself. The hostess's bubbly personality returned as she quickly closed the distance and handed him a menu. He gave her a half-smile and set the menu aside. He pulled out his phone, checked that he had no messages and laid it next to the menu. He closed his eyes for a moment and when he opened them a waitress was standing next to the table.

"Hi, hon," she smiled. "I'm Bridget. Can I get you something to drink?"

"I'll take a classic cheeseburger, medium, everything on it," he said. "Fries and a dark ale."

"Okay, hon," she said picking up the unopened menu. "I'll put it in."

Hawke scanned the dining room watching families interact over their meals. They fell into three categories. There were those whose heads were bent over their smartphones scrolling through social media or exchanging text messages with people not at the dinner table. Others sat silently chewing their food, looking as though they would prefer being anywhere but where they were and who they were with. The remainder appeared to be enjoying friendly conversations and the occasional laugh. This last group appeared to be genuinely happy.

Hawke wondered if he would ever find someone he could settle down with and have a family. If he did, would they be truly happy? Or would that just be something they told each other? He had a girl before he joined the military. They had exchanged the words, made the promises. Serve his country, save some money, return to her and start a life together. It was a plan and it lasted almost six months. That was how long it took for her to fall for some guy she met at college. Truth be told, it was better that way. The military changed him and he would never have returned to her. Better she didn't wait four years to find out.

He heard she was a nurse, married with a couple kids. He was happy for her. He wondered, if they crossed paths at some point, would they recognize one another. For all he knew, she could be sitting in this very restaurant.

A wail drew his attention to the right where a three or four-year-old boy was bawling his eyes out. The boy's mother was speaking to him in a hushed voice while the father ate his meal without a glance at the child. The screaming stopped abruptly and the boy nodded his small head, tears still streaming down his cheeks. Whatever promise or threat she had made had struck home.

He did give marriage a try. Twice. The first time was Sonia, a woman he met while in the military. They met at a bar in the small town where he was stationed. Everything happened so fast. She was looking for a way out of that small town. He was looking for a way not to be lonely. And it worked for a year or so. Then came the diagnosis, something to do with the large industrial plant upstream dumping chemicals. They had worked their way through the soil and into her hometown's water supply. The sickness was swift and deadly. A quarter of the town ended up in the hospital within two years. About half of them never came out, including Hawke's wife.

The second go-round was just after he left the military. Linda was like a breath of fresh air. Until she wasn't.

Bridget set his drinks in front of him and moved on without slowing, a tray filled with glasses and appetizers balanced on one arm. Hawke lifted the ale to his lips and sipped the dark liquid. Deeming it worthy, he tilted the glass and downed about half its contents. Maybe he had more than two vices.

Losing interest in the other patrons, he tapped his phone and started searching the news feeds for something to read. He was halfway through a story about the financial woes of the city when Bridget appeared again with his burger and fries. She flashed him a smile and asked him to check the doneness. He obliged, assured her it was correct and ordered another ale.

He took a large bite and was savoring the flavors of meat cheese and condiments when the headlights of a car parking outside the window to his left washed across his face. The years he had spent in the military and as a cop had trained him to be fully aware of his surroundings, so motion always got his attention. He glanced out as the headlights went dark and saw a black car with the BMW logo on the hood.

The lawyer stepped out of the car and walked down the sidewalk, at a leisurely relaxed pace, toward the entrance. Hawke wondered what the odds were of this man coming to this restaurant at this time. He could be meeting with a client, another investigator, or any number of other persons. One thing Hawke was sure of, the man was not here to eat. There was no way this place was anywhere the lawyer would choose to have dinner.

Hawke downed the last of his ale just as Bridget dropped off the next. He thanked her, never taking his eyes off the lawyer as the man stepped inside. Bypassing the hostess, the lawyer moved into the dining room with the same confidence he had demonstrated when Hawke first met him. It was obvious to Hawke by then that the man was coming straight toward him.

"Mind if I join you?" the lawyer said, sitting across from the PI before he could answer.

Hawke sat with his burger in hand, his eyes locked onto the lawyer's.

Reaching across the table, the lawyer snatched a fry from Hawke's plate and popped it into his mouth. He chewed briefly before swallowing. He said, "Those things will kill you, you know."

Hawke took another large bite of his burger and took his time with it.

"You may wonder why I'm here," the lawyer said.

Hawke swallowed. "The thought had crossed my mind."

"You see," the lawyer said, "I'm confused. I paid you a retainer toward a contract of your services and you haven't delivered."

"It's only been two days," Hawke said. "I can't force her to cheat on her husband."

"But instead of following Mrs. Rochester to get compromising photos," the lawyer said, "you rescue her. Twice."

"Is that a bad thing?" Hawke asked.

"And now," the lawyer continued, "instead of following her at all, you are riding around with her, following her husband, your client."

Hawke narrowed his eyes. The only way for the lawyer to know what he was doing was if the man was having him or the woman followed. Hawke didn't like either possibility. Either the lawyer never trusted that Hawke would do his job or there was something else going on.

"I'll tell you what," Hawke said, his voice low and menacing. "I'll keep the retainer as full payment for the two days' work. You keep the rest and consider our agreement finished. Then you get your ass out of that seat and your face out of my sight."

The lawyer's confident demeanor faltered. As he stood he said, "Tell Mrs. Rochester I hope she enjoys her stay at the Ritz. I hear it's quite lovely."

Hawke watched the lawyer leave and used his phone to snap a picture of the man's license plate as he drove away. Taking the shot through the window in the dark resulted in a distorted image that only revealed a partial number.

He ate the rest of his meal as quickly as he could without choking and ignored the rest of the ale, a damn waste if ever there was one. He caught the waitress for his ticket and paid her in cash.

The lawyer knew that Maddie had been with him all day and where she was staying. Someone was reporting back to him, someone who had been there to witness both kidnapping attempts, someone who watched them watching Ricky. And Hawke never saw them.

As he was climbing into his truck to leave, it occurred to him that the lawyer knew where he was dining. It wasn't Maddie being followed. It was him.

14

As Hawke drove to the hotel where Maddie was staying he watched every car on the road, looking for a tail. Either there wasn't one, or whoever was following him was very good. If they were that good, they were pros, which gave Hawke pause. Why hire a PI to follow your wife to get compromising pictures then hire another professional to follow the PI? Why not have the latter do the job in the first place?

Hawke pulled into the parking lot and chose a spot where he had a clear view of both the main and the side entrances. He lit a cigarette and sat back, watching for anyone who didn't belong. Every person approaching the door he scrutinized with a cop's eyes. How much luggage were they carrying? How many people were they with? Did they look around too much? How were they dressed? What were they driving? Did they tip the valet?

There was no way of knowing who might be a true threat unless they pulled out a gun and attached a silencer right in front of him. There was no way to keep Maddie one hundred percent safe. Anyone entering the parking lot Hawke saw as a potential threat.

He took out his phone and called Roger. He only had to wait a couple of rings for the detective to answer.

"What do you want, Hawke?" the aggravated man said.

"What are you so pissed about?" Hawke asked.

"This is my family time, if you must know," Roger snapped. "Why are you bothering me at home?"

"Didn't know you were at home," Hawke said. "I just have a quick question."

"Nothing is quick with you," Roger grumbled. "What is it?"

"When they impounded my car," Hawke said. "Did they take a folder out of it?"

"A folder? What folder?"

"The moron that hired me gave me a file on Maddie," Hawke replied. "Photos, addresses, dates and times. It wasn't in my car when I went to clean it out."

"So you found your car?" Roger said. "I didn't even have to draw you a map."

"Screw you, Rog," Hawke said. "Did they take the folder or not?"

"This is the first I'm hearing of it," Roger said. "So, I'm guessing not. A file that made it appear you were stalking the woman would definitely have been brought to my attention."

"Where the hell did it go then?" Hawke asked. "Thing's been in impound since the incident."

"The incident where you shot two men?"

"Two armed men in the process of an attempted kidnapping."

"That's why you aren't in jail," Roger said.

"Fact is," Hawke said. "The folder was in my car when I rammed that van. Then the car was taken to impound. And now it's gone."

"Did you check under the seats?" Roger asked. "Maybe it fell during the crash."

"Yes," Hawke said. "I checked under the seats, between the seats. It wasn't in the car."

"Maybe you took it out without remembering," Roger said.

"I'm not senile," Hawke said. "I would remember if I took it out."

"You sure?" Roger said. "You are getting up there."

"I'm thirty-two," Hawke said.

"Really?" Roger said. "You really should take better care of yourself. I thought you were around forty."

"We were partners for over two years," Hawke said. "You didn't know how old I was?"

"Never cared," Roger said. "And on that note, I don't care about your folder either. I'm getting back to my family."

Roger hung up and Hawke brought up the internet, searching for articles to read while he waited. There was one about the shooting in the park. The few details provided were vague. It was good to know the police department could still keep a secret. There was also a small story about the attempted abduction the day before. No connection was made between the two crimes.

A little past eleven he made a perimeter check, walking around the free-standing building as if he worked security for the hotel. He checked the side doors to be sure they were locked as the sign on the glass promised they would be at that hour. Satisfied Maddie was as safe as she was going to be, he returned to his truck and drove home for some much-needed sleep.

Six and a half hours later he was back, this time parking in the closest available parking space and entering the lobby. His clothes wrinkled from sleeping in them, he was greeted with disapproving glares and disgusted looks from hotel guests. He scowled at them until they turned away. At the front desk a man in business attire, reminding Hawke of the lawyer, was arguing with the clerk about the charges on his room. The clerk, a young woman, was holding her own and only offered a cursory glance in Hawke's direction as he passed.

He rounded the corner toward the elevators and stepped into one behind a woman in athletic wear and a towel around her neck. She pushed the button for the fourth floor, same as Maddie's, and stood staring at the doors as they closed. Hawke moved to the back of the car and leaned against the wall admiring the woman's athletic build, wondering if she hit the gym every morning. He could not remember the last time he had stepped inside one.

The doors opened and Hawke followed the woman out and down the hall to their left. He noticed her glancing over her shoulder and slowed to allow her the space to feel secure that he was not stalking her. The woman's room, 416, shared an alcove with Maddie's, 418, so Hawke continued down the hall until she was safely inside before doubling back. A man his size, looking the way he did, in a fancy hotel was sure to make some people nervous.

He knocked on Maddie's door and waited. When he got no response, he knocked again, more forcefully. The door to room 416 opened, with the safety bar thrown. The woman peered out through the gap. Hawke gave her a grin and nod, and knocked on Maddie's door again. The woman closed the door as Maddie opened hers.

"Oh, Mr. Hawke," Maddie said. "Come in."

She pulled the door open and let Hawke enter. She wore a fluffy white robe and a matching towel wrapped around her head. Hawke stopped mid-stride. "You want me to wait downstairs?"

"Don't be ridiculous," Maddie smiled. "There's plenty of room. Make yourself comfortable and I'll be right out."

She turned and vanished through a door leading to the bedroom suite. Hawke stood in a sitting room with a desk and chair tucked into one corner. He guessed that one night's stay in the room probably cost a month's rent at his apartment. He crossed to the couch and sat facing the entrance.

When Maddie reappeared, she wore dark jeans and a black turtleneck. She was brushing her red hair in long deliberate strokes. Hawke stood and watched.

"How are things, detective?" she asked.

"Just call me Hawke, ma'am," he said. "I'm no longer a detective."

"Okay, Hawke," she said. "How are things?"

He held her gaze for a moment trying to decide how to answer the question. "The lawyer, the one your husband had hire me, paid me a visit last night."

"What did he want?"

"Wanted to know why I wasn't doing what he paid me to do," Hawke said. "Which was a legitimate question."

"But?"

"But he knew you had been with me yesterday," Hawke said. "He knew where to find me last night. And he knew that you were staying here."

"How?"

"My best guess is that he has someone following me," he said. "But I never saw a tail. Even after I started looking for one."

"Then me?"

"Following you wouldn't have told him where I was having dinner last night," Hawke said.

"So what do we do?"

"I assume he's warned your husband that we're following him," Hawke said. "It's unlikely he'll be doing anything, um, embarrassing."

"You're saying we shouldn't follow him anymore?"

"I didn't say that," Hawke said. "But we may want to wait a day or two. Give him a chance to think we stopped watching him."

"Then I guess I'm going to work," Maddie said.

"You think that's a good idea?" Hawke said. "Following your regular routine makes it easy to find you, assuming they haven't given up."

"I have to do something," she said. "You want to come with me? You can be my bodyguard. I'll even buy you lunch."

"How could I say no to that?"

"Let me change real fast," she smiled, retreating to the bedroom.

True to her word she was back out in a matter of minutes. This time she wore a grey suit with the same black turtleneck. She was carrying the briefcase she took to her lunch meeting. Hawke caught a glimpse of his own attire in a mirror behind her. She looked like a million bucks. He looked like pocket change.

"I should take you shopping," Maddie said, apparently reading his mind. Or maybe just speaking her own.

"No. You shouldn't," Hawke said. "You ready?"

"I don't look ready?" She turned to the mirror, checking herself at different angles. "What's wrong?"

"Let's go," he said. "Sooner we get you there, sooner you can get done and I get you somewhere safe."

"Somewhere safe?" Maddie said. "Where in the world would that be?"

"I'll think of something," he said.

They left the room and walked side by side down the hallway to the elevators. Pressing the down button, Hawke stood slightly in front of her as they waited for the car to arrive. The doors started opening and his hand moved to his sidearm. The elevator was empty. He let out the breath he hadn't realized he was holding and waved Maddie inside.

A busy time of the morning, the elevator stopped at the third and second floors on the way down. Both times Hawke posed ready to defend his charge. Both times hotel patrons stood ready to enter and take the ride down. Hawke refused them.

"Was that necessary?" Maddie asked after the doors closed the second time.

"Yes," he answered, offering no further explanation.

"Are you sure you don't want to go back up and frisk them?" she said. "That six-year-old looked especially menacing."

Hawke turned to her. She was grinning. He said, "Six-year-olds are devious indeed."

The elevator reached the lobby and Hawke turned his attention back to the doors as they opened, one hand on his weapon. It takes less than two seconds for elevator doors to open. In that time, Hawke assessed the situation in the lobby. As with the other two floors, there was someone waiting to enter, a man of muscular build in casual attire. The jeans were new, the button-down starched. A loose-fitting jacket completed the ensemble.

As the doors completed their motion, Hawke glanced down at military-style boots. His head snapped up and his eyes locked on the man's as they shifted from Maddie to him. Simultaneously their arms raised, pistols at the ready. Maddie screamed.

The doors started to close and the man in the lobby kicked a foot forward to block it. "What gave me away?"

"Boots," Hawke said.

"Figures," the man said. "Whatcha gonna do?"

Hawke's eyes narrowed, focusing on the man's face. "Woodrow? Is that you?"

The man stared at the PI's face trying to see through the stubble. "Lieutenant? I heard you were a cop. Why are you doing private security?"

"Long story," Hawke said. "What's it been? six years?"

"Eight," the man said.

"Really?" Hawke said. He motioned toward the other's gun. "What are you doing man?"

"My transition to civilian life wasn't as smooth as yours, sir," Woodrow said. "A man's got to eat."

"But a hired gun?"

"They trained me to be a killer," Woodrow said. "It's what I'm good at."

"You're good at killing unarmed women?" Hawke said.

"I don't choose the target," he said. "I get a name and location. She's supposed to be alone in her room upstairs."

"Sorry to disappoint," Hawke said. "What now?"

"I'm not going through you, sir," Woodrow said. "Just a warning. They'll send someone else."

"Who?" Hawke said. "Who are they?"

They heard sirens in the distance and Woodrow shrugged. "Gotta go."

He pulled his boot back and let the elevator doors slide shut. Hawke hit the open button and the doors obeyed, exposing the lobby again. Woodrow was gone.

Hawke looked back at Maddie who had made herself small in the corner of the car. Tears had ruined her makeup. He offered her a hand and helped her to her feet.

"I changed my mind," Hawke said. "Let's go find your husband."

15

They arrived at the Rochester home just as Ricky was backing down the driveway. Hawke slowed to allow the man time to pull into the street. At about two car lengths, he followed the sports car as it sped through the neighborhood. Ricky did not turn toward the coffee shop as he had the day before, nor did he take the route that would lead him to Derek's house. Instead, he turned south toward the river district.

The river district was made up of small businesses and restaurants, mostly local. It was also home to museums, art galleries and historical landmarks. It was a popular area for tourists and therefore had several hotels overlooking the water.

It was to one of those hotels that Ricky steered his Camaro. He parked on the street in front and bounded into the lobby. Hawke parked a half a block away.

"Looks like someone's in a hurry," he observed.

"That asshole," Maddie said. "I knew it."

"Wait a minute," Hawke said. "Could be he's having breakfast here. Or meeting with someone. You said he's an artist. Could be a buyer."

Maddie gave Hawke a look that suggested he might be insane. He said, "You wait here. I'll go in and see if he's in the lobby or dining room. If not, then we can jump to conclusions."

"I'm not waiting in the car," Maddie opened her door.

"Maddie," Hawke put a hand on her arm. She pulled away but stayed in the vehicle staring at him. "If this turns out to be innocent, you could cause irreparable damage to your relationship. Remember the lawyer knows we are following him.

So odds are he knows. Why would he chance a romp in the hay if he knows we might catch him?"

"The damage to our relationship occurred the minute he hired you to follow me," Maddie said. "And he sent someone to my hotel to kill me. As for the rest, he may just be that stupid. Did you think of that?"

She exited the truck and slammed the door. Hawke climbed out and followed her to the hotel entrance. As they neared the building, it occurred to Hawke that if her husband knew he was being followed he may be luring Maddie into a trap. With that in mind, he did something that was against every part of his being. He jogged. Only for the short distance to catch up to her before she entered, but jogging is jogging.

He opened the door and stepped into the lobby, scanning the occupants as he had from the elevator in her hotel. There was no immediate threat, but any of the dozen or so people he saw there could easily be a hired killer, with the exception of the toddler who stood at the front desk with his arms wrapped around his mother's leg. Hawke quickly ruled out the mother as well, hoping an assassin wouldn't bring her kid to work. Ricky was nowhere to be seen.

Maddie did not slow as she barged through the open space, clearly determined to get what she wanted. Hawke fell into pace with her and followed. She rounded a corner and stopped so suddenly that Hawke ran into her. Ricky was standing in front of the elevators. Hawke managed to step around his client and block her from view just as her husband turned their way. The PI nodded at the man who turned away when the elevator doors opened.

Stepping inside, Ricky put an arm out to keep the doors from closing and looked back at Hawke. "You going up?"

"No thanks," Hawke said.

Ricky and his arm disappeared inside.

"You let him get away," Maddie swatted at Hawke's back.

Ignoring her, he stepped up to the elevator and watched the small panel above tick off the floors as it ascended. When it reached the seventh floor, it stopped. With a quick glance at Maddie, he pressed the up button and waited. It was only a few seconds before the other elevator opened. Hawke took a step forward and then back again to allow an elderly couple to exit. Once they were clear he and Maddie stepped into the car. Hawke pressed the seven and they rode up.

The two of them stood side by side in silence until the doors opened. As had become his habit, Hawke moved to shield Maddie from any threat. The hallway was empty.

Cautiously, Hawke stepped out with Maddie right behind him. According to the plaque on the wall, the seventh floor had twenty-two rooms, ten to the left and twelve to the right. There was no sign of anyone on the floor.

"What now?" Hawke said.

"We need to know which room he's in," Maddie stated the obvious.

"And how do we do that?" Hawke said.

Maddie looked up and down the hall, her eyes landing on the small red box on the wall opposite her.

"No," Hawke followed her gaze. "We're not doing that."

"It would work," she insisted.

"It's illegal," Hawke said.

"Then we knock on every door until we find him," she said.

"I'm not doing that either," he said. He stared down the hall for a moment. "I have an idea. Go halfway down the hall in that direction and wait."

"Wait for what?"

"Just go," he said.

She hesitated but eventually turned and moved to the place he had indicated. He turned the other direction and walked halfway down the other hall. There, he pulled out his phone, searched for the hotel's phone number and pressed call. It rang twice before being answered.

"Riverside Hotel," the woman said. "How may I help you?"

"Can you ring Ricky Gillihan's room please?" he said.

"Just a moment," she said. Her voice was replaced by ringing.

Hawke held the phone away from his ear and listened. He didn't hear anything but he saw Maddie turn her head sharply then move toward one of the rooms. He walked back down the hall to where she stood staring at the door to room 722.

"Hello?" Ricky's voice came through Hawke's phone. "Hello? Who is this?"

Hawke disconnected the call. "How do you want to play this?"

Maddie stepped forward and pounded on the door with her fist. She waited a couple of seconds then began again. The door flung open.

"What do you want?" Ricky demanded. He stood in the doorway shirtless, a towel wrapped around his waist. When he saw Maddie his jaw dropped. His eyes became ping pong balls with irises. "Maddie?"

She pushed past him into the room. Hawke followed, taking Ricky by the arm as he went. Inside Maddie stood at the end of the bed gazing on the woman whom her husband was there to screw. "Penelope?"

"Maddie?" her best friend said. "Let me explain."

"Explain?" Maddie shrieked. "Explain what? You're sleeping with my husband, Penelope. How can you possibly explain that?"

"Maddie," Ricky said, "it's not what you think."

"So, you're not screwing my best friend?" she turned on her husband. "What? You're planning a surprise party for me? Naked?"

"I just," he started. "I mean . . ."

"What I don't get," Maddie said, "is why you would hire someone to follow me. To get pictures of me cheating on you. When you're the one cheating."

"I what?" Ricky said.

"And when you find out we're following you," she continued, "you still meet up with . . . with her."

"What are you talking about?" Ricky said. "Hired who to follow you?"

"You hired a lawyer who hired Hawke to follow me," she said.

"Hawke? Who's Hawke?" he said.

"That would be me," Hawke said.

"And a lawyer?" Ricky said. "I didn't hire a lawyer. Or anyone for that matter."

"You didn't hire anyone to kill me?" she asked.

"Kill you?" he stepped back. "God, no. Why would I do that?"

"You didn't hire a lawyer?" Hawke said.

"No," he shook his head. "I wouldn't. I couldn't. I love you, Maddie."

"What?" Penelope said. "What do you mean you love her? You said you were tired of her. You said you loved me."

Ricky looked at Penelope and then Maddie. His jaw moved but no sound emerged. The panic-stricken man made Hawke smile.

"Apparently he lies to everyone, Penelope," Maddie said.

"I just," Ricky said.

"Save it," Maddie snapped. "You may not have hired a lawyer, but I suggest you do. I want you out of my house by the end of the day."

"It's our house," Ricky said.

"Not anymore," she said.

"Where am I going to go?" he whined.

"I don't know?" Maddie turned to Penelope. "Maybe you can call your buddy Derek and see if he'll let you stay with him."

"Maddie, I'm sorry," Penelope said.

"You deserve each other," Maddie threw up her hands and walked out of the room.

Hawke stood there a moment longer then followed his client.

"You know what this means, don't you?" Hawke said as they stepped onto the elevator.

"I'm getting a divorce," Maddie said.

"Besides that," Hawke said. "If Ricky didn't hire the mystery lawyer, someone else did. And someone else wants you dead."

"Oh, God," she said. "I didn't think about that."

"You have any enemies, Maddie?"

"I guess I do," she said. "But I have no idea who."

"You need to think," Hawke said. "Someone is angry enough to want you dead. Who have you wronged? Who did you screw over in a business deal? Who have you fired lately? What competitor have you put out of business?"

"Jesus, Hawke," Maddie said. "I just found out that my husband has been sleeping with my best friend. This is all too much."

"I know," Hawke said. "And I'm sorry. I will protect you as well as I can. But it would be a lot easier if we could identify who is doing this and put a stop to them."

"I can't think right now," she said. "Can we do this tomorrow?"

"I don't think we should wait," he said. She looked up at him, her eyes welled, the confidence missing. "Okay. Fine. But tomorrow we go at this hard."

"Okay," she said. "I promise."

The doors opened to the lobby and Hawke scanned the area. No one appeared to be watching. No one seemed to be out of place. He gestured to her to go and they walked out together. Leaving the building, Hawke searched the street.

The first thing to catch his eye was a man sitting in a pickup, facing their general direction. As he neared he saw the man was not facing them at all. He was asleep. Second, he saw two men sitting in a black sedan. Unlike the sleeping driver, they were watching intently. Hawke led Maddie to his truck and opened the door for her. Once seated he rolled her window down a crack before shutting it. He said, "Wait here."

"Hawke?" she was suddenly alert. "Where are you going?"

"Just wait here," he repeated. "I'll be right back."

He changed directions, walking straight for the black sedan. He put his hand inside his jacket, resting it on his weapon. As he neared, he heard the engine start. When he was about ten feet away, the car sped off. He had been right. They were following him. But he had been extra careful. He had watched for tails and never saw anyone. Yet here they were.

He walked back to the truck, slowing as he came closer. They weren't following him. They were following his truck. It was too old school to have a GPS to hack. He walked around the vehicle reaching under bumpers and wheel wells. Above the right rear tire he found the magnetic tracking device. He pulled it off and walked to the driver's side. As he did, a furniture truck was slowing for a red light. He reached out and attached the tracking device to the truck box.

"We need to get you somewhere safe," he said.

"Where?"

"Somewhere I know," he said. "Somewhere I can control the environment."

"Where?" she asked again.

"It's a step down from the suite you were in last night," he said.

"Are you going to tell me where?" she asked.

"My place," he said. "It's not much, but I can protect you there."

"Okay," she said.

"I think it's our best option for tonight," he said.

"I said, okay," she said.

He started the truck and pulled into traffic behind the furniture truck. He followed it for about a mile before steering away. "You need anything?"

"Something to eat," she said.

"Oh, I know just the place," he smiled.

88

16

The Uptown Deli was crowded and loud. The owners, the Spiros, were boisterous and friendly, the type of people who never met a stranger. "At least no one stranger than me," the husband, George, would say. They had founded the establishment in their early thirties. They had college degrees and high paying jobs, but were as unhappy as they had ever been in their lives. They would eat often at the pizza joint that occupied the space before them. When that establishment closed due to the owner's health issues, they joked about taking it over. For almost a year they would walk by the empty building and talk about what they would do with the place. Then another pizza restaurant opened across the street and they stopped talking about it. After another six months and a particularly bad day they walked by again. This time George stopped and stared at the dark storefront window. "This place needs a good deli," he said. That was nearly twenty years ago.

Hawke pushed the front door open and guided Maddie through. A chime above the door announced their arrival and a man's booming voice called out, "Welcome to Uptown."

George never raised his head as he was busy creating the next customer's desired sandwich. His wife, Margarete, was talking to a woman over the counter while her hands moved quickly to finish the order she was preparing. She glanced toward Hawke and Maddie and her face lit up. She did not, however, miss a beat in the conversation she was having.

Stepping to the end of the line, Hawke turned to Maddie, "You're in for a treat."

Maddie took in everything around her and inhaled. "They just do sandwiches. Right?"

The man ahead of them in line snickered.

"Oh, Maddie," Hawke said. "They no more just do sandwiches than Picasso just paints."

It was Maddie's turn to snicker. "You're telling me their sandwiches are works of art?"

"Exactly."

"And you're comparing them to Picasso?"

"I am."

"Well, this I have to try," she said.

The line moved forward at a steady pace as satisfied customers left with their purchases. An almost exact number of new patrons entered and cued up behind them. Maddie watched the couple interact with each person as they took and prepared the orders. She was amazed with the ease at which the two owners spoke to every person as if they had been friends for years.

In some instances it seemed that was the case. The couple would greet people with their names and ask questions about family, friends and jobs. It was like walking into a family reunion. When Hawke and Maddie reached the front of the line, Margarete beamed.

"Detective Hawke," she said. "What do you want today? Who is your friend? Why do you bring her here and not to a nice restaurant?"

"Are you with Detective Hawke?" George said to Maddie. "He must really like you. He's never brought anyone in before. What do you like? I'll make you something special."

"I've told you," Hawke said, "I'm not a detective anymore."

"All those questions," Margarete said, "and that's what I get from you?"

"You have your work cut out for you with that one," George said to Maddie.

"Do I now?" she smiled.

"Ignore them," Hawke said. "We're here for lunch. Nothing more."

They placed their orders and paid. On their way out, the couple wished them well and suggested Maddie return again soon.

Out on the sidewalk Maddie sighed. "How is it they know you so well? It seemed like you must come nearly every day."

Hawke opened a door next to the deli revealing a stairwell. "This way."

They climbed. At the top was another door, this one with frosted glass and no markings. Hawke produced a keyring, thumbed through until he found the right one and unlocked the door. Holding it open, he allowed Maddie to enter before him, following closely. He pulled the door shut behind them, sliding the deadbolt back into place.

"Welcome to my office," he said. The space was barren. A rickety chair stood behind a desk at an angle that suggested it might fall at any moment. The desk, faded and stained wood, held a lamp, a computer and a stapler. Facing it were two more chairs, worn from use. Hawke set his food on the desk and directed Maddie to one of the two chairs. He circled the desk and sat heavily in the one facing her.

"Your office is above their deli?" Maddie said.

"To be fair," Hawke said. "I was eating there long before I took the office."

She took in the bare walls and the only other piece of furniture in the room, a tall metal file cabinet. "How long have you been here?"

"A couple months maybe," Hawke said, unwrapping his sandwich.

Maddie scooted to the front of the chair and mimicked his motions to free her lunch from its wrappings. "This isn't the safe place you were telling me about is it?"

"No," Hawke said. "I thought we could spend some time here while I try to figure out who our lawyer friend is."

He took a bite of his sandwich and closed his eyes to savor the flavor before turning to his computer. He pulled out his phone, opened the photo gallery and selected the picture he had taken of the lawyer's BMW the night before. He logged into the license plate database and entered what information he had; partial plate, make, model and color of the car. Hitting the enter button, he reached for his sandwich.

He was still chewing when his search spit out two hundred twenty-nine possible matches. He let out a long, exasperated sigh. At his best he could follow up with a dozen or so a day. The list on his screen would take all month. And he hadn't been at his best for some time.

"I can't get over the fact your office is above a deli," Maddie said.

She set her sandwich down and stood. Moving to the window she admired the colors of the waning rays of sunlight against the sky. Her face was aglow with the neon yellow of the business sign mounted just below the sill. Hawke was to his feet in seconds, moving swiftly to usher her away from the glass, saying, "You shouldn't be standing there."

He turned and stared out onto the street. He searched the scene below for anyone who appeared to be out of place. From his vantage point he could see nearly everything outside. Of the dozen or so faces, none stood out.

"Do you think they know we're here?" Maddie asked.

"I don't know," he said. "But I prefer to be cautious. Their original plan was to kidnap you. I assume I was to be the witness that would say it wasn't your husband because I was hired to get pictures for a divorce. After nabbing you they would demand an unreasonable amount and make negotiations a nightmare. When an agreement couldn't be reached, you would be killed. When I interfered with that plan, they switched to a more direct approach. Woodrow was there to kill you in your hotel room. No more subtleties. I don't want them taking a shot at you through the window."

"I don't want that either," she said. "But what are we going to do? I can't hide forever."

"Which is why I'm going to find the lawyer," Hawke returned to his desk.

"And how is that going?"

"I have it narrowed down to two hundred twenty-nine potentials," he said.

"So not well?"

"Not yet," he said. His fingers moved over the keyboard and he struck enter again. "Removing the female owners brings us to one hundred thirty-two."

"What other filters do you have?" Maddie said, pulling a chair to the side of the desk.

"White males," he said. A few keystrokes and he said, "Seventy-four."

"What about age?"

"Okay," Hawke said. "Eliminate anyone under thirty and anyone over, let's say, fifty."

"You were a cop," she said. "You can't narrow it down any more than that?"

"Fine," he said. "Under thirty and over forty-five."

"Better."

"That leaves us with thirty-eight," Hawke said.

"That's doable," Maddie smiled.

"That's still a lot of names to follow up on," Hawke said.

"Then I guess we better get started," she said.

17

Hawke printed the list of names and addresses using a pen to quickly mark through two of them because he knew the area where their homes were located. There was no way the lawyer would be caught dead living in a lower-class neighborhood. He was pretty sure the man wouldn't be in a middle-class home either, but Hawke wasn't ready to mark them out just yet.

The two of them finished their sandwiches and gathered their things. As they exited the office Hawke handed the list to Maddie, turning back to turn out the lights and lock the door. She scanned the pages as they made their way down the stairs.

"I know one of these," she said. "Well, I don't know him, but he lives down the street from me."

"Have you spoken to him?" Hawke asked. "Maybe run over his dog and pissed him off enough to want you dead?"

"No," she said. "At least I don't think so. I didn't even know his name. But I know the house. And I've seen him a few times. Seems nice."

"We'll start with him," Hawke said taking the list. "It would be great if it were that easy to find him."

At the bottom of the stairs Hawke told Maddie to wait. He stepped through the doorway onto the sidewalk, his hand resting on the handle of the pistol inside his jacket. Just as the search from the window of his office had set off no alarms, at ground level no one stood out as a threat. He tried to remember if any of the faces he had seen earlier were among those he was looking at now. Satisfied they weren't, he motioned for Maddie to follow him.

He held the door to the truck open for her then made a sweep of the vehicle checking the bumpers and wheel wells again for a tracking device. Coming up empty-handed, he joined Maddie in the cab of the truck and drove in the most direct route to her neighborhood.

Her street was mostly deserted. Very few of the residents parked vehicles on the curb making it a difficult place to try to blend in. Hawke cruised down the main drive scrutinizing every car he saw. He took his time passing side streets, taking in everything.

"Stop!" Maddie shouted.

Hawke slammed on the brakes and reached for his weapon. "What?"

"What the hell is he doing?" she said staring past the PI.

Hawke turned his head to follow her gaze. They were in front of her house, the windows dark and lifeless. "What is who doing?"

"My husband," she said.

"It doesn't look like he's doing anything," he said.

"Exactly," she said. "I told him to get the hell out of my house today. His car's there, but it doesn't look like he's packing his things."

"No," Hawke said. "It doesn't."

"Pull in," she said.

"Are you sure you want to do that?"

"Pull in."

Hawke put the truck in reverse and backed into the driveway. Maddie had the door open and was halfway to the front porch before he came to a full stop. Hawke rolled out and was in pursuit in seconds. When he caught up to her, she was just pulling the keys free of her pocket.

"Don't try to stop me," she said, sliding the key into the lock.

"I know we said he isn't the guy behind all of this," Hawke said, pulling his gun out. "I would just feel better knowing you aren't alone with him."

She turned the knob and pushed the door open, revealing the entry hall beyond. Hawke moved with the practiced motions of the trained cop he once was. Maddie moved with the anger of a wife having been cheated on. He was forced to give up his efforts to clear rooms and instead rushed ahead to be at her side as she climbed the stairs to the second floor.

The upper level was dark save a line of light shining beneath a single door at the end of the hall like a beacon calling to Maddie. She did not slow and Hawke was forced to increase his speed to keep up with her. He managed to pass her halfway down the hall, determined she not walk into an ambush. At the same time, he didn't want to walk into one either.

"Are you sure?" Hawke whispered.

"Don't ask me again," she snapped, her voice barely audible. She sprang forward with an unexpected burst of speed, reaching the door at the end of the hall just ahead of Hawke.

As she pushed the door open, he had visions of her husband and best friend, but inside Ricky was standing in the middle of the room with a painting canvas on an easel. His back was to the doorway and he wore headphones so he did not react to them entering. He held a paintbrush in one hand making large strokes with bold colors, pausing to examine each before making the next. In the other hand he held a blowtorch, which he would use to scorch the edges of the colors. Hawke leaned against the door frame and studied the canvas. He was no expert, but what he saw was simply hideous.

Maddie walked up behind her husband and pulled the headphones from one of his ears. "What the hell are you doing?"

"Painting," he said.

"I told you to get out," she said.

"You were serious?" He turned, saw Hawke and said, "What is he doing here?"

"Pack your stuff and get out," she said. "Tonight."

"Maddie," he pleaded. "We can fix this."

"You slept with my best friend, you jackass," she said. "There's nothing left to fix. Get out tonight, or I'll have someone come haul all your crap away."

"You can't be serious," he said. "I can't get everything out tonight."

"Get your clothes out of my bedroom," she said. "Show you're making the effort and I'll give you another day to come back for your, your," she indicated the canvas, "art?"

"Are you mocking my work now?" he said.

"Tonight, Ricky," she said. "If you don't, I change the locks and dump everything."

"You wouldn't," he challenged. "Really, why is he here? Why are you here?"

Ricky took a step in Hawke's direction. Hawke straightened and held up a hand. "I wouldn't do that."

"Do what?" Ricky said. "Assault a stranger in my home? What are you going to do?"

"Probably break something," Hawke said. "Probably an arm. Or maybe a couple fingers. Which hand do you paint with?"

Ricky backed away, keeping his eyes on the PI. He said to Maddie, "Is this what you're hanging out with now?"

"Tonight," Maddie repeated. She walked toward Hawke who stepped aside to let her pass. "Let's go."

"You're the boss," he said. He nodded at Ricky and followed his client out of the house. In the truck he asked, "You okay?"

"I'm fine," she said.

"If he doesn't get out," Hawke said, "I know some people."

"I don't want him killed," she said, surprised.

"That's good," Hawke said. "I was saying I know some people who'll take his things out for you."

"Oh," she said.

He started the truck. "But if you change your mind, I know some of those people too."

She turned her head to him sharply. He grinned and pulled out onto the street, driving the half block to the home of the registered black BMW.

The house, like Maddie's, was a large modern home with a massive entry. Hawke pulled into the circular drive and parked directly in front of the walkway. There was no sign of the BMW, but Hawke suspected the owner kept it in the garage. Most of the windows were lit with a blatant disregard for energy conservation. The two of them exited the vehicle and approached the door.

"You were kidding, weren't you?" Maddie said. "About what you said."

"I do know some people like that," Hawke said. "But I don't arrange hits. Goes against my principles."

She visibly relaxed and Hawke hammered the door with his fist. After a brief moment a voice came from the video doorbell.

"Mrs. Rochester?" the man said. "Is that you?"

"Yes, uh . . ." Hawke held out the list for Maddie to see. "David, it's me."

"What can I do you for you?" the voice said.

"Could you come to the door?" she asked.

"Can the big guy step back?" David said. "He makes me nervous."

Hawke shrugged and moved to the steps. The door opened slowly and David peered out.

"Do you own a BMW?" Maddie asked.

"That isn't him," Hawke said, spinning on his heels and walking back to the truck.

"I do," David said. "What's this about?"

"Never mind," she smiled. "So sorry to bother you."

She returned to the truck leaving David to wonder on his porch.

18

"Thirty-five to go," Hawke said.

"What do we do next?" Maddie asked.

"Now we pick three or four names from the list and pay each of them a visit," Hawke said. "Detective work at its finest."

"That's really how you find people?" she asked.

"Sometimes," Hawke said. "Just depends how much information you have."

"No wonder you charge so much," she said. She held out her hand. "May I?"

Hawke handed her the list. She perused the names and addresses, using a pen to cross through her neighbor's. She made few more marks and handed the page back to Hawke.

"These three are only a few miles from here," she said.

He looked at the names she marked. "In different directions."

"But they're close," she said.

"Let's check them out," Hawke said, dropping the list onto the seat between them.

They drove through town silently as Hawke maneuvered traffic. He turned into a middle-class neighborhood and slowed. Unlike the roads around Maddie's home, these were filled with activity. There were joggers, cyclists and walkers. Singles and couples. With children. With dogs. With both. Kids played with balls of every type and occasionally ran into the street.

Hawke followed the signs leading him to their destination. When they arrived, Hawke took one look at the BMW in the driveway and drove on without slowing. Maddie protested until the PI explained the car was too old to be the one they were searching for.

The second proved more difficult to locate, as the road ended a half block before the street address indicated on the registration. Hawke sat with the engine idling, staring out the windshield at the "Dead End" sign. He picked up the list and read the address again to be sure he had it correct.

"Either the DMV mistyped this guy's address," he said. "Or he lied to them."

"And we don't know which?"

"Not without talking to him," Hawke said.

"What now then?" Maddie asked.

"We move on to the next name," Hawke said, picking up the list. He typed the next address into his phone's GPS and made a U-turn. The dead-end had been two blocks outside the last residential area. Driving back through, they both searched the driveways for black BMWs. They did not see any, but they had no way of knowing what was parked inside garages or who simply wasn't home.

The next address was a high dollar neighborhood, the kind where Hawke would expect the lawyer to live. The GPS led them to a large estate complete with a separate garage that was larger than the PI's apartment. Hawke parked on the street.

"You should stay here," he said without taking his eyes off the house.

"Why?" Maddie said.

"If it's not him," Hawke said, "then it's a quick in and out. If it is him, I would rather he didn't know you were here."

"But . . ."

"Humor me," he said.

She looked at him for a long moment. "Okay. I'll wait here."

"Good," he said. He opened his door and stepped out onto the street. "I'll be right back."

He closed the door and followed the walk up to the front porch of the house, ringing the bell and stepping back. He watched shadows moving on the other side of the translucent glass panels of the door. A moment later, the door opened.

"May I help you?" The man was in his late twenties or early thirties, round face and body with very little hair to speak of. His eyes were half-closed and dull, almost lifeless.

"I'm looking for," Hawke checked the list, "a mister Theodore Peterson."

"That's me," the man focused on the paper in Hawke's hand. "What's this about?"

"It's about your car," Hawke said. "But I think I have the wrong place."

He nodded at the man and turned to leave.

"Which car?" the Theodore said. "Is it the BMW?"

Hawke stopped and turned back. "How did you know?"

"Did you find it?" he asked. "I reported it stolen a week ago. Haven't heard from you guys since."

"You guys?"

"Aren't you a cop?" he said. "You look like a cop."

"I'm not," Hawke said. He didn't see the need to explain that he used to be. "Was it stolen from your home?"

"No," Theodore said. "Work. Got off and went outside. No car."

"Where do you work?" Hawke asked. "If you don't mind."

"I own a software firm," the man said. "In Lake Point Corporate Park."

"Do you have surveillance cameras on the building?"

"Yes," he said. "But the police already went through them."

"Mind if I take another look?" Hawke said. "I think the guy who took your car may be the same person I'm tracking. I'd like the chance to confirm."

"If it will help me get my car back," he said. "Sure. When do you want to check them out?"

"Now," Hawke said. "If that's all right with you."

"You want to go down there now?"

"If you don't mind," Hawke said. "It's a rather pressing matter."

"I guess so," Theodore said. "Just a second."

The man disappeared into the house. He returned a moment later wearing a jacket. An ID badge hung around his neck. He stepped out onto the porch and pulled the door closed behind him, testing to be sure the lock was engaged.

"Okay," he said. "Good to go."

"Do you need a ride?" Hawke asked.

"No," Theodore said. "You can follow me."

He turned toward the garage and Hawke made his way back to the truck.

"Anything?" Maddie said.

"Maybe," Hawke said. "We're going to check out some video footage."

"We are?"

A bright yellow corvette came down the driveway, pausing at the street for just a second before speeding off. Hawke pulled in behind the sports car and accelerated well over the limit until he caught up. He then slowed to match the other's speed.

"Where are we going?" Maddie asked.

"Theodore owns a BMW," Hawke explained. "But it was stolen from his business a week ago."

"You think the lawyer stole his car?"

"I think it's possible that whoever stole Theodore's car is posing as a lawyer," Hawke said.

"And you're sure it isn't Theodore?" Maddie asked.

Hawke frowned at her. "I met with the so-called lawyer. I just spoke to Theodore. I'm positive they are not the same person."

"Yeah," Maddie nodded. "Okay."

They followed Theodore's taillights for about twenty minutes before the Corvette turned into an office park. He followed the road to the last building on the left and parked next to the front entrance. Hawke pulled up next to him and parked.

The three of them exited their vehicles and started for the doors. Theodore was thumbing through his keys as he walked until he found the one he wanted. He held it up triumphantly and turned to the others.

"Got it," he said. When he saw Maddie he stopped dead in his tracks. "Madeline Rochester? Is that you?"

Hawke stepped between them defensively. "You know each other?"

Maddie shifted her weight to look around Hawke's large frame. "Teddy Peterson? God I can't believe it. Last I heard you were developing some breakthrough financial software program."

"You heard right," Theodore said. "And you founded Rochester-Kinsley."

"The two of you know each other?" Hawke repeated.

"We were in college together," Maddie smiled. "Teddy was my main competition."

"You made me a better programmer," Theodore said.

"You definitely made me sharpen my skills," Maddie said.

"I guess we helped each other succeed," he said.

"I guess so," Maddie said. She looked up at the building and the sign above the door. "TPi? This is you?"

"Theodore Peterson, inc.," he nodded.

"Well, good for you," she said.

Hawke watched the interaction for as long as he could. "Can we get to the video?"

"Oh, yes," Theodore said. He stepped up to the door, unlocked it and pulled the door open. He held it while the others entered. "What brings you out here, Maddie?"

"Just a personal interest," she said.

"In my car?"

"In the person who may have taken it," she said.

The next door they came to required Theodore to wave his name badge over a panel to disengage the lock. Hawke watched the man every step of the way while the two former classmates continued their small talk.

They came to a door marked 'Security' and Theodore waved his badge again to gain entry. Inside the wall was covered with small screens showing footage from a number of cameras that were monitoring the interior and exterior of the building. Theodore sat in a chair in front of a computer and started typing. A short time later an image of the parking lot, full of cars appeared on the screen. He said, "This is the day my car was stolen."

He clicked a button and the video began to play. Hawke leaned over the man, watching the screen. The BMW was parked in the same space in which Theodore had parked the Corvette. People were coming and going, but no one paid any attention to the BMW.

"Can you play it faster?" Hawke asked.

"Of course," the man said. He clicked a button and engaged the fast-forward.

The people on the screen began moving quickly, jerking about as they did. They watched this for several minutes until the BMW suddenly moved back and out of the frame.

"Stop," Hawke said, but Theodore was already doing it.

The car's owner backed the video up until the BMW was back in its place. He hit play again and they watched the video at normal speed. A grey sedan pulled up behind the BMW and a man exited the passenger side. He walked up to the BMW and a moment later opened the driver's door and entered. The grey sedan drove away, followed by Theodore's BMW.

"Back it up," Hawke ordered.

Theodore complied.

"Stop," Hawke said. "Can you enlarge the thief's face?"

Theodore manipulated the image and filled the screen with the man's face.

"Is that him?" Maddie said.

"No," Hawke said. "That's Richard Hendrix."

104

19

The sun had given up on the day when they left TPi. Hawke sat in the truck with Maddie until the yellow Corvette was long gone. Only then did he start the engine and back out of the parking space.

"What's bugging you?" Maddie said. "Other than your friend stealing the BMW?"

"First of all, Richard Hendrix is not my friend," Hawke said. "But more than that, don't you find it at all odd that your former classmate's car was stolen and then used by someone who is trying to have you killed?"

"Well," Maddie said. "When you put it that way. But Teddy wouldn't have done this."

"How well do you know him?" Hawke asked. "I mean really know him."

"We went to school together," Maddie said. "We had a lot of the same classes. We competed against each other a lot, always trying to outdo the other."

"And now your company is how much bigger than his?"

"I don't know," Maddie said. "Besides, it isn't the size of the building. It's what you produce in the building. I'm always telling Jevon that."

"Jevon?" Hawke said. "Who is Jevon?"

"Jevon Kinsley," Maddie said. "My partner. He's the one that wanted the big flashy building. Said it projected success. He thought it would be good for generating future business."

"And you disagree?"

"Most of our sales are word of mouth or internet searches," Maddie said. "The majority of our clients never set foot in this city, let alone our building. I wanted to keep it simple. But I let Jevon have his way."

"Do you compromise for him often?"

"Only when it doesn't affect the product," she said. "In that I always have the final word."

"Interesting dynamic," Hawke observed.

"You have to know Jevon to understand," she said.

"Like what?"

"When we were in college we became friends because we had the same classes," Maddie said. "We soon found that our interests were the same. Our programming skills were similar. It was easy for us to collaborate on projects."

"That doesn't explain the different way of looking at things," Hawke said. "If anything it suggests your views would be similar."

"I chose my education path and my father wrote a check," she said. "My family had money. Jevon's family was poor. He was at school on a scholarship. A well-deserved scholarship. But it was an opportunity he otherwise wouldn't have had. We came from different worlds. Had it not been for school and programming, we would never have become friends. When we talked about starting our own company I had money to invest. He didn't, at least not until he got lucky betting on a horse race."

"A horse race?"

"Crazy, huh?" she said. "Had that horse not won, everything would have turned out differently."

"What about Teddy?"

"What about him?" Maddie said.

"Family money or scholarship?" Hawke asked.

"Scholarship," Maddie said. "I think."

"And you don't think it's possible that your former college classmate saw your projected success and decided that he had fallen behind in your competition?"

She shook her head slowly. "I can't imagine he would do anything like that."

"I hope you're right," Hawke said. "But for now, he's on my list of suspects."

"All right," she said. "But it's not him."

Hawke pulled out his phone, scrolled through his contacts and pressed Roger's name. It rang a half dozen times before his old partner answered.

"What do you want, Hawke?" Roger growled, not even trying to hide the irritation in his voice.

"You wake up on the wrong side of life?" Hawke said. There was no response, so Hawke continued. "I was wondering if you had any leads on who tapped out Hendrix."

"No leads," Roger said. "Is that all you want? Or are you going to ask a favor too?"

"What's eating you, Rog?" Hawke said.

"Sorry," his old partner said. "Rough day. We had four homicides today."

"Four?" Hawke repeated. "What is the world coming to? But hey, I don't want to ask a favor. I want to give you some information."

"What kind of information?"

"Turns out the guy who hired me to follow Mrs. Rochester," Hawke said, "He was driving a car stolen by Hendrix. The same guy who tried to kidnap her."

"So, not a lawyer," Roger said.

"That's what I was thinking," Hawke agreed. "I was also thinking that if he's not a lawyer, he might be a con."

"You think he might be in the database," Roger said.

"Worth a try," Hawke said.

"It is," Roger said. "Come down tomorrow. I'll get you in front of a sketch artist."

"Sylvia," Hawke said.

"You'll get whoever is available," Roger said.

"Sylvia," Hawke said. "She's the best. I want the best."

"And yet you'll get who you get," Roger said. The call disconnected before Hawke could say anything more.

"Who's Sylvia?" Maddie asked. "Girlfriend?"

"Sylvia?" Hawke said. "A girlfriend? Don't let her hear you saying that. She's just a damn good sketch artist."

"So what do we do now?" Maddie said.

"It's getting late," Hawke said. "We need to get off the streets and bunker for the night."

"You said something about staying at your place," Maddie said.

"You'll be my guest tonight," he said.

"Well aren't you charming?"

"It'll be safe," he said. "You'll take my room. I'll sleep between you and the door. They won't think you would be there. But if they do come, they'll have to go through me."

"Are you sure you want to give up your bed?" Maddie asked.

"I sleep in cars," Hawke said. "I'll be fine on the couch."

"Okay."

"I will warn you," Hawke said. "It's not like your home. Or even your hotel."

"I'll be okay," she said.

Hawke drove an indirect route to his apartment. He watched the rearview mirror intently, trying to find any sign that they were being followed. In the end, he did not spot a tail and felt confident they were safe for the time being. He circled the block one last time just for good measure before pulling into the parking lot of his apartment building.

The two of them stepped out into the night air and Maddie stared up at the four-story building. "This is where you live?"

"I told you it's not the Ritz," Hawke said.

He led Maddie to the entrance, producing a key to unlock the security door, allowing them entry to the lobby. Hawke stopped at the wall of mailboxes and retrieved a thick stack of envelopes. Tucking them under his arm, they continued to the elevator. The doors opened immediately and they stepped inside. Hawke pushed three, watching the doors slide shut.

"I need to warn you about one more thing," Hawke said.

"I notice you waited until I was trapped in the elevator before you mentioned it," Maddie said. "It must be bad."

"It's Mrs. Mancini," Hawke said.

"Mrs. Mancini?" Maddie turned to Hawke. "You're warning me about a woman?"

"She's not just a woman," he said. "She's my neighbor, and when you meet her you'll understand."

"I'm just staying the one night," she said. "Do you really think I'm going to meet her?"

The elevator door opened to the third-floor hallway. Hawke led Maddie to the right where there were four doors leading to their respective apartments. Hawke's was the last door on the left. As he slid the key into the lock, the door across the hall swung open.

"Sebastian Hawke," a shrill woman's voice said. "You didn't come home last night."

"Hello, Mrs. Mancini," Hawke said. "How are you this evening?"

"I'm fine," Mrs. Mancini said. She eyed Maddie with a scrutiny she could feel. "Is this young woman the reason why?"

"Mrs. Mancini, this is Maddie," Hawke introduced.

"Maddie," the woman said. "Lovely name for a lovely girl."

"Thank you," Maddie said.

"You hang on to this one, dear," Mrs. Mancini leaned into Maddie. "He's a little rough, but a fine catch."

"Mrs. Mancini," Hawke bent and kissed the woman on the cheek. "You know my heart belongs to you."

The woman blushed and retreated to her apartment. Just before closing the door, she said, "You be good to her, Sebastian Hawke."

Hawke guided Maddie into his apartment and locked the door behind them. "Sorry about that."

She turned back to him sharply and her red hair flared like a cape. "So, 'Sebastian' is it?"

"It is," Hawke said. "And no. You may not call me that."

Maddie scrunched her face and pushed her lower lip out. She turned again to take in the apartment. It was sparsely furnished with no decorations at all, much like his office. The small wood dining table had a pile of mail on it where Hawke added his latest bounty. The kitchen was simple, but clean. A single plate, fork and glass sat in the drying rack next to the sink. An old television sat on a crate opposite the worn couch with a matching chair that appeared brand new.

"This place needs a woman's touch," she said.

"It most certainly does not," Hawke said.

Maddie laughed and removed her jacket. She held the garment in one hand looking around the apartment and then to Hawke.

"No coat rack," he said. "No coat closet."

"Where do you put your coat?"

"I use the chair," he pointed at the armchair next to the couch.

Maddie scrutinized his choice, opting to drape her jacket over one of the dining chairs instead. She strolled into the kitchen and opened the refrigerator door. Seeing the nearly empty appliance, her eyebrows raised. She reached in and took two bottles of imported dark ale.

"You want one?" she asked, holding the bottle out to Hawke.

He took the bottle, popped the lid off and drank. "We should talk."

"About sleeping arrangements?"

"We've already established that," Hawke said. "No. We need to discuss your enemies."

"My enemies?" Maddie frowned. "What makes you think I have enemies?"

"Someone has gone to a lot of trouble to make you dead," Hawke said. He pulled out one of the chairs and sat at the table. He pointed his bottle to the chair closest to Maddie. "So you have at least one."

She followed Hawke's lead and sat. She had the same defeated expression she had when Hawke told her she could not call him by his first name. "Why would anyone want me dead?"

"That's what we're going to discuss," Hawke said. "Think of everyone you've wronged and tell me about them. Don't leave anything out. And be sure you convey exactly how angry they were."

"You know," Maddie said. She drank from the ale before continuing. "As far as . . . wow, this is really good. Anyway, as far as first dates go this one really sucks."

"This isn't a first date," Hawke said. "It isn't any date. You're paying me."

"That makes you my escort," she grinned.

"It makes me your bodyguard," he said.

"Oh, come on," she said. "I haven't been on a date in a long time."

"You're married," Hawke reminded her.

"To Ricky," she said. "You're right about his name."

"Can we talk about your enemies?"

"Can I have another beer?"

"Talk to me and finish the one you've got," Hawke said. "Then you can have another."

"Fine," Maddie said. "It's just the idea of talking about people who hate me enough to want me dead is kind of depressing."

"I know," Hawke's voice softened. "But it's the best way to figure out who is behind this so I can put a stop to it once and for all."

"Where do I start?"

"Most recent," Hawke said. "It's unlikely the guy you dumped in high school waited this long to get back at you."

"I didn't dump him," Maddie said. "Oh, wait. You were just using an example."

"That's right."

"Most recent," she pondered. "Well apparently there's Teddy, who I still say isn't the one."

Hawke took a notebook from his pocket and wrote Theodore Peterson's name. "Let's assume you would say that none of them would do this and just give me the names."

"Okay," she said. She sat silent for a long time staring at the bottle in her hand. "Ambrose Sinclair."

"Who is he?"

"Ambrose was a programmer that worked at my company about a year ago," she said. "Only he kept missing his deadlines. His work was inferior and we had to let him go. He didn't take it well."

Hawke added the name to the list. "Did he threaten you or make any hateful comments?"

"He cried."

"He cried?"

"Like a baby," she said. "It was heartbreaking."

"Anyone else?"

"Raymond Vallance," she said. "About six months ago my company was in a bidding war with his to get a lucrative national account. We edged him out. I heard his company folded shortly after."

"Sounds promising," Hawke said. He wrote down the name.

"Oh, and there's my neighbor," she said. "Not the one we talked to. Mr. Burns from next door. He wanted to install a pool but it was going to be too close to my property so I protested."

"What happened?" Hawke said.

"He had to install a smaller pool," she said.

"Rough," Hawke smirked.

"Hey," she said. "At the time he was livid."

Hawke put the name on his list.

"And Jamie Simmons," she said. "Before I got married, I dated a guy who turned out to be Jamie's boyfriend. He forgot to tell her they were done. She made all kinds of threats. I dumped the guy and went on to meet Ricky."

Hawke jotted down the name.

"Wow," Maddie said. "This is easier than I thought. Thinking of people who hate me."

"Anyone else?" Hawke asked. "Maybe someone you overlooked for a promotion? Someone who didn't get the raise they thought they deserved? Someone jealous of your success?"

"I can't think of anyone," she said. "We're really like a family."

"Except for Ambrose."

"Except him."

"Any other bad breakups?"

"Just Ricky."

"What about friends?"

"Like Penelope?" Maddie said.

"Like her," Hawke said. He added her name, followed by Ricky's.

"I don't make friends easily," Maddie said. "I work all the time. The only people I meet are employees and clients. Doesn't make a great friend pool."

"I guess not," Hawke said.

"Speaking of work," Maddie said. "I have to go in tomorrow. I have some meetings set up that I can't get out of."

"You being where they expect you to be isn't the wisest thing," Hawke said.

"I understand," she said. "I just can't miss these meetings."

"Okay," Hawke nodded. "But I'm going with you."

"Works for me," she said. "You can break things up if they get out of hand."

"What kind of meetings are these?" Hawke said.

"I was just kidding," she said. "One is a finance meeting. The other is a client presentation. I'm expected to be at both."

He examined the seven names on his list. It was a start. But he also knew it was very possible none of them were involved.

"When are the meetings?" he asked.

"Both are in the afternoon," Maddie said. "Why?"

"I need to go see Roger first thing," he said. "Going to have a sketch artist try to capture the lawyer's image."

"That's right," Maddie said. "Sylvia."

"Right," Hawke said. "We can go to your work after that."

"Okay," she nodded. She set the empty beer bottle on the table. "Now, how about that other beer?"

20

Morning came way too early for Hawke. He opened his eyes. Disoriented at first, he was quick to identify his living room. On the kitchen table nearly a dozen empty bottles stood guard. He sat up and stretched his upper body muscles. He checked his phone. It was a little after seven. No missed calls. He considered waking Maddie but decided to make coffee first.

He pulled himself to his feet and finished his stretches. He walked quietly to the kitchen and loaded a filter with grounds and the brewer with water. With the coffee started, he leaned against the counter and waited.

"Smells good," Maddie said.

Hawke looked up to see his houseguest using one of his towels to dry her hair.

"Hope you don't mind," she said. "I used your shower. You think there might be time to stop by my place for a change of clothes?"

"We can probably do that," Hawke said. He poured himself a cup of coffee, raised it to his face and inhaled the aroma. He sipped at the hot dark liquid he used to bring him out of his morning comas. This morning it had its work cut out for it. "Let me change and we can go. Help yourself to the coffee."

He stepped around her, his sheepish eyes meeting her bright ones, before moving on to his room. He closed the door behind him and began stripping away the wrinkled clothes he had been wearing for the past two days and tossed them in the general direction of the hamper. He considered taking a shower but didn't feel there was enough time. He pulled a shirt and slacks from his closet and dressed before heading to the restroom to groom himself. In less than ten minutes he emerged clean-shaven and refreshed.

"You ready?" he said.

"Sure am," she said.

They stepped into the hall and Hawke pulled his door closed and locked it. Before he could get the deadbolt to slide into place, he could hear the door behind him opening.

"Good morning," Mrs. Mancini said. To Maddie she continued, "Isn't that what you were wearing last night?"

"Hello, Mrs. Mancini," Hawke said, wrapping his arm around Maddie, guiding her down the hall and away from his neighbor. "You have a good day."

In the parking lot, Hawke searched the truck for GPS trackers and other devices, finding none. Either they had given up on that tactic or they had hidden them much better this time. He unlocked the passenger door and held it for Maddie.

"Such a gentleman," she said as she climbed in.

"Not something I'm accused of very often," Hawke said. He shut the door and moved around to the driver's side.

"So, Mrs. Mancini," Maddie said.

"Sorry about that," Hawke said.

"She thinks we're sleeping together," Maddie said.

"That's what happens when you spend the night in a man's apartment," Hawke said.

"She's kind of nosey," Maddie said.

"Kind of?"

"Does she just stand at her door and wait for you to come in or out?"

"It does feel that way doesn't it?" Hawke said. "Don't worry. She's harmless."

At Maddie's home, they did a quick check. No strange cars on the street. Ricky's Camaro was nowhere to be seen. Just to be safe, once they were inside, Hawke did a room by room search of the house. When he gave the all-clear, Maddie barricaded herself in her bedroom to get ready for work.

Hawke stood guard in the hallway. He studied the family pictures that lined the walls. There were several of Maddie and Ricky that he suspected would not hold their places of honor much longer. Many were clearly of Maddie at different stages of her life, often holding trophies or awards. There were similar shots of Ricky, but only a few. The rest were of people Hawke assumed were family and friends. A lot of work had gone into the layout of the different sized frames to create an evenly spaced collage.

The bedroom door opened and Maddie stepped out in a smart professional pantsuit, navy blue with grey pinstriping. Her shoes were practical yet stylish. Her red mane was pulled back into a bun that made Hawke wonder how long they had been there.

"How do I look?" she asked.

"You look good," Hawke said. "Professional."

"Wow," she said. "You really know how to flatter a girl."

"What? You look good."

She laughed at his discomfort. "Never mind. Are you ready?"

"Seriously?" he said. "I was ready before we got here."

"Most of his clothes are gone by the way," she said as they descended the stairs.

"That's what you wanted, right?"

"Yeah," she said. "Just didn't think he'd actually go. Not this easy anyway."

They filled the drive to the police department with small talk. Maddie did most of the actual talking and Hawke provided his skill of artful listening, grunting at all the appropriate places. They arrived fifteen minutes early and took their time walking in. Hawke had to stop and check his gun and talked to the officer at length. The two men shook hands and Hawke returned to Maddie's side.

She followed as Hawke led the way to the elevators and up to the third floor where homicide was located. A number of officers and detectives stopped to speak with the PI, usually curious about his and Maddie's relationship. One female detective, in particular, prodded more than once for the truth. Maddie got the impression the detective did not want the door closed on the Hawke possibility.

Roger was waiting at his desk. As soon as he saw them, he rose to his feet and met them part way. The two men shook hands and the detective exchanged pleasantries with Maddie.

"Sylvia's in three," Roger said. "She said something about you already owing her."

"I forgot about that," Hawke said. "I guess I better figure out how to pay her back."

Hawke turned and disappeared through a door, closing it behind him.

"We're in two," Roger said to Maddie.

"Pardon?" Maddie said.

"I thought we could talk about your situation," Roger said. "Two attempted kidnappings, and Hawke tells me a hitman came after you. Seems we should get some more details."

"You sound like Hawke," Maddie said.

"He was a good cop," Roger said. "But I will deny saying it."

They entered room two and sat across from one another.

"What would you like to know?" Maddie asked.

"Enemies," Roger said. "Trouble at work or home? Anything that might help identify who is doing this to you."

"Hawke and I tried that last night," she said. She told him about the names she had given the PI and the reasons they made the list. He asked for more details on each of them and took extensive notes.

"Anyone that didn't make the list that might warrant a look?" Roger asked. "Sometimes it only takes a small thing to set someone off. You might not even know you did it."

"Then how would I know to put them on the list?" she said.

"Just think through recent interactions," Roger said. "Anyone react in a way you didn't expect but didn't raise a big red flag?"

Maddie thought about all the people she could remember talking to over the past few weeks. None of them spurred a memory of misunderstanding or confusion. She knew there were probably others she couldn't remember. She shook her head, "I just can't think of anyone."

"It's okay," Roger said. "But if you think of anyone, call me. Meanwhile, I'll follow up with the names you gave me."

"I appreciate it, detective," Maddie said. "It's nice to know someone is looking into it."

"Attempted kidnapping and assassination plots tend to catch our attention," Roger said.

"I suppose they would," she smiled.

Roger stood and Maddie rose with him. "How are you doing, by the way? That's a lot for anyone to go through."

"Surprisingly well," she said. "It helps that Hawke is watching over me."

"Speak of the Devil," Roger said, opening the door. "Looks like they're finished."

Maddie stepped into the main room and saw Hawke standing next to a dark-haired Mediterranean beauty who cradled a notebook in her arms. The two of them were talking when Maddie approached. Hawke turned to her and smiled.

"Show her the drawing, Sylvia," he said.

The woman turned the notebook around and held it out to Maddie. The face staring back at her was remarkably realistic.

"Ever see him before?" Hawke asked.

"No," she said. "I'm guessing I don't want to."

"Probably not," he said. "This is the so-called lawyer who hired me to follow you. And you're sure you've never seen him?"

"Never," she confirmed.

"Okay," he said. "They're going to run the composite through a database and see if they get a hit. Maybe we can get a name."

"How will that help us?" Maddie asked.

"It will help me locate him," Hawke said. "Once I find him, I can convince him to tell me why he's after you. Or he can tell me who hired him to do this to you."

"Do you really think he'll tell you?" Maddie said.

"I can be very persuasive," he said.

"He can be," Sylvia agreed. "I once saw him convince a man to turn in his own mother."

"That's not a good example," Hawke said. "He didn't like his mother and he wanted her out of the house. I'm not so sure he didn't make it all up to get her locked up."

"She embezzled over two hundred thousand dollars from her employer," Sylvia said.

"True," he said. "But that wasn't what her son turned her in for."

"What did he turn her in for?" Maddie asked.

"According to the son," Hawke said, "the woman killed a neighbors' dog. Allegedly not the first time either."

"That's horrible," Maddie said.

"Couldn't really prove it," Hawke said. "Never found the dog. But while we were looking into that, we stumbled on the embezzling."

"Holidays must be fun at that house," Maddie said.

"They won't know for five or ten years," Sylvia said. "That's when she gets out."

"If we're going to get you to your office we should probably be on our way," Hawke said. "Sylvia, thanks again for taking the time to do this."

"My pleasure," she said. "You know I'll do anything for you. Miss your ugly mug around here."

The two of them hugged briefly and Hawke led the way out of the department with Maddie following closely. Within a few minutes they were in the truck, headed toward Rochester-Kinsley Inc.

21

They arrived at Maddie's company just before ten o'clock. She directed Hawke to park the truck in her reserved space. A couple of passers-by looked on with interest as they climbed out of the vehicle and Maddie retrieved her briefcase from behind the seat.

This time she led the way as they approached the building. She held out her name badge to a scanner to gain entry to the building. A security guard sitting behind a small desk stood when he saw her.

"Hello, Thomas," she said with a smile. "How are Isabel and the kids?"

"They're doing great, Ms. Rochester," Thomas said. "I'm glad to see you're okay."

"It was just a scare," she reassured. "This is Mr. Hawke. He is going to be with me for a while."

Hawke nodded at the man. Thomas gave him the once over.

"Like a bodyguard?" Thomas asked.

"Something like that," she said.

"No offense, but he ain't in shape," Thomas said, puffing out his chest. "Wouldn't you rather have someone more fit to protect you?"

"I'm in shape," Hawke said. "A shape anyway. Just not a good one."

"I'll be fine, Thomas," Maddie said. "Especially knowing that you're here at the door."

"Yes, ma'am," Thomas said. "No one will get to you on my watch."

"Thank you," she said.

They walked down the hall to the elevator, but Maddie passed it by and took the door to the stairwell. Hawke gave a side glance to the elevator as they moved through the door. On the second landing, Maddie stopped to let Hawke catch up.

"You trying to prove his point?" the PI asked between breaths.

"I'm sorry," she said. "Did you want to take the elevator? I wasn't even thinking. I always take the stairs. Helps me clear my head."

"I'm all right," he said, eyeing the large '2' on the door behind her. "What floor are we going to?"

"Fourth," she said.

"Okay then," he said. "We should get going,"

Maddie started up the stairs again and Hawke took a deep breath and followed at a much slower pace. He toyed with the idea of swearing off cigarettes but concluded that was just too extreme. Instead he decided to swear off stairs. After all, if man was meant to climb stairs, why would elevators exist?

Hawke reached the fourth floor and found Maddie leaning against the wall, phone in hand. As he struggled to catch his breath, her fingers flew across the small screen. She finished, put the phone away and made eye contact with the PI.

"You okay?" Maddie asked. "Need anything?"

"A smoke," he said, between gasps.

"I think that's the last thing you need," she said. "You should really give those things up. They'll kill you."

His breathing began to even out and he stood upright. "I appreciate your concern, but you aren't the first person to tell me that and you won't be the last."

"Don't you think you could stop?" she asked. "There are some effective programs available."

"Oh, I can stop any time," Hawke said. "In fact, I stop several times a day, right after each cigarette."

"Funny," she said, dismissively.

They opened the door to the fourth floor and stepped out of the relative quiet of the stairwell into a chaotic harmony of voices and electronics. Almost immediately the staff saw Maddie and swarmed on her with outpourings of concern and congratulations. Word of her attempted kidnapping had escaped no one. Graciously, Maddie thanked each of them personally, returning hugs to those who wanted to give them. The whole scene made Hawke uncomfortable. Not just the excessive show of affection, but also the fact that any one of these people could be the person he was looking for in connection to her attacks. He wanted to stand between her and them but knew she would not allow it.

When everyone had returned to their stations and to whatever it was they did, only one woman remained at Maddie's side. She was the woman who had accompanied her employer to the meeting at the restaurant. The woman stared at Hawke with an intensity that made him feel she was mentally criticizing everything about him. He gave her his best "same to you" smile.

"Delia," Maddie said. "This is Mr. Hawke. He's going to accompany me today. This is my assistant, Delia."

Hawke nodded.

"We have some sensitive things to go over," Delia's expression changed to distrust.

"Hawke knows how to keep secrets," Maddie said. "Don't you?"

"Been doing it for years," Hawke said. "Besides, I usually just don't listen."

"But Mrs. Rochester," Delia protested.

"Ms. Rochester," Maddie said. "And while I'm thinking of it, I need you to track down a good divorce attorney. Maybe the one Kim used. She seemed happy with him."

"Ma'am?" Delia said.

"You heard right," she said. "Track the lawyer down and set up an appointment. Soon."

"Yes, ma'am," the assistant said. "But first, we have a lot to go over. Starting with the Red Moon account."

"What's wrong now?" Maddie took a paper that Delia held out to her. The two women walked away and Hawke fell in behind them.

"They say the delivery was late and they are refusing to pay," Delia said.

"It was late because of the last-minute changes they wanted," Maddie said.

"I told them that," the assistant said. "Didn't help."

They reached a door in the corner of the building. Her office was modern with clean lines and sparsely decorated. Aside from two awards hanging behind her desk, there were only a few generic pieces of artwork. On her desk stood a phone, a computer and a single stack of papers. Maddie walked in and around the desk taking a seat in the plush executive chair, the only suggestion of her stature in the company. Delia stepped in front of the desk facing her employer. Hawke stepped up to the floor to ceiling windows and peered out at the city.

"Get Edward on the phone," Maddie said.

"Right away," Delia said. The assistant moved from the large office to a small desk just outside the door. A moment later the phone on Maddie's desk beeped and Delia's voice said, "Mr. Yang is on line one."

Maddie snatched up the phone and pressed the button for the appropriate line. In an unnaturally sweet voice she said, "Edward, so good to speak to you."

She paused as she listened to the man on the other end of the call.

"I understand your concern," Maddie said. "But I would like to point out that when you made changes to the scope of work, that changed the terms of the contract. If you have your lawyers read the agreement you will see that was addressed in the contract that you signed."

She waited again, her jaw clenching as the man spoke.

"Edward," she said, "do you really want to pull this? No company will do work for you if word gets out that you don't pay your obligations. And have no doubts, I will sue you, very publicly."

A brief pause, then, "Edward."

Hawke stepped up to the desk with his hand out. "May I?"

Maddie looked at Hawke with confusion, but handed the phone to the PI.

"Mr. Yang?" Hawke said. After a moment he continued, "My name is not important. What is important is that I have the ability to find things, particularly things that people don't want found. I'm guessing that a man willing to cheat another company has a history of, let's say unsavory actions, both business and personal."

Hawke stopped for a minute.

"I'm doing no such thing," Hawke said. "I never threaten. What I'm telling you is that if you do not pay Ms. Rochester for the work she provided, every dirty secret you have will be plastered over every news outlet, social media outlet and possibly a few billboards."

Hawke paused, then held the phone out to Maddie. "He wants to talk to you."

Maddie took the phone and listened. "No. He's not an employee of Rochester-Kinsley. I couldn't stop him if I wanted to."

She grinned at Hawke. Into the phone she said, "Yes, sir. I'll be looking for your payment. And Edward. Don't ever try to hire my company again."

Maddie hung up the phone and smiled at Hawke with her head tilted to one side.

"What?" he said.

"Would you really have done those things?"

"I'm not exactly up to speed on social media," Hawke said. "But I would have dug up enough to pass on to the police anonymously. Businessmen who try these tactics always have shady dealings in their past. And if he has a girlfriend? His wife might have found out, along with any secret accounts he's keeping from her."

"Remind me not to get on your bad side," Maddie said.

"You think he should be on your list?" Hawke asked.

"He didn't have reason to be," Maddie said. "At least not until today."

"Okay," Hawke said. "But I might look into him anyway."

Maddie pushed a button on her phone. "Delia, Mr. Yang is going to make payment by end of day. Please let me know when it hits our account."

"Yes, ma'am," Delia said. "Very good, ma'am."

"You want to get me that list of things we need to address? I'm feeling very productive today."

"Just a moment," Delia said. As promised, she soon came through her doorway and held out a stack of papers. "These are the most pressing."

"Where is Jevon?" Maddie said as she thumbed through the pages. "He should have addressed some of these."

"He isn't in yet," Delia said.

"He isn't?"

"No ma'am," Delia said. "He had a meeting this morning. He said he would be in before noon."

"Okay," she said. "Let me know when he arrives."

"Yes, ma'am," the assistant returned to her station guarding Maddie's door.

"What's up?" Hawke said.

"Pardon?" Maddie said.

"You seem troubled by something," he said.

"For someone who doesn't listen," Maddie said, "you sure hear a lot."

"I didn't hear a thing," he grinned. "So, what's up?"

"It's nothing," Maddie said. "I just hate dealing with things Jevon usually handles for me."

22

Over the next couple hours, Hawke alternated his time between sitting in the corner, leaning against the wall and staring out the window. Maddie busied herself with phone calls, emails, and paperwork. She held three small meetings with various staff members, receiving progress reports, hearing idea pitches and troubleshooting problems.

Delia entered the office numerous times to get signatures and to remind Maddie what was on her agenda. One such appearance was to announce that Mr. Yang's payment had cleared the bank. A few minutes after that Delia used the intercom on the phone to announce that Jevon Kinsley was in his office.

"Would you ask his assistant to have him call me when he has a moment?" Maddie said.

"Of course," Delia said.

Hawke, standing by the window, made his way back to the chair in the corner and settled into the over-stuffed cushions. His stomach growled and he realized he hadn't eaten since the previous evening. He had the sensation of being watched and raised his eyes to Maddie who was staring back at him.

"What?"

"We need to get you fed," she said.

"I'm fine," he said.

"I heard you from over here," she said. 'Besides, I promised I would treat you to lunch."

Her phone buzzed and Delia's voice came through the speaker. From Hawke's position he could hear her through the doorway as well. "Jevon is on line one."

"Thank you," Maddie said. She reached across and pressed a button on the phone. "Jevon."

"So glad you're in the office," Jevon said. "We were all worried about you."

"Thank you," she said. "I was a little worried about me as well."

Hawke cleared his throat. Maddie made a face at him and he mouthed, 'sorry'.

"Who was that?" Jevon asked.

"That's Hawke," Maddie said.

"Hawke?"

"Just think of him as my bodyguard," she said. "Or my shadow. Can't get rid of him."

"Is it really that serious?" Jevon asked. "I thought it was a wrong place, wrong time kind of thing."

"They've tried to take me twice," Maddie said. "Or three times. Wasn't sure if that last guy was there to kidnap me or kill me."

"You sound so calm," Jevon said. "Like you're ordering coffee or something."

"I'm shaking on the inside," Maddie assured him. "Delia said you had a meeting this morning. Anything I need to worry about?"

"Oh, you know how clients can be," Jevon said. "Happy one second, needing reassurances the next. It's handled. The team is already working on it."

"Good," Maddie said. "Did you hear about Yang trying to screw us over?"

"I got a message about that," Jevon said. "Do you need me to call him?"

"No," she said. "It's all taken care of. Payment has already been made."

"Really," he said. "That's good. From the sound of it, I didn't think he was going to give in."

"Well he did," Maddie said. "And I told him not to contact us for any future projects."

"You what?" Jevon said.

"I'm not doing any more work for that man," she said.

"We can't just turn away business," Jevon said. "We can't afford to."

"I'm not wasting time and resources on clients who don't want to pay," she said.

"But he paid," Jevon pointed out. "Surely he wouldn't try it again."

"That's right," Maddie said. "He won't. Because we won't be working with him again."

"You should have consulted me, Maddie," he said.

"You should have been here," she said.

With that the line went dead. Maddie's face was nearly as red as her hair. She sat behind her desk and composed herself. Hawke sat silently and waited for her to relax.

"You two always like that?" he asked when she appeared to be normal again. "Arguing about things?"

"Sometimes," she said. "We usually get along fine."

Hawke's stomach growled again, maybe even louder than the first time.

Maddie said. "We need to get you fed."

After lunch, Maddie spent the rest of the day working, doing all the same things she had done earlier in the day but with much less enthusiasm. As she had said, she sat in two meetings without contributing much. She took notes during the finance meeting and watched as her team made the presentation for the potential client. Her expression came alive while interacting with the head of the other company. Smiling, laughing, making assurances and creating connections. In the end, contracts were signed and the team had a brief celebration after the new client had left. Hawke watched everyone, but mostly, Maddie.

She celebrated with the team, but without her usual confidence or sparkle. The team took notice and the festivities died down quickly. Everyone shuffled out to their cubicles. Maddie thanked each one of them for a job well done as they left. Apparently, having someone out there who wanted her dead and finding her husband in bed with her best friend was taking its toll on her.

The staff began to thin as the workday drew to an end. Maddie was reluctant to leave, but knew Delia would not leave until she did. With that in mind, she packed her briefcase and rose to her feet. Hawke was already leaning against the wall by the door.

"I'm ready," she announced. "You can take me home."

"Let me carry your case," he said, taking it from her before she could protest. "And we need to talk about where you're going to stay tonight."

"Home," she said. Her voice projected a strength that was challenged by the exhaustion in her eyes. "I want to sleep in my own bed tonight."

"Maddie," Hawke said. "I don't know if that's safe."

"I don't care," she said. "I need to have something in my life be normal right now. Sleeping at home is it."

Hawke started to protest again, but the determination in her face stopped him. "Okay. We'll work with it."

"You can have the guest room across the hall," Maddie said. "It's very comfortable."

"I'll be sleeping in the hallway," Hawke said. "Until this all blows over, I won't be more than one door away."

As they left the office, Maddie told Delia to go home. The assistant thanked her, gave her a small hug and was out the door ahead of her boss. Maddie, followed by Hawke, walked to the elevator.

Just before they got there, Maddie said, "Wait a minute." She turned to continue down the corridor and around the corner.

Hawke followed at a comfortable distance. She walked to the far corner, knocked on the door, opened it and leaned inside.

"Heading out," Maddie said. "See you tomorrow."

"Take care of yourself," Hawke heard Jevon say.

"I will," she said. "You should think about getting out of here soon."

"Just have a couple things to finish up," Jevon said. "Then I'll be on my way."

"Promise?"

"Promise."

"Hey, Jevon?"

"Yeah?"

"We're okay, aren't we?"

"Sure," Jevon said. "Why wouldn't we be?"

"You know," she said. "The disagreement earlier. Just thought I should check in."

"We're good," he assured her.

"Okay," she said. "Goodnight."

Maddie turned to Hawke and the two of them made their way back to the elevator. While they waited, Hawke's phone rang. He took the call, spoke for a short time, then returned the phone to his pocket just as the elevator arrived.

"That was Roger," Hawke said as they descended. "They got a hit on my sketch. Want us to stop by and see if we recognize him."

23

Back at the police department, Roger took Hawke and Maddie to an interrogation room. Under his arm, he carried a manilla folder. He sat on one side of the table in the room and the other two sat across from him.

"Thanks for coming in," Roger said.

"You said you got a hit on the sketch," Hawke said.

"We did," Roger said. "And we'll get to that. First I want to ask some more questions."

"What kind of questions?" Hawke asked.

"Ms. Rochester," Roger squared his shoulders toward her. "Is there anything you aren't telling us?"

"What do you mean?" Maddie said.

"Is there anything in your life or your business that we should know about?" Roger asked. "Anything that up to now you haven't felt comfortable sharing?"

"I don't understand," Maddie said.

"What are you getting at, Rog?" Hawke said, purposely using the nickname his ex-partner hated.

"Hawke," Roger said. "I'm allowing you to be in here out of professional courtesy. But I can change that. Understand?"

Hawke clenched his jaw followed by an almost imperceptible nod.

"Have you gotten yourself mixed up with something that maybe you shouldn't have?" Roger turned back to Maddie. "Maybe you've gotten yourself in over your head."

"I haven't," Maddie said. She glanced at Hawke then back at the detective. "What is this about?"

"Roger," Hawke said in an even, nonchallenging tone. "Why don't you tell us what you have that initiated this line of questioning."

Roger slid the manilla folder to the center of the table and opened it. "Do you know this man?"

The photo was a grainy head and shoulder shot of a middle-aged man looking somewhere off-camera. The neck was thick and the facial features strong. It was an older image, Hawke knew. The man was not as solid as he was in this photo.

"That's him," Hawke said. "That's the lawyer who hired me."

"What about you, Ms. Rochester?" Roger asked. "Do you know this man?"

"No, detective," Maddie shook her head. "I don't know him. I've never seen him."

"Are you sure?" Roger pressed.

"Positive," she said.

"Who is he?" Hawke asked.

"We don't know," Roger said. "We do know he isn't a lawyer."

"Thought so," Hawke said.

"He is wanted for questioning in connection to at least a dozen murders in the past ten years," Roger said. "Problem is this is the only photo we have of him. And several of the cases have been solved, so nobody is searching for him."

"Solved as in the killer is behind bars?" Hawke asked. "I thought this guy was wanted for questioning?"

"The triggermen are behind bars," Roger said. "But this guy was involved. We just don't know to what extent. And even given the opportunity to shorten their sentences, nobody will talk."

"So you want to know how someone like Maddie ended up on this guy's radar?" Hawke said.

"Exactly," Roger said. "She doesn't exactly fit the profile of the victims in the other cases."

"You think I did something that pissed this guy off bad enough to want me dead?" Maddie stared at the grainy image.

"So, I need you to try again," Roger said. "Have you ever seen this man? It may have been a chance encounter. It's possible you didn't even speak to one another."

"I don't remember ever seeing him before," she said.

Roger sat back in his chair, no longer in attack mode. "Okay. But if you think of anything, I don't care how small the detail or what time of the night, you call me. Is that understood?"

Maddie continued to stare at the image of the man who apparently wanted her dead. She couldn't imagine what she could have done to warrant such a harsh sentence.

"Is that understood?" Roger repeated.

"It's understood, Rog," Hawke said. "Now, unless you actually have something useful to tell us, we're leaving."

He rose to his feet and offered a hand to Maddie who accepted it without realizing it. Roger stood as well, making no move to stop them. The three of them emerged from the interrogation room and the atmosphere changed drastically.

"Hawke," Roger said. "Be careful with this one. This guy has helped a lot of people get dead. Don't get in his crosshairs."

"Already there," Hawke said. "But thanks for the concern."

"What can I say?" Roger smiled. "I hated having you as a partner, but you were still the best one I ever had."

"Same to you, Rog," Hawke said. "Roger."

Hawke put his hand on Maddie's arm and steered her toward the elevators. His perception of their situation had now changed. They were dealing with someone who was experienced at having people killed. But his methods were unusual. Hiring Hawke threw suspicion on the husband, but also provided a witness to the intended abduction, in what would surely have ended as a ransom demand gone bad. The man obviously didn't expect Hawke to interfere, at least not successfully.

Sending Woodrow to the hotel clearly showed a change in motive from money to murder. Had the kidnapping gone as planned, police would have been looking for opportunists. Now they were looking for someone with a direct tie to Maddie. Whether that connection was personal, business or random would determine how easy or difficult it would be to find them.

"Roger?" Hawke called back to his old partner. "You said this guy was wanted for questioning in several murders."

"Yes."

"Were they all around here?"

"Across the country," Roger said. "Only one of them was committed locally."

"So, he could be from anywhere," Hawke thought aloud. "The murder that was from this area? When did it occur?"

"Almost a year ago," Roger said. "June."

"Then that's not it," Hawke said.

"Not what?" Maddie said.

"I thought you may have witnessed something he didn't want you to share," Hawke explained. "But if that were the case, he wouldn't have waited a year to come after you."

"What I did to make this man want me dead," Maddie said, "happened recently?"

"I would suspect a week or two ago," Hawke said. "Recent enough to make him pursue it, yet far enough back to give him time to organize the kidnapping crew."

"All I have to do now is figure out who I pissed off one to two weeks ago," Maddie said.

"And how," Hawke added as the elevator doors opened.

24

The doors opened on the ground floor as the last rays of daylight receded into dusk. Hawke and Maddie left the building and strolled toward the old truck. As they neared the vehicle, she ran her hands through her red mane, pulled out the bun and let it fall to her shoulders.

"What a beautiful night," she said. "Don't you think?"

"Not bad," Hawke agreed.

"Not bad?" Maddie said. "Are you kidding? Look at that sky. The temperature is almost perfect. I would love to take a walk by the river."

"That's not a good idea," Hawke said.

"Just for a little while," she said.

"It's too exposed," he said. "The river would prevent a fast escape if something went down. It would be too easy to get trapped."

"I need some air, Hawke," she said. "I've been cooped up in the house, the hotel, the office and your truck for two days. I usually drive a convertible. I need the wind in my hair."

"If they catch us in the open," Hawke said, "I can't guarantee your safety."

"Just fifteen minutes," she negotiated.

"Maddie," Hawke said.

"We're at a police station," she said. "You can drive around and make sure no one is following. We don't have to stay long. I promise."

Hawke closed his eyes and breathed deeply. When he opened them, she was staring at him with hers, pleading with him. He opened the passenger door of the truck, "Get in."

"Are we going?"

"Get in," he repeated. She complied and he shut the door. He spent the next ten minutes checking the wheel wells, bumpers and undercarriage of the truck for tracking devices. Finding nothing, he climbed into the driver's seat.

"Are we going?" She asked again.

He looked at her, studying the features of her face. He said, "Fifteen minutes."

She smiled and settled into her seat. Hawke started the truck and backed out of their space. A few minutes later he was driving down the street erratically. He took turn after turn without slowing. Accelerating quickly and braking suddenly, he watched mirrors and scanned the streets for any sign they might have a tail. Positive they weren't being followed, he turned onto a side street and made two more quick turns before pulling into a small park by the river. Maddie had her door open before he could come to a full stop.

He reached into the glove box and withdrew two extra clips of ammunition which he put into the pocket of his jacket. He joined Maddie who was following a path down to the water's edge. With more than just a little skip in her step, Maddie forced Hawke into a half jog in order to keep up with her. Ever vigilant, Hawke moved his head constantly, scanning the area for threats.

After a short distance she slowed to a stroll, holding her head high, rotating it from shoulder to shoulder so her hair waved from side to side. Hawke fell in step beside her and the two of them walked along the river together. He couldn't help but notice the smile on her face.

"Tell me about yourself, Hawke," she said.

"What?" he was caught off guard.

"Tell me about Sebastian Hawke," she said.

"I was a cop," Hawke said. "And now I'm a private investigator. I've told you this before."

"No," Maddie shook her head. "I want to know about you. Why did you become a cop? Have you ever been married? Do you have kids? I want to know the man I'm spending my time with."

Hawke did not immediately respond.

"Seriously?" Maddie turned to him. "I get nothing at all?"

"I'm not really the sharing type," he said.

"So, divorced?" she said.

"Once," he said.

"Once?" Maddie said. "What does that mean?"

"Married twice," he said. "Divorced once."

"So you're married?" she said. "Where is she?"

"No," he said. "I'm not married."

"But you said . . ."

"My first wife died," he said. "About a year after we married."

"I'm sorry," Maddie said.

"Don't be," Hawke said. "It was a long time ago."

"And you remarried?" she said.

"Yep," he nodded. "Lasted a little longer than the first marriage."

"What happened?"

"Let's just say we had different expectations of marriage," Hawke said.

"You wanted her to be your first wife," Maddie said. "She wanted you home with her?"

"Something like that," Hawke said.

"Any kids?"

"No," Hawke said. He saw movement and spun, gun in hand, as a squirrel scurried to the nearest tree. Maddie made herself small behind the man's larger frame. Deeming the squirrel non-threatening Hawke holstered his weapon.

"Don't you want some?" Maddie said when they were walking again.

"Some what?"

"Kids," Maddie said. "You know, some day?"

Hawke paused, his pace slowing. "I never gave it much thought."

"You're kidding?" she said. "I think about it all the time."

"Well that's . . ."

"Don't you dare tell me it's a woman's thing," she said. "Or that it's my biological clock."

"I wasn't," Hawke said. "All right. Maybe I was."

"I knew it," Maddie laughed.

"What about you and Ricky?" he said. "If you thought about having kids, why don't you have kids?"

"First it was school," she said. "Then it was my career. Then the whole starting a company thing. Eventually it came down to waiting for Ricky's art to become a success. Like that was going to happen."

"And now?"

"Now I'm getting a divorce," she said. "Not exactly the best time to have a baby."

"I don't know," Hawke said. "I've heard having kids fixes everything."

"You've heard that, have you?"

Hawke grinned. "We should head back."

"You haven't told me why you became a cop," she said.

"I tell you that," Hawke said, "and we head back. Agreed?"

"Agreed."

"It was the next step," he said. "Now let's go."

"Wait," she said. "That's no answer. I want to know the real reason."

"I was a soldier," Hawke said. He took a deep breath and let it out slowly. "Did my years and came home. They tell you that serving is hard and it is. What they don't tell you is stopping is even harder. Over there you're on constant alert. You fight when you have to. You kill when you have to. Then they send you home and tell you to get a job and become a civilian. Be normal."

"That must have been awful," Maddie said.

"It wasn't easy," Hawke said. "But unlike Woodrow, I got through it. I managed to land on my feet. I had a buddy that got out a year before me. I looked him up and he suggested I become a cop. Said it was a good fit; still wearing the vest and carrying the gun. Just had to focus on bad guys."

"And that's what you did?"

"What he didn't mention is how much time you spend with normal citizens having normal everyday problems," Hawke said.

"But that's a good thing," Maddie said. "Right?"

"Sure," he said. "But it took adjusting. Eventually, it was all good."

"Not all good," Maddie said. "You told me you punched your superior. Was that because of your time in the service?"

"Partly," he said. "Partly because he was an ass that needed to be punched."

"I'm sure he was," Maddie said.

"We do need to head back," Hawke said.

They turned and started back to the park.

"Thank you for this," Maddie said.

They walked to the truck silently, enjoying the view of the last of the evening's sun rays dipping below the horizon. The night air was brisk and Hawke offered his jacket to Maddie who refused. By the time she climbed into the truck, she was shivering. He started the truck and turned the heat on.

"I have another favor to ask," Maddie said.

"You want to stay in your house tonight," Hawke said. "We already discussed this."

"No," Maddie said. "I mean yes. I want to stay at home. But that isn't the favor."

"Then what is it?"

"I want to make one more stop on the way home," she said.

"We've already pushed our luck," he said. "It's dark out. Much harder to spot dangers. Can't this wait until tomorrow?"

"No," Maddie said. "It has to be this evening."

"And what is this stop that is too important to wait until daylight?"

"Ice cream," she said. "I want, no, I need ice cream."

"You're kidding," Hawke said.

"I never kid about ice cream," she said.

Hawke backed out of the parking space and steered toward the park exit. "Which way?"

"What?"

"I assume you have a favorite ice cream parlor or something," Hawke said. "Which way?"

"Turn left," Maddie said. "You're really going to let me get ice cream?"

"They didn't attack while we were alone and in the open," Hawke said. "We should be safe getting ice cream. But we take it to your place to eat."

25

The local ice creamery Maddie led Hawke to specialized in fresh-made, uniquely flavored ice creams. Sitting in Maddie's kitchen, she worked diligently on her triple scoop bowl while the two of them made small talk.

Hawke finished the single scoop he had gotten at Maddie's insistence then took a walk through the ground floor of the house checking doors and windows to ensure they were closed and locked. Everything secured, he climbed the stairs and did the same thing on the second level. He returned to the kitchen as Maddie was rinsing the spoons to put in the dishwasher.

"House is clear," he said. "Does your security system work?"

"It does," she said. She walked to the main hall, followed closely by Hawke, and set the alarm. "There. It's all set."

Hawke checked his watch. It was only a little past eight. "Kind of early to call it a night. What do you normally do in the evenings?"

"Watch a little TV, read, exercise, or work," she said. "What do you do?"

"TV and read," he said. "It's obvious I don't exercise."

"What'll it be?" she asked.

"You do what you want," he said. "I'm going to keep an eye on the entry points. Focus on keeping you safe."

"Thank you for that," she said. "I feel safe with you here."

"I'm glad you do," Hawke said. "And I intend to make sure you aren't putting your faith in the wrong place."

"I guess I'll take advantage of the time to catch up on some reading," Maddie said. She went to a small room off the foyer, pulled a book from a shelf and sat in an overstuffed chair.

Hawke followed, constantly scanning windows for movement. He stopped by one of the two windows in the room where she was and peered through at the darkness. He was not happy about them being in her home. There were too many points of access. It would take a team of three or four to properly monitor the perimeter. The back of the house was a security nightmare. Floor to ceiling windows made up seventy-five percent of the back wall, with three sets of French doors. Nothing to prevent a determined killer from gaining entry.

Over the next three hours, Hawke walked the perimeter of the house dozens of times, checking doors and windows with each pass. On each side of the structure, while checking locks, he searched the night for motion before moving on. He moved about quickly, trying to cover as much distance as he could without alarming Maddie, alternating his path so that anyone watching from outside would not identify a specific pattern. Even then, he felt it wasn't enough, not if there were a real threat.

Nearing eleven, Hawke passed through the room and noticed Maddie had closed her book and set it on the table beside her chair. He continued on the same path, looking outside and searching for the danger he knew had to be out there. Nothing appeared out of place. Nothing was any different than the previous fifteen times he had checked. Yet it still didn't look right. He stared a couple more minutes before turning to the red-headed woman he was charged with protecting. "You finished?"

"The book?" she said, stifling a yawn. "No. But I did get most of the way. My eyes were getting tired. I'm tired for that matter."

"You ready for bed then?" Hawke asked.

"Let me get a glass of water from the kitchen," she said. "Then, yes."

"I'll get the water," Hawke said. "You stay here. I'll walk you up."

He gave a glance to the windows then moved to the kitchen checking rooms and windows as he went. The third cabinet he opened revealed the glasses. He pulled one down and held it under the flow of cold water from the faucet. With just over a half a glass of water in hand, he returned to the reading room where Maddie was not.

He spun quickly and continued up the stairs, taking two steps at a time. He passed the glass from his right hand to his left, pulling his weapon free of its holster. Reaching the second floor, he held the gun before him, cautiously moving down the hall to the light that shone through the door of what he knew was her bedroom.

He rounded the opening and saw her facing away from him. He brought the weapon down and put it away just as she turned to him.

"I told you to wait downstairs," he said.

"Sorry," she said. "I'm just so tired. I wanted to come up."

"I understand," he said walking into the room. "But next time, wait for me."

He checked the bathroom, the closet and the windows. When he was sure they were secure, he excused himself and returned to the hallway.

"Goodnight, Hawke," she said.

"Lock the door and sleep well," he responded, shutting the door. He stood in place until he heard her engage the lock.

He turned the light on in the room across the hall. There was a chair in one corner next to a window. He dragged the chair into the hall and pushed it up to the wall. Turning the light out again, he let the darkness wash over him, allowing his eyes to adjust before he sat where he could keep an eye on either end of the hall with a turn of his head.

Having Maddie set the alarm was for her benefit. It would be enough to stop an everyday intruder. But a professional hitman, the kind he was expecting, would know how to bypass the alarm and gain entry.

From time to time, he stood and paced the length of the hall. Every third or fourth time he would descend the stairs and check the entry points there. Each time, he returned to the chair outside Maddie's room. The hours ticked by and he became drowsy. His pacing became more frequent in order to stay alert.

It was after three in the morning when he was on yet another pass through the ground floor that he saw one of the French doors standing ajar. He pulled his weapon, adrenaline kicking in. He cleared the rooms as he moved back through the house to the stairs. He saw a shadow ascending the steps and jumped back just as two muffled shots in close succession hit the wall inches from his head. The would-be assassin had gotten between him and Maddie.

26

Using the layout of the house to his advantage, Hawke made himself small against the foyer wall until he reached the stairway. Turning with his weapon out, he searched for a target. There was no one there. Taking the steps two at a time he closed the distance rapidly, gun at the ready.

He reached the second floor just as the shadow was about to breach Maddie's room. The intruder's foot smashed into the bedroom door, splintering wood. Maddie screamed and Hawke fired three shots into the upper body of the attacker. The shadow fell away from the doorway and behind the chair. Hawke dove to the ground as a single flash sent a bullet over his head. He fired twice into the chair. Another bullet passed over him and struck a wall somewhere in the darkness. Bounding to his feet Hawke ran and jumped over the chair, landing hard on the man who lay there. The intruder tried to turn his weapon on the PI, but Hawke grabbed his wrist.

"Maddie!?" he yelled out. "Are you okay, Maddie?"

"I'm here," she called back.

"Turn on a light," he shouted as he struggled to control the man's gun hand.

Light burst through the dark and allowed Hawke to see the man beneath him. The face was shrouded in a mask, the large eyes peering through the small holes. The gun tumbled out of his hand as he tried to fight off Hawke's assault. The other arm remained limp at his side, bleeding from just above the elbow. Hawke used the butt of his gun and coldcocked the guy, who went still.

"Do you have any rope?" Hawke called to Maddie.

"In the garage," she answered.

He did not relish the idea of sending her to the garage alone. "Anything up here?"

Maddie appeared in the doorway holding a lamp. "I have an electrical cord. It's Ricky's lamp. I always hated it."

Hawke took the lamp and cut the cord off. He pulled his prisoner into the chair and tied the man's hands to its arms. He asked for another and Maddie brought him the charging cable for Ricky's razor. Hawke used it to tie the man's legs to the chair. He then leaned down and picked up the silenced pistol the man had intended to use on Maddie.

Hawke checked the man's wounds. He had hit him all three of the first shots he had fired. Once in the arm and twice in the upper body. He was bleeding quite a bit. He would need a doctor soon. Hawke pulled the man's mask off and slapped his face twice to bring him around. When he was sure the man was awake, he slapped him again, only much harder.

"Who hired you?" Hawke said.

The man sat silently with a smirk on his face. Hawke formed a fist and punched the man in his gut, doubling him over.

"You're going to bleed out," Hawke said. "We can get you some help, but you need to talk. Tell me who hired you."

"You won't let me die," the man said. "I ain't telling you nothing."

Hawke showed him the weapon and then rested the barrel on top of the man's knee.

"You wouldn't," the man said. "You don't have it in you."

Hawke pulled the trigger and the man wailed in pain. Maddie flinched. Hawke calmly moved the gun barrel to the man's other knee. "Who hired you? And how do I find him?"

"Are you insane?" the man said. "You're a cop."

"Used to be," Hawke said. "Now? Not so much."

"Tell me what I want to know and Maddie will call 911," Hawke said. "We'll get you all fixed up. If you don't, I'm going to shoot out your other knee. And then we'll decide what other body parts you don't mind bleeding from."

"I don't know who hired me," the man said through clenched teeth.

"You know something," Hawke said.

"He didn't share his name," the man said.

"What do you know about him?"

"He's a fixer," the man said. "He makes other people's problems disappear."

"Did you meet with him?"

"Once."

"What did he look like?"

"A big dude," the man said. "Comfortable in a suit."

"What did he drive?"

"I don't know," the man said. Hawke moved the gun slightly and the guy said, "Wait. I remember. It was a . . . a black sedan. I think it was a BMW. Yeah. It was a black BMW."

"And how do you get ahold of him?" Hawke said. "You know. To tell him you were successful."

"You don't just call this guy," the man said. "He calls you."

"That's too bad." Hawke stood straight and aimed the silenced weapon at the man's chest.

"Hawke!" Maddie cried out.

"I swear that's all I know," the man pleaded.

Hawke lowered the gun. He turned to Maddie, "Make the call."

27

"What did you do to this guy?" Roger asked.

"I asked him a few questions," Hawke said.

"He's been shot four times," Roger said. "The shot to the knee appears to be a contact wound."

"I may have encouraged him to answer," Hawke said. "Didn't take much."

"If he presses charges . . ."

"He won't," Hawke said.

"What makes you so sure?"

"I shot him three times," Hawke said. "Stopping him from murdering my client. The shot to the knee was with his own gun. I think it was self-inflicted."

"You think anyone's going to buy that?"

"It's all I'm selling," Hawke said. "Now if you'll excuse me, I need to get my client somewhere safe."

"I'm not done with you," Roger said. "Besides, she's still giving her statement. Now, tell me what happened."

"I've told you," Hawke said, looking across the driveway where Maddie was talking to another detective. "I've told you. I've told the first officer on scene. I think I even told one of your rookies. I'm tired. I need sleep, and I need to get Maddie somewhere safe."

"Where are you going to take her?" Roger said. "Where can you possibly keep her safe?"

That was a question Hawke had begun to ask himself. It seemed there was an endless flow of killers coming after Maddie. Of course, if they kept getting killed, it didn't cost much to keep hiring more. Dead men don't get paid.

"I've kept her safe up to now," Hawke said. "Why would I tell you where I'm taking her?"

"Because you know you can trust me," Roger said. "And I'm assigning a car to watch the place when you get there."

"We're going to my place," Hawke said.

"That dump?" Roger said. "You sure you want to take a woman there?"

"She's already seen it," Hawke said. "And I don't know why you're saying anything. I've seen the shithole you live in."

"I like my place," he said.

"So do the rats," Hawke said. "First one I saw, I thought it was a cat."

"You're just jealous because you can't have pets," Roger said.

"If you two are finished," a female officer said, "the witness has given her statement."

"Thank you, officer," Roger said. "Would you bring Ms. Rochester over here?"

"Don't bother," Hawke said, shouldering himself between the two of them. "I'll get her. We need to be going."

"Hawke," Roger said. "Wait until I can arrange an escort."

"I told you where we will be," Hawke said. "We'll be fine there."

"You're stubborn," the detective said.

"You're right," Hawke said. "See you around."

Hawke walked up to Maddie slowly. She was still shaking inside the blanket someone had given her. He wrapped his arm around her and led her away from the crime scene that was her home. She did not resist, only walked alongside the PI with her head tilted slightly into his large chest.

He guided her to the truck and helped her inside then circled the vehicle without checking for devices. It was a pointless effort. They seemed they would be found no matter what he did. He was pretty sure they wouldn't send anyone else for at least several hours. First, they would try to contact the man who had just failed. Unable to do so they would come up with their next plan of action. Maddie would be safe for the rest of the night.

He drove to his building and the two of them entered his apartment without a peep out of Mrs. Mancini. Apparently the woman did sleep sometimes. Hawke quickly cleared the rooms then took a few things out of his room before relinquishing it to Maddie. Exhausted, she was asleep within minutes. Hawke pulled the door closed and turned to the living room. He too was ready for some rest. He shoved the couch under the windows. He took the matching chair and used it to block the door to the hallway. There would be no entry without his knowledge.

He lay down, gun in hand, and closed his eyes. The events of the day ran through his mind, threatening to keep him awake. He pushed them all away and slept. Not the deep sleep he truly needed, it was filled with dreams he would barely remember. But it was sleep.

28

Hawke opened his eyes to sunlight shining brightly through the window above his head. Far too much light for a breaking dawn, he checked his watch. It was past 11:00 am. He sat up searching for signs of a breach. Instead he saw Maddie sitting on the arm of the couch with the blanket they gave her earlier that morning pulled around her shoulders.

"You cold?" he asked.

"We left my place in a hurry," she said. "I don't have much on under here."

"Oh," he said, unable to stop himself from looking down.

"Eyes up here," she said.

"Sorry," he said. "Power of suggestion."

"Sure," she said. "What are we going to do about this?"

"I can loan you a shirt," he said. "It would be long enough to cover you."

"Any shirt in particular?"

"My closet is yours," he said.

"I'll be back," she grinned. She hopped off the couch, went to the bedroom and closed the door.

Hawke took advantage of the time to return the furniture to where it had been. He started a pot of coffee and leaned against the counter waiting for it to brew. He was pouring himself a cup when Maddie reemerged from the bedroom.

"What do you think?" she asked, posing in her new outfit.

She wore one of his dark blue button-down shirts cinched at the waist with one of his belts wrapped around her body twice.

"I think I'll never be able to wear that shirt again," he said. "Looks much better on you."

"You are a very good liar," Maddie smiled. "Maybe we can swing by my house and get some clothes? And my purse?"

"It's an active crime scene," Hawke said. Maddie's shoulders fell. "But I will see what I can do."

"I would appreciate it," she said. "What's on the agenda today?"

"There are six names on our list," Hawke said. "We're going to start checking them out. We'll either find whoever is behind this, or we'll eliminate them all as suspects."

"You're not going to question them like you did that man last night are you?" Maddie said.

"I won't shoot anyone's knees," Hawke said. "He was a pro. He wasn't going to be persuaded to give up information. I did what I had to in order to get him to tell me what he knew. The names on your list aren't professionals. They'll crack. I won't shoot anyone who doesn't prove an immediate threat to you."

Maddie nodded. The confidence Hawke was used to being in her eyes was not there. He put his hand on her shoulder. "I'm going to protect you."

"I know that," Maddie said. "I'm just scared. They just keep coming."

"And we'll keep stopping them," Hawke said. "Okay?"

"Okay," she said. "So where do we start?"

"Let's start with the two we can find the fastest," Hawke said. "Penelope and Mr. Burns."

Maddie visibly stiffened.

"Unless you want to save Penelope for later?" Hawke said.

"No," she said. "Let's get it over with. The sooner we do, the sooner I don't ever have to talk to her again."

"That's the spirit," Hawke said.

They drove to Derek and Penelope's house without much conversation. Hawke was watching for threats at every intersection and in every car that passed. He was missing his Taurus that blended in with traffic. But he appreciated the fact that if trouble did arise, the truck had the power to get them out of it.

When they arrived at the house they had once followed Ricky to, Hawke parked the truck across the driveway, blocking in the cars there. He stepped out and turned back at Maddie. "You want to wait out here? So you don't have to see her?"

"No," Maddie said. "I'll go. I want to hear what she has to say."

The two of them approached the door side by side. On the porch, Maddie stepped to one side and Hawke stood square to the doorway. He used his fist to announce them, hammering the wooden door hard enough to make the windows vibrate.

The door swung open and Derek stood there in a t-shirt and boxers. His chest heaved and his face was red with anger at the intrusion. He sized Hawke up and his demeanor ratcheted back a couple notches. When he saw Maddie he almost deflated.

"What the hell, Maddie?" he said. "Where's Ricky?"

"You don't talk to your wife much, do you?" Hawke said.

"What?"

"Never mind," Maddie said. "Is she here?"

"In the kitchen," Derek said, stepping to one side.

Maddie walked into the house, followed by Hawke. Derek looked from the PI to Maddie then returned to his perch on the couch where he continued his paused video game. Maddie led the way through the small house to the kitchen. Penelope was standing at the sink trying hard to look like she was doing the dishes.

"Penelope?" Maddie said.

The woman turned so suddenly, Hawke thought she might have a weapon. His hand instinctively went for his sidearm. When her turn was complete, she only had a plate in her hands which she held on to with a death grip.

"Maddie?" she said in a very timid voice. "I'm so sorry."

"Save it," Maddie said. "Hawke has some questions."

A confused Penelope shifted her gaze to the large man beside her once best friend. "Questions?"

"When did you start sleeping with Ricky?" Hawke said.

"Shhhh," Penelope said. "He'll kill me."

"He has his damned headphones on," Maddie said. "Just answer him."

Penelope looked at Maddie for a long moment.

"When?" Hawke said.

"I," she stammered. "It's just, I mean . . ."

"When?" Maddie yelled out.

"Four years ago," Penelope cried. "I'm so sorry, Maddie. You have to understand. You have to forgive me."

"Four years?" Maddie said. "You were my best friend, and you've been sleeping with my husband for four years?"

"She's what?" Derek said from the doorway. "Pen? What is she talking about?"

"It's not what it sounds like," Penelope said to Derek.

"It sounds like you've been cheating on me," Derek said. "With my cousin."

The couple started to argue, talking over one another. Maddie added something from time to time when prompted. Hawke stood in the middle growing less and less patient.

"Everybody shut up!" he shouted.

The room went silent and all eyes were on him.

"I don't care about your marriage," Hawke said. "I don't care about your relationship with Maddie. All I care about is how far down the hole you've crawled."

"What does that mean?" Derek said. "Who are you?"

"Penelope," Hawke said. "Look at me. Did you hire someone to have Maddie killed? And don't lie. I'll know."

"Killed?" Penelope said. "Maddie? Why would I have Maddie killed? She's my best friend."

Maddie stared at Penelope, then turned to Hawke. "Well?"

"She's clear," Hawke said. "Let's get out of here."

"Maddie?" Penelope said.

"God, Penelope," Maddie said. "What could you possibly say to me?"

She left the kitchen with Hawke close behind. Before they reached the front door the couple was screaming at one another again. They could hear the argument all the way to the street.

"He's not going to really kill her is he?" Hawke said.

"Are you kidding?" Maddie said. "Without her, he would have to get off his ass and get a job."

They climbed into the truck and drove away.

29

Mr. Burns was standing in his manicured front yard watering his meticulously cared for flower beds. Hawke chose to park in Maddie's driveway and the two of them walked across her lawn to confront the neighbor. Mr. Burns did not acknowledge them as they approached.

"Are you Mr. Burns?" Hawke said.

"Who's askin'," Mr. Burns said.

"My name's Hawke," he said. "I would . . ."

"Hawke?" Mr. Burns said half turning. "You don't have a last name?"

"That is my last name," Hawke said. "I . . ."

"So no first name?" Mr. Burns said. "Your parents didn't see fit to name you?"

"No, sir, they didn't," Hawke snapped. "I'm here to ask you some questions. Then we'll be on our way."

"You don't have to yell," Mr. Burns said. "I'm not deaf."

"You may have noticed the police over there," Hawke pointed to Maddie's house.

"Don't surprise me," Mr. Burns said. "That woman's not a very good person."

"I'm right here, Mr. Burns," Maddie said.

"I'm not blind either," the man said.

"I understand that you and Ms. Rochester had a run in a while back," Hawke said.

"Is that what she told you?"

"It is," Hawke said.

"Well, then," Mr. Burns said. "Why are you asking me?"

"She says you were very angry at the time," Hawke said.

"I was," the man confirmed.

"Are you still angry?" Hawke asked.

"You could say that," Mr. Burns said.

"So you're holding a grudge?"

"A grudge?" the man said, looking down at his feet. "I guess you could call it that."

"Enough to do her harm?" Hawke said.

"Harm?" Mr. Burns said. "I never hurt her. I never hurt you."

"But did you hire someone else to hurt her?" Hawke said.

"Hire someone?" Mr. Burns said. "What are you trying to say? What are you accusing me of?"

"Did you hire someone to kill Ms. Rochester?"

"Kill her?" Mr. Burns said. "First you say I hurt her. Now you're saying I'm trying to kill her? You have some nerve coming onto my lawn and accusing me of things I didn't do. I have half a mind to . . ."

Mr. Burns turned the water on Hawke, who stepped forward and yanked the hose from the man's hands.

"Unless you want an enema with this I suggest you stop."

Mr. Burns shied away from the PI. Hawke threw the hose to the ground.

"Let's go," Hawke said. "If his idea of an outburst is spraying me with water, I doubt he's plotting revenge killings."

Maddie grinned and followed Hawke back to the truck. The two of them climbed into the cab where Hawke turned on the heat in an attempt to dry his clothes.

"Well, two down," Maddie said. "Who do we see next?"

"Why don't we pay your friend Peterson another visit?" Hawke said.

"Teddy?" Maddie said. "Sure, why not? It's not like he and I were close."

30

The building that housed TPi looked drastically different in the light of day. In darkness the structure had appeared gray and gloomy, almost ghostly. Pulling up in front of the entrance, the white and steel walls were bright and alluring. Even the logo mounted above the door appeared more inviting than it had the night before.

Hawke and Maddie entered the building and stepped up to the security guard who had his head bowed. Hawke couldn't tell if he was sleeping or reading. When they were directly in front of the man's desk Hawke saw the man was texting. They stood silently for a moment but when the guard made no attempt to acknowledge them Hawke cleared his throat to get his attention. When that failed the PI reached across the desk and yanked the phone out of the man's hands.

"Hey," the guard raised his head at last. "What the hell? Give me my phone or we're going to have a problem."

"We already have a problem," Hawke said. "Get Peterson on the phone."

"Mr. Peterson is in a meeting," the guard said. "He's not taking visitors."

"I didn't ask if he was available," Hawke leaned over the guard. "I told you to get him on the phone."

"I don't work for you. I work for Mr. Peterson," the guard said. "He told me not to disturb him, so I'm not. Now give me my phone or I'll call the cops."

"You want your phone? I'll . . ."

"Hawke," Maddie put her hand on the PI's arm and used her other to take the phone. She held it out to the guard and said, "Just call Teddy and tell him Maddie is here about the BMW."

The guard snatched the phone from her hand. "Lady, I don't care who you are. You aren't going to see Mr. Peterson."

Maddie turned to Hawke, "So much for being nice."

"Nice doesn't get you anywhere," Hawke said.

"Isn't that sad," Maddie said. "Used to be nice was the best way to get through to people. Now you have to insult them, yell at them or hurt them just to get them to listen."

"That's what I find to be true," Hawke said. He hooked his thumb at the guard. "Take this guy. I tried nice, or at least kind of nice."

"You did take his phone," Maddie said.

"Only because I don't like being ignored," Hawke said. "But I wasn't rude. Just asked to see Peterson. But that went nowhere. So now I'm left with insult, yell or hurt."

"Just like I said," Maddie said.

"But this guy," Hawke said. "Insults won't go anywhere. He's too tough for that. And yelling, well, that just isn't my style. So, I guess I have to hurt him."

The two of them turned to the guard who, up to that point, sat listening to their banter. "You wouldn't."

"I would," Hawke said.

"He would," Maddie nodded.

"Besides," Hawke stepped to the side of the desk. "I'm already going to get, what would you say, five years for that last guy?"

"At least," Maddie said.

"What's a few more years?"

"How much could they add?" Maddie said.

"Fine," the guard said, reaching for the desk phone. "I'll let him know you're here. But when he says he won't see you there's nothing more I can do."

"Fair enough," Hawke said.

The guard pushed the number for Teddy's office and waited. He let it ring for some time before Teddy finally answered.

"Hey, boss," he said. He was silent for a while, then, "Yes, sir. I know, sir. It's just . . . Yes, sir. There's someone here to . . . Yes, sir. A Maddie and a big guy. Yes, sir. Okay, sir."

He hung up the phone and looked at the two intruders in his space.

"Well?" Maddie said.

"He'll be down in a minute," the guard muttered.

"I knew it," Hawke said. He and Maddie stepped away from the desk to wait. He leaned close to Maddie. "These intellectuals, who think they're smarter than everyone else, always want to talk. Especially the guilty ones. They get off proving they are smart enough to get away with it."

"So, he's guilty because he wants to talk?"

"No," Hawke said. "But if he is, he'll be trying to play games with us just to prove he can get away with it."

"That just doesn't sound like Teddy," Maddie said.

"How long has it been since you two were in college?" Hawke said. "People change. Or maybe you didn't know him as well as you thought you did back then. You said the two of you were competitive. Did you ever have things go missing? Or maybe you wrote some code that worked one day but not the next? He could be the reason why."

"Sure I lost things," Maddie said. "But I can't blame him for everything I ever misplaced. And as far as code goes, everyone knows how easy it is to make a mistake that makes it stop working. But I could always backtrack and fix it."

"Did you have a thing for this guy?"

"What?"

"You're awfully quick to defend him," Hawke said. "Is he an old crush?"

"Teddy?" Maddie said. "Not at all. I just like to see the good in people, I guess."

"Yeah," Hawke said. "In my line of work, you don't get that luxury."

They waited about ten more minutes before Teddy appeared. He came through the locked door a few feet from where the security guard sat. He smiled at them, or at least at Maddie, leaving Hawke to wonder if maybe he had been the one with the crush. When he reached them, he held his hand out to shake. Hawke clasped it in an iron grip that made Teddy cringe a little. He moved on to Maddie who had a much softer touch. He held her hand a bit longer.

"Well, twice in as many days," Teddy said. "To what do I owe this pleasure?"

"Hawke has some questions for you," Maddie said.

"He does?" Teddy turned to the investigator. "About the car?"

"No," Hawke said. "These are more about you."

"Me?" Teddy tilted his head. "What could you possibly want to know about me?"

"The two of you mentioned being competitors in college," Hawke said.

"Sure," Teddy grinned at Maddie. "Why?"

"Was it ever more than competition?"

"What?" Teddy said. "I don't understand what you're asking."

"Were you ever jealous of Maddie?" Hawke said. "Maybe obsessed with her?"

"No," Teddy was taken aback. "I mean sure, I was jealous at how easy everything seemed to be for her. But it made me work that much harder. She's the reason I became so good at what I do."

"So you don't have any pent-up grudge because her success came so easy to her?" Hawke said. "Or maybe her company stole a contract you were after? Pissed you off. Enough so that you wanted to get rid of that competition you say you're so fond of?"

"Hawke," Maddie said.

"Okay," Teddy's voice became more forceful. "First of all, I don't know where all this is coming from, but let me get one thing clear. I have no reason to be jealous of Maddie anymore. Sure she's successful, but my company outperforms hers by millions. Second, we are both in the programming business, but we do entirely different things. Her company would not be looking to steal any contract I might be working on."

"You sure know a lot about her company for someone who isn't obsessed with her," Hawke observed.

"I kept track of my college friends," Teddy said. "And I did look into her company to see if it would be competition, but it wasn't, as I said. Maddie, I don't know what all this is about. Whatever it is, I'm sorry if someone is doing you wrong, but it isn't me."

"I know, Teddy," Maddie spoke softly. "I'm sorry. Hawke's just talking to everyone."

"Well," Teddy looked at her and his body became less rigid. "Just take your thug and go."

He turned back to the locked door. He said something to the guard who stood, then scanned his access card and disappeared to the back. The guard came around his desk and approached Hawke and Maddie.

"Let's go," Hawke said.

The two of them left the building just ahead of the guard, who had a smirk on his face.

"That doesn't take him off my list," Hawke said when they were outside.

"I figured as much," Maddie said.

31

"Who next?" Maddie fastened her seatbelt and looked at Hawke as he did the same.

"That leaves us with Ambrose, Raymond and Jamie," Hawke said. "You don't happen to know an address for any of them?"

"No addresses," Maddie said.

"We can swing by my office and see what we can find on them," Hawke started the truck. "Probably start with Raymond. If you made my company go under, I might feel the need to take it out on you."

"I'll remember that," Maddie said.

Hawke gave the TPi building one last glance in the rearview mirror before merging into traffic. Something about Teddy had rubbed him the wrong way. That wasn't unusual. A lot of people got on Hawke's nerves. Sometimes all it took was being in the same room. That wasn't enough to assume guilt, but it had moved the man to the top of Hawke's suspect list.

At the office, Hawke sat behind his desk using the internet to search for Raymond Vallance while Maddie sat and stared at the bare walls. The search produced more results than the investigator expected. He tried localizing the search and came up with two possibilities. Hawke jotted down the addresses in his notebook.

Not to waste time, he entered Ambrose Sinclair's name. It was much easier to find the programmer's address. He wrote it down and moved on to Jamie Simmons.

The woman's name produced hundreds of results. Even narrowing the parameters left him with dozens of options. He turned the computer to Maddie who scrolled through the long list of profiles.

"Her," Maddie stopped on a photo of a woman about her age with gaunt features and artificially black hair. Below her picture her likes were listed as running, biking and mountain climbing.

"You picked a fight with her?"

"I did not pick a fight," Maddie said. "I accepted an invitation to dinner. I didn't know he had forgotten to tell her that he had dumped her and moved on."

"You said you dumped him right after that, didn't you?" Hawke leaned back in his chair.

"I did," Maddie said. "But she blamed me. She harassed me for months after."

"Did you report it to the police?" Hawke asked.

"No."

"Why not?" Hawke said. "What if it had escalated? Or did?"

"Honestly, I felt bad for her," Maddie said. "The jerk didn't even break up with her. He just moved on. That had to hurt. I didn't want to call the police and add to her problems."

"I guess we'll find out if that was the right move or not," Hawke said. He worked the keyboard for a little while and came up with an address for the woman, adding it to the list. He put all four addresses into a GPS program. "Raymond number one is closest and to our west. The other Raymond is a couple of miles farther but to the south. The other two are equally distant, Ambrose to the north and Jamie to the northeast. We could hit those two first, then Raymond one and finish with Raymond two. There's someone I want to see out in that area of town anyway."

"Sounds good to me," Maddie said. She stood and stretched. "You should really do something with this place."

"This place is fine," Hawke said.

"If you came in here, would you hire you?" Maddie asked.

"You hired me," Hawke said.

"That's different," Maddie walked toward the door. "I had seen you at work. You saved me twice. But others would come here and their first impression of you would be . . . this place. What does that say?"

"It says I don't waste money on crap," Hawke said.

"It says you have no imagination," Maddie said. "And apparently no license."

"I have a license," Hawke said.

"Then why don't you hang it up somewhere?"

"It isn't a medical degree," Hawke opened the door for her. "Nobody cares if it's on the wall or not."

"You would be surprised," Maddie said. She looked at Hawke's impassive expression. "Think about it."

Hawke grunted, closed and locked the door, then followed the woman to the bottom of the stairs.

32

Turning the corner into Jamie Simmons' neighborhood, the duo was caught off guard by what they saw. The address was not a home, but rather a trailer park. There had been no indication of a unit or lot number when Hawke had done his search. He coasted to a stop just shy of the first trailer on the road.

"Well, this isn't good. Do you have any idea what she drives?" the investigator asked. Maddie wrinkled her brow. He said, "Didn't think so."

"How many do you suppose there are?" Maddie said.

"We're not going door to door," Hawke said.

Off the road to the left there was a bank of mailboxes presumably for the entire park. Just beyond it stood a trailer with a well-manicured lawn and an "Office" sign in front. They were unlikely to share, but it was worth a try. Hawke pulled up and parked in front of the building.

Hawke walked up the drive and followed the sidewalk to the front door, following the suggestion on the door to enter. Maddie wandered over to the mailboxes and started reading the names under the lot numbers. Inside, Hawke waited in a room that doubled as an office and a living room for the onsite manager. After a couple minutes he tapped the bell on the composite board desktop.

"B'right there," a woman said.

Hawke turned, trying to discern where the voice had come from. The size of the structure should have made it easy to pin down sound, but somehow made it seem to come from all directions at once.

The woman appeared in the hallway leading to the bedrooms. She was a heavyset woman in her fifties or sixties leaning laboriously on a walker. She made the painstaking journey to where Hawke stood. He felt he should offer his assistance, but didn't know what he could do for her.

"What kin I do fer ya?" she said, her breathing as burdensome as her movements.

"I'm sorry to bother you ma'am," Hawke said.

The woman inhaled deeply and let it out in a rush.

"I'm looking for a woman who is supposed to live here," he explained. "But I only have an address. No lot number."

"Name?" she said forcefully.

"Name's Sebastian Hawke," Hawke introduced himself.

"Sebastian?" the woman inhaled name. "Strange name for a woman."

"No," Hawke said. "My name is Sebastian Hawke."

"What do I care what your name is?" the woman turned herself with a great deal of effort and sat hard on a lopsided recliner.

"Her name is Simmons," Hawke corrected. "Jamie Simmons."

"Oh, Jamie," the woman nodded. "Lovely girl."

"That's what I've heard," Hawke lied.

"But what a bitch," the woman continued.

"Heard that too," Hawke grinned.

"Lot fifty-six," she said. "If you're thinking of takin' her out of here she owes me two months' rent. You understand?"

"Yes ma'am," Hawke said. "Two months' rent."

He bowed his head and backed out the door. Outside he turned to the truck where Maddie stood leaning against the front fender. He walked out to join her.

"Did you get the lot number?" she asked.

"As a matter of fact," Hawke said. "I did. It was remarkably easy."

"Was it fifty-six?" she smiled.

Hawke looked at the mailboxes then back to her. "Seriously? They have their names on the boxes?"

"Not all of them," Maddie said. "But fifty-six had the name J. Simmons."

Hawke shook his head and the two of them climbed into the truck. "She's behind on her rent."

"So she probably didn't hire a hitman," Maddie said.

"Unless she used the rent money to hire him," Hawke suggested.

Finding lot fifty-six proved to be a challenge in itself as most of the markers were worn to the point of being illegible. When they found the right trailer they parked between it and the neighbor's. The parking pad had two cars on it, one an old Buick with two flat tires and the hood popped up, though not open. The other was a Chevy truck with rusted out wheel wells and a dent in the bed just behind the driver's door.

The two of them stepped up to the door and Hawke knocked. They waited a minute and knocked again.

"Get the damn door!" a man's voice yelled.

"You get the damn door!" a woman shouted back.

"I'm busy," the man said.

"You're busy sittin' on your ass!" the woman shouted again, though she sounded closer.

The door opened and Jamie Simmons appeared.

"What do you want?" she said. Her gaze fell on Maddie and her expression changed. "Hell no. You get out of here."

"Jamie Simmons?" Hawke said.

"What's it to you?" she said. "She knows who I am. What? You want to steal another man from me?"

"God, no," Maddie said. "I didn't want to steal the other one."

"So, now you admit it?" Jamie said. "What is this? You in AA? Need to make amends?"

"We need to ask you some questions," Hawke instinctively stepped between the two women.

"I don't have to talk to you," she said. "Especially not her."

"It will just take a minute and we'll be out of your life," Hawke reasoned.

"Leave now and you'll be out of my life," Jamie countered.

"I would just come back," Hawke said.

"Fine," Jamie huffed. "What do you want to know?"

"Landlord says you're behind on your rent," Hawke said.

"That's not your business," she said.

"That depends on why you're behind," Hawke said.

"I'm behind 'cause I ain't paid her," Jamie smirked.

"Is it because you fell on hard times?" Hawke said. "Or because you hired someone to kill Ms. Rochester?"

"Kill . . .?" Jamie looked at Maddie. "Why would I do that?"

"You said she stole your boyfriend," Hawke said.

"Hell, that was nearly ten years ago," she said. "And that a-hole wasn't worth the time."

"You harassed Ms. Rochester for several weeks," Hawke said.

"Yeah," she said. "Well, I was young and stupid."

"Can you tell me why you weren't able to pay your rent?"

"I couldn't pay because," Jamie leaned back and shouted into the trailer, "because that nimrod lost his job because he's too lazy to get off his ass and go to work!"

"Go to hell!" the response came back.

Hawke glanced at Maddie and rolled his eyes. He cocked his head toward the truck and the two of them left the trailer with the couple screaming inside. It was unlikely she was who they were looking for.

33

Ambrose Sinclair lived five miles away and a world apart from Jamie Simmons. His stately home sat on a sprawling ten acres complete with stables and a pond. The driveway was approximately a hundred yards from the street to the home. There were two other structures besides the house and the stable. One appeared to be a guest house, smaller but similar to the main building. The other was a garage, with four overhead and two regular doors. For a man who had lost his company, he was doing very well for himself.

Hawke slowed to a stop at the entrance. It was gated, but the gates stood open, inviting them in. "You sure this man suffered because of you winning that bid?"

"No. I'm not sure of anything," Maddie said. "I just heard that shortly after losing out on that contract he lost the company."

"What was the company called?"

"From Mind to Reality," Maddie said.

"Okay," Hawke accelerated down the drive. "Let's see what he has to say."

There was a large circular drive directly in front of the house with a half dozen vehicles parked with no particular organization. Hawke pulled up behind the last one and parked. The two of them stepped out of the truck and scanned the acreage. It would be a beautiful place to wake up to.

"You think he has guests?" Maddie was looking at the cars.

"No idea," Hawke said. "Only one way to find out."

They stepped onto the large wraparound porch and up to the door. It opened just before Hawke could knock. There was a woman standing behind a screen door wiping her hands on a towel. "Hello. What brings you to our home?"

"Mrs. Sinclair, I presume?" Hawke said with a touch of sweetness that took Maddie by surprise.

"You presume right," the woman said. "And you are?"

"Name's Sebastian Hawke, ma'am," Hawke almost bowed. "I'm a private investigator and I need to talk to your husband. Is he here?"

"He was down for a nap," she said. "Have a seat and I'll see if he's up."

The woman shut the door leaving Hawke and Maddie standing on the porch. They followed her suggestion and sat in a couple of matching rocking chairs just to the side of the door.

"What was that?" Maddie asked.

"What was what?" Hawke said.

"That voice?" Maddie said. "I thought for a minute you might kiss her hand or something."

"People of money like to feel important," Hawke said. "Talk to them like that and they are more willing to talk to you."

"You don't talk to me like that," Maddie said. "I'm people of money."

"You've already told me what I need to know," Hawke shrugged.

The door opened, followed by the screen. The woman leaned out. "He'll be right down. Can I get you some tea or lemonade?"

"Lemonade would be great, thank you," Hawke said.

"And you, miss?"

"I'm good, thank you," Maddie smiled.

The screen closed, but the door remained open. A moment later Mrs. Sinclair stepped out and handed Hawke a glass. He nodded and sipped the cool liquid. "Oh, my. Haven't had fresh squeezed in years."

"Glad you like it," she said. "Well, I need to get back to things. Just leave the glass on the table when you're done."

The woman vanished again. Maddie watched Hawke take a long drink.

"She's like a southern lady, or something," Maddie said.

"Makes a mean lemonade," Hawke said. He downed the rest of the beverage and set the glass on the table next to him as she had requested.

The screen opened again and a man in a suit and tie stepped out. He held the screen as it closed to keep it from slamming, then walked to where his unexpected guests were waiting.

"I'm Ambrose Sinclair," the man introduced. "My wife said you wanted to see me?"

There was none of the southern charm that embodied his wife. He was a straightforward, get to the point kind of man. As such, Hawke took a direct approach with him as well.

"I need to ask you some questions about a company you owned," Hawke said.

"Which one would that be?" Ambrose leaned against a porch post. "I've owned several."

"I'm interested in From Mind to Reality," the investigator said. "Closed recently, I understand."

"If you call eighteen months ago, recently," Ambrose said. "Then, yes. What could your interest possibly be in F.M.R.?"

"I was told that the company closed shortly after losing a contract bid to another firm," Hawke said. "Is that true?"

"I suppose it's possible," the man reached into his pocket and withdrew a pipe and a handkerchief. He started polishing the pipe with the cloth. "Don't really keep track of those things."

Hawke got the impression the man kept track of everything. "So, you don't remember losing a contract to Rochester-Kinsley Incorporated?"

"Oh," Ambrose drew out the word, something coming to mind. "You're talking about the Livingston contract."

Hawke looked at Maddie who nodded. He said, "Yes. That's the one."

"I still don't understand your interest," Ambrose said, stuffing the pipe with tobacco. "That was some time ago. Who are you working for?"

"My client is Rochester," Hawke said.

"Rochester?" Ambrose looked off as he lit the pipe, puffing clouds of smoke into the air. "Madeline wasn't it? Never met her."

"That's her," Hawke said. "I must say, you remember a lot about the details."

"Rochester-Kinsley was my main competition at the time," Ambrose said. "I learned all I could about them."

"But you never met?" Hawke asked.

"Obviously not," Ambrose said, pointing at Maddie. "Or I would have known who she was right away. Pictures don't do you justice, Ms. Rochester. What exactly is it you think I did to you and your company on that bid? I didn't exactly force you to underbid me."

"We're more interested in what you've been up to since that time," Hawke said. "You know, after your company folded."

"Folded?" Ambrose raised an eyebrow. "Who said the company folded?"

"Shortly after we won that bid," Maddie spoke for the first time. "I was told you lost the company."

"I didn't lose the company," Ambrose sucked on the pipe and blew smoke over Hawke's head. "I sold the company. New owners changed the name to . . ."

"Digital Art Forms," Maddie said. "They bought it from you?"

"Yes ma'am," Ambrose said. "Made a fortune on that deal."

"So you weren't financially devastated?" Hawke asked.

"Does it look like I'm financially devastated?" Ambrose gestured to the property around him.

"No, it doesn't," Hawke said. "But looks can be deceiving, as they say. For all I know, you could be in foreclosure."

"Could be," Ambrose said. "But I'm not. Listen, I'm not going to show you my finances. They're none of your damn business. But whatever it is you're looking for, you won't find it here."

"So, you never had a desire to hurt Ms. Rochester?" Hawke said. "Or to have someone hurt her?"

"Never," the man said. "I respect Rochester-Kinsley. If I tried to hurt every company that edged me out on a contract, let's just say I have much better things to do with my time. And with that in mind, I would ask you to leave now. I'm rather busy."

Hawke and Maddie stood. The two of them walked to the steps leading to the driveway and started to leave.

"Thank you for your time, Mr. Sinclair," Hawke called back to the man.

"My pleasure," the man said. "It was . . . enlightening. Have a good day Ms. Rochester."

Maddie nodded silently then continued to the truck. Hawke climbed in and they were on the road again in a matter of minutes.

"What'd you think?" Hawke asked.

"I don't know," Maddie said. "He didn't seem to want to hurt me."

"I don't trust him," Hawke said. "But his wife sure makes good lemonade."

34

Hawke found two Raymond Vallance's in his search. One had a very small social media presence with very poor-quality pictures that Maddie could not identify as being her former employee, nor could she say he wasn't. The second had a huge presence, but did not have a single photo of himself anywhere, choosing instead to use slogans and symbols as his profile pics.

Given that the man worked in the programming field for a living, Hawke chose to believe the second was the man they were searching for. The only way a tech-savvy person would create the first profile would be to throw people off his scent. That would mean the man was hiding from someone. Which of course meant they would still need to take a look at him.

Even so, Hawke chose Raymond Vallance number two to be the next interview. They drove through town making small talk to fill the awkward silence and pass the time.

Number two lived in an apartment complex in a lower-middle-class part of town. Unlike the trailer park, Hawke had an apartment number at the ready. Raymond lived on the third floor. The layout of the complex made finding the correct building a breeze and Hawke parked the truck just a few spaces from the entrance.

They got out and climbed the stairs to apartment 2308. Once there they knocked and waited. After a short time they knocked again. They waited a little longer the second time before knocking again. They were waiting after the third knock when a twenty-something woman climbed the stairs behind them. She stepped up to 2306 and unlocked her door.

"He won't answer," she said before going inside.

"Is he home?" Hawke asked.

"Usually is," the woman said. "But he never comes to the door for anyone."

"Not even you?" Maddie asked.

"Especially not me," she grinned. "He thinks I called the manager on him for something, which I didn't do. But there's no telling him that."

"He doesn't work?" Maddie asked.

"I don't know," she said. "If he does, he must work from home, because I never see him leave. Not for very long anyway. Usually comes back with groceries when he does."

"Okay, thanks," Hawke said. He turned back to look at the door he had been knocking on while the young woman disappeared behind hers.

"What do we do?" Maddie said.

"Chances are he's in there," Hawke said.

"And that he won't come to the door," Maddie added.

Hawke balled his hand into a fist and banged on the door with so much force the door frame shook. "Mr. Vallance! Step away front the door! We're coming in!"

"Hawke," Maddie scolded. She pulled the investigator back and stepped up close to the door. "Raymond? It's me, Maddie Rochester. Can we talk, please?"

There was a crash within the apartment. A couple minutes later they could hear a chain slide from its perch. A series of deadbolts were disengaged one at a time, a total of five. Tentatively the doorknob was unlocked and the door was opened just a couple of inches.

"Raymond?" Maddie said to the eye looking back at her through the opening.

"It is you," the eye proclaimed. "You have some nerve showing up here."

"Can we ask you some questions, Raymond?" Maddie said.

"First you fire me for things that I didn't do," the eye said. "Then you show up here to finish me?"

"Nobody is finishing anybody," Maddie said. "We just want to talk."

"You ruin my life and then you want to talk?" the eye said. "You didn't want to talk when I was explaining my situation. When I was explaining why your expectations were so unreasonable. You didn't want to talk then."

"She doesn't want to talk now," Hawke kicked his foot into the opening, preventing Raymond from being able to close the door on them. "I do."

"Who are you?" Raymond squealed. "I'm going to call the police."

"Go ahead," Hawke said. "Want to use my phone?"

"Hawke," Maddie scolded again.

"Right," Hawke said. "Listen. We both know you're a nut job. We both know that if you were to call the police I would have to tell them about the illegal things you're doing on that computer of yours. Just answer a few questions and I'll leave you alone."

"Are you spying on me?" Raymond said. "I'll . . ."

"You'll what?" Hawke waited a moment. "Thought so. Answer this: Why are you trying to hurt Maddie?"

Raymond looked at Maddie. "Hurt her? I didn't try to hurt her. I didn't touch her. You can't say I hurt her."

"I know you didn't hurt her," Hawke said. "You're a sniveling weasel. You wouldn't hurt her yourself. But you might get on that computer of yours and find someone who would do it for you. Isn't that right?"

"What?" Raymond said. "I didn't. She cheated me out of my job and she lied to do it. And I hate her for it. But I didn't. I wouldn't."

"I think you did," Hawke said. "And when the police get here and search your computer they'll find the evidence they need to prove it. Isn't that right?"

"I didn't!" Raymond yelled. "Now go away and take that redheaded bitch with you!"

"You're not helping your case there, Ray," Hawke said.

"For the record," Maddie said. "The woman we hired to replace you has no trouble getting the work done to standard and on time."

"Lying bitch," Raymond spat.

Hawke pulled on his foot, but Raymond was pushing the door hard enough he couldn't get the boot free. He smacked the door with the palm of his hand, popping Raymond in the face with the wood. He yanked his foot out and let the door slam. From inside they could hear cursing and threats to call the police and to sue. Hawke rolled his eyes and the two of them started down the stairs.

"Okay," Hawke said. "We can skip the other Raymond Vallance and move on to my stop."

35

"Where are we going?" Maddie asked when they were on the road again.

"To a bar," he said.

"It's a little early for that isn't it?" Maddie said. "Not that I couldn't use a drink."

"We're not going to drink," Hawke said. "I need to talk to someone."

"A bartender slash therapist?"

"No, a criminal slash confidential informant," he said. "At least he used to be. He knows just about everything that goes on in this city. Everything illegal anyway."

"You think he can help us find who is trying to kill me?" she asked.

"I don't know what he'll be able to tell us," Hawke said. "That's why I need to talk to him."

"And he's going to be in a bar at this hour?"

"He's always in a bar," Hawke said. "He owns it."

"Well, then," Maddie said. "Let's go to a bar in the middle of the day."

Half an hour later, they walked into The Frosted Mug, a small hole-in-the-wall bar located in the center of a high-traffic business district. Inside, the dim lighting was just enough to illuminate the few patrons who had come in to get an early start to their day of drinking. Maddie was shocked anyone was there. Hawke didn't give them a second glance as he weaved through the maze of tables in the center of the floor space. Similarly, the bartender seemed to not even notice their presence.

Maddie looked at the back of the establishment where Hawke was going and only saw a pool table not currently in use. It wasn't until they were almost to the table that she saw a middle-aged man sitting in the corner booth staring at a laptop screen with a cellphone to his ear. He glanced up at Hawke as the PI neared. The recognition in his eyes suggested he was not happy to see the large man. He leaned back and spoke into his phone just before disconnecting the call and laying it on the table.

"Hello, detective," the man said. "It's been a long time. To what do I owe this pleasure?"

"Not a detective anymore, Leland," Hawke said.

"Then what the hell are you doing here?" Leland's manner changed from forced cordiality to outright disdain.

"I need some information," Hawke slid into the booth opposite the other man. Maddie remained standing next to him.

Leland looked up at the woman and then back to Hawke. "I'm not the internet. Look it up yourself."

"What I need isn't on the internet," Hawke said. "I need a name."

"How about Sally?" Leland said. "You've always struck me as a Sally."

"I'm looking for a fixer," Hawke ignored the man.

"A fixer?" the man said. "Did you break something, Hawke?"

"Don't play stupid, Leland," Hawke said. "You know what I mean. Now give me a name."

"You're not a cop anymore," Leland glanced up at Maddie. "So I can only wonder what you've done to bring you to the point of needing the services of a fixer. What have you done, Hawke?"

"A name," Hawke said.

"Why would I give you anything?" Leland said, looking down to read a notification that appeared on his phone. "What's in it for me if you can't offer me the protections you could as a detective?"

"You want protections?" Hawke said. "How about this. If you don't give me a name and something happens to this woman, I will come back and feed that damn phone to you."

178

Leland looked at Hawke, his eyes shifting to Maddie once more. "Who is she?"

"Not your concern," Hawke said. "You only need to concern yourself with what happens to her. Give me a name."

"If you need a fixer for his services, I can give you a name," Leland said. "If you are looking to stop a fixer who has their sights on this woman, you would need three names."

"What are they?"

"If I give them to you," Leland said. "I place myself at risk. If they found out I gave you their names, my life would be forfeit."

"Give me the names," Hawke leaned closer. "Or you will wish they were the ones coming for you."

Leland's right eye twitched, so he looked away from the man sitting across from him to the woman standing next to the booth. He had known Hawke for a number of years. As a detective the man was by the book. They had a good relationship. There was no pushing for information that would endanger his confidential informant. Leland stared at Maddie, wondering what the relationship was between the two.

What he knew of Hawke wouldn't fill a shot glass. But two facts stood out in his mind. Hawke was relentless in his pursuit of a suspect. And he was a man of his word. His threat could not be taken lightly.

"You can't tell them who gave you the names," Leland turned back to Hawke. "They will kill me."

"You have my word," Hawke said.

"Give me your notebook," Leland held out a hand. "I'll write them down."

The PI pulled out his small notebook, thumbed to a blank page and placed it along with a pen in front of Leland. The middle-aged man slid his laptop to the side and leaned over the notebook as he wrote out the names and what information he had on each of them. He checked his phone twice for accuracy before finishing. He pushed it back across the table.

Hawke skimmed the names and returned the notebook to its rightful place in his pocket. With a nod he slid to the edge of the booth and pulled himself to his feet.

"Hawke," Leland said.

The investigator looked down at the man.

"Don't come back here," Leland warned.

"You threatening me, Leland?" Hawke said.

"No threat," Leland said. "Just don't come back."

Hawke turned away and taking Maddie's elbow led her through the maze of tables to the exit.

36

Hawke sat at his desk in front of his computer with the notebook opened to the list of three names Leland had given him. The first name on the list, Johnathan Feldman, was a man Hawke thought he knew. He typed the name in just to be sure and hit the search button. The results were extensive.

"What are you going to do when you find him?" Maddie said from over his shoulder.

"Ask him some questions," Hawke said. He clicked on the first result and looked at the face of an aged balding Johnathan Feldman. He quickly closed the window and clicked the next.

"Like you asked that Leland fellow?" she asked. "Or like you asked the man that broke into my home?"

"That will be entirely up to him," he said. The second Feldman was a young college-aged boy. He closed it.

"I would think men like this would avoid having their pictures on the internet," she commented.

"True," Hawke said, clicking the third result on the list. "Sometimes you don't have control over what is there."

He looked at the image on the screen. A Johnathan Feldman in his thirties stared back at him with a headline about the man being found innocent in his trial for murder. He was the man Hawke thought he was but he was not the man the PI was looking for. He took a pen and marked Feldman off his list.

The next name was Trey Morgan. Hawke typed in the name and started clicking through the results. After two pages, he gave up and moved on to the third name, Victor Osterman. Much like Morgan, Osterman produced a number of results, but none of the pictures were that of the lawyer who had hired Hawke.

"What now?" Maddie said, noting the PI's frustration.

"Now I pay them a visit," he said, standing. He stretched his back and put on his jacket.

"You mean we pay them a visit," Maddie corrected.

"No," Hawke said. "You're not going with me. It's too dangerous."

"You can't leave me here," she said. "What if they come after me while you're gone?"

"I don't intend to leave you here," he said. "I'm taking you to your office. They won't try anything there. Too many witnesses."

"They sent someone to my hotel room," she reminded him. "There were a lot of witnesses there too."

"That was supposed to happen in your room," Hawke said. "No witnesses. You'll be safe at your office. I'll be back before the end of business."

"What if you're not?" she said. "What if you meet this guy and something happens to you? What then?"

Hawke saw the fear in her eyes. Concern for him or herself he wasn't sure. "I'll be fine. But if I'm not there by five, call Roger. He'll protect you."

"I'd feel safer being with you," she said.

"And if we meet this guy and something happens to me?" Hawke used her words against her. "What then?"

"You are worried then," she said. "That you might be killed."

"There's always a possibility in my line of work," he said. "But I'll be fine. Now, let's go."

"I can't go to the office dressed like this," she said, posing in his shirt for emphasis. "I need to go by the house."

"It's a crime scene," Hawke said. "Police won't let you in."

"I need clothes," she said. "My purse and my briefcase. I can't work without my papers."

"You're not going there to work," he said. "You're going to be safe."

"If I'm there," she said, "I'm going to work."

"Fine," he said. "I'll call Rog on the way. Let's go."

After some argument, Roger agreed to meet the two of them at Maddie's home. Roger would escort the woman to her room where she could get what she needed. Hawke would have to wait outside where he couldn't contaminate the scene. Hawke wasn't sure what he could contaminate since he was there when the crime in question occurred.

They arrived at the house before the detective and sat in the truck in the driveway. Maddie sat staring at the front door of her home.

"It doesn't look the same," she said.

"What doesn't?" Hawke said. He did not look up from his phone, where he was searching the contact information Leland had given him for the two men he needed to find.

"The house," she said. "It looks different somehow."

Hawke raised his head and studied the front of the building. "Looks the same to me."

"It doesn't look like home," she said. "I lived here with my husband. Now, I'm getting divorced and it just looks like the place someone tried to kill me."

Hawke continued studying at the building before them. "Look at it this way. It's a house. It has walls to protect you from the elements and from those who would you do you harm. It has a roof to keep out the weather. It's a place to sleep, to eat, and whatever else you may do there. It isn't defined by one event, or by who lives there, or did. It's just a house."

Maddie stared at her home, considering what Hawke had said. "Nope. That didn't help."

"Then I say let's burn it to the ground," Hawke said.

"What? No." Maddie sat up straight. "I meant I was probably going to move. I don't need to burn it down."

"That works too," he said.

Roger pulled into the driveway and parked beside them. The two men acknowledged one another with a nod and the three of them piled out of their vehicles.

"You're not going," Roger said.

"I'm stretching my legs," Hawke said. "Is that all right with you?"

"As long as you don't go inside," Roger said. "I don't care what you do."

Hawke reached into his pocket and withdrew a pack of cigarettes. He slapped it against his palm then took one in his mouth. Leaning against the front fender of the truck, he lit the cigarette and blew clouds of smoke over Roger's head. "I'll be right here."

Roger shook his head then led Maddie through the crime scene tape into the house. The two entered cautiously as if danger lurked within. Maddie paused in the entryway taking in what she could see from there. It looked exactly the same as it had every day since the last time they painted. Even the bright yellow paint could not counter the dark feeling of gloom she felt.

"Let's get this over with," Roger said. He pushed past her and took the lead as they climbed the stairway to the second level.

As they neared the bedroom, Maddie slowed. The blood spatter in the light of day was daunting. It was going to take a lot of work to make things appear normal again. It would take a lifetime for them to actually feel normal again. She diverted her eyes as she skirted around the devastation into her room. There, under the watchful eyes of the detective, she retrieved an overnight bag and packed it full of clothing, toiletries and makeup. The zipper had to be forced closed before she slipped the strap over her shoulder, followed by her purse. In her other hand she gripped her briefcase. She was ready to go. Her gaze fell on the bloodstained doorway.

"They're going to kill me, aren't they?" She said.

"What? No," Roger said. "Hawke won't let that happen. And we're pursuing every lead trying to identify who's behind all this. We'll catch him."

"I appreciate that," Maddie said. "But Hawke can't be there for me twenty-four seven and the odds that you'll find who's responsible before they get me are pretty slim."

"Don't underestimate Hawke," Roger said. "He's a royal pain in the ass. But he's good at what he does. He's protected you up to this point. He'll keep you safe."

"I hope you're right," she said as they left the room and approached the stairs.

The unmistakable roar of the truck's engine shook the windows of the house. Arms full, Maddie took the stairs at a run with Roger close behind. She burst through the front door onto the porch, just as the taillights of the old Chevy disappeared around the corner.

"Hawke!" she screamed to no avail.

Roger stepped up next to her. "I guess you're with me."

37

The decision to leave Maddie with Roger had been an easy one. The detective would see that she got to her company safely. Meanwhile, Hawke could get to business without wasting a moment. His first stop was in the opposite direction. Even ignoring all the speed limits it would take an hour to get there.

Trey Morgan, according to the information provided by Leland, worked out of a pawn shop in a small town thirty miles north of the city. It was an unlikely choice which is probably why he chose it.

The drive gave Hawke time to think. The rush of wind coming through the cracked window that allowed him to expel smoke and ash blocked out all other sound and eliminated distractions. He cleared his mind and let the thoughts flood in.

Hawke was on his way to meet a fixer who may or may not be the so-called lawyer who had hired him. He was definitely a man who arranged, among other things, hits. A man such as Hawke, knowing the identity of a man like that, would have a target on his back the minute the fixer was made aware of that knowledge.

If Trey Morgan proved to be the lawyer, it was likely Hawke was already in his crosshairs. If he turned out to be a previously unknown individual, he may become an additional threat, not just to Hawke but to Maddie as well. Hawke would have to take measures to protect them both.

Joe's Pawn occupied the corner space of a row of storefront businesses that faced the main street. Hawke drove by on the first pass, circling the block before finding a parking space in front of a drugstore two doors down. Lighting another cigarette, he watched the comings and goings of the pawnshop customers. In the hour that he watched there were three.

The first was a rough-looking man in his late forties or early fifties. He entered the shop empty-handed and stayed inside for nearly a half-hour before exiting with what appeared to be an electric drill under his arm.

The second was a younger man, early to mid-twenties. He arrived with several items including a flat-screen TV and a laptop computer. After fifteen minutes the man came out stuffing some bills into his wallet. The items could just as easily be stolen as they could be the property of the young man, which made Hawke wonder if fencing was one of the services the fixer provided.

The third was a man wearing a suit and carrying a briefcase. He walked with the confidence of a man who was sure of who he was and where he stood in life. He glanced around as he approached the pawnshop, not nervously, but like a man who thought he might be followed. Of the three, he was the first to enter the shop and the last to leave. He exited with as much confidence as when he entered, with maybe a little more swing of his arms. He was no longer toting the briefcase. An unusual item to pawn, Hawke wondered if it had been a payment for services rendered.

Hawke opened the truck's door and dropped his cigarette butt to the ground. He lowered his foot and crushed it beneath his heel. Three quick rotations of the manual crank closed the window. Shifting his weight, he rose to his full height beside the vehicle, shut the door and checked to be sure he had locked it. He stretched to loosen muscles that had not moved in almost two hours.

He walked with a leisurely stride to the pawnshop and made a silent entry, ruined by a chime on the door. He looked up at the offending device then searched for a clerk. There was no one in the room with him.

"May I help you?" The voice was small as was its owner. Standing no more than three feet tall, he could barely see over the counter. Even as he spoke, he bounded upward onto what Hawke imagined to be an overturned wooden crate. Once settled, the man leaned forward with his hands on the glass top of a display case.

"Just looking," Hawke said, taking a position next to a shelving unit filled with miscellaneous tools. He made a point of handling a couple of items in feigned interest. Lifting a third item and turning it in his hands, he half-turned to the small man. "You Joe?"

"Me?" the man said. "No. I'm Paul. Just Paul."

"Nice to meet you, Just Paul," Hawke said. "Maybe you could help me after all."

"You lookin' for something specific?"

"You could say that." Hawke put the tool back in its place and approached the counter as nonthreateningly as he could. "I'm looking for somebody."

"We're a pawnshop," Paul said. "Not an escort service."

"That isn't what I meant," Hawke said, wondering if maybe escort service was indeed on their menu. "I'm looking for someone who I'm told works here."

Paul cocked his head to one side. "Who might that be?"

"Name's Trey Morgan," Hawke said. "Probably stays in the back."

"Nope," Paul said. His demeanor changed slightly, more focused, more cautious. "No one here by that name."

"You sure?" Hawke said. "I was told he would be here."

"You were told wrong," the man said. "Now, if you're not here to buy something, maybe you should be on your way."

"How about you tell Mister Morgan that I'm here to see him."

"How about . . ." the small man started.

"I'll handle this, Paul."

Hawke turned to the voice. A stocky man with a head full of thick, black curly hair stared at him without expression. It was not the lawyer. But then, Hawke didn't know if this man was Trey Morgan, Joe or someone else sent out to handle the situation.

"Do I know you?" the stocky man asked.

"Are you Morgan?"

"So you don't know who you're looking for." It was a statement, not a question.

188

"I know his face," Hawke said. "Yours ain't it. Are you Morgan?"

"How did you come by my name?" the man said. "My place of business?"

"That's a yes," Hawke said. "I guess I can be on my way."

"I'd say that would be a good idea," the man shifted his weight. "And I would suggest you never return."

"I've been hearing that a lot lately," Hawke said. "Now, why do you think that is?"

The stocky man only stared at him. Paul said, "Cause you're a . . ."

Hawke pushed his way through the door onto the street. The sun was starting its journey toward the western horizon. He had just enough time to get to Maddie's office to pick her up.

38

Hawke drove into the parking lot of Rochester-Kinsley a half hour before closing time. He found a space near the front doors and sat finishing the cigarette he had started while on the highway. When he finished, he left the truck and entered the building. The security guard, Thomas, was at his station. He stiffened as the PI approached but waved him on.

"She's expecting you," Thomas said.

Hawke took the elevator since Maddie was not there to encourage the stairs. The doors opened and he turned toward her office but motion drew his attention in the opposite direction.

Maddie was walking toward him along with the woman she had taken with her to the restaurant meeting. The two of them were deep in conversation and did not look up as they passed Hawke by. He fell in step behind them, following at a modest distance so he wouldn't startle them. They spoke in hushed voices, glancing about the large open space that contained the majority of the staff, looking for eavesdroppers. It was all very mysterious to Hawke. Maddie turned slightly to take in the dozens of desks and their occupants. From the corner of her eye she saw the large man following them.

"Hawke?" she said. "I didn't realize you were here. Any luck?"

"Depends on how you look at it," he said.

"How do you look at it?"

"I'll update you later," he said. "Everything okay? You seem upset."

"Everything is fine," she said.

They arrived at Maddie's office and Hawke followed the two women inside. Maddie circled to her side of the desk and Becky stepped up to face her. Hawke pulled the door closed and moved to the corner.

"Now what is it you wanted to tell me?" Maddie asked.

"I found another discrepancy," Becky said sheepishly.

"Another one?" Maddie sat heavily in her chair.

"Yes, ma'am," Becky said. "This time the difference is greater than the other times."

"How much are we talking about?"

Becky checked her notes to be sure she was accurate. "Twenty-five thousand six-hundred thirty-two dollars."

Hawke's head tilted slightly. "That's not a small number."

"No it isn't," Maddie said. "We need to figure out what's going on and stop it."

"I tried to track it down," Becky said. "Just like the other times, I couldn't figure out when it went missing. Whoever it is, they're good at covering their tracks."

"Are you sure it isn't just a clerical error?" Hawke said, shifting his eyes to Becky.

Becky stiffened. "It's no clerical error."

Maddie was silent for a long moment. She said, "Becky, will you wait outside? I'll be right with you."

"Yes, ma'am," she said. As she turned to leave her eyes caught Hawke's. He saw tears forming just before she turned away.

When the door closed, Maddie said, "Becky has been with us for ten years. She isn't the problem."

"I didn't mean to suggest," Hawke said. "But mistakes can be made."

"She has never made an error," Maddie insisted.

"How do you know?" Hawke said. "And twenty-five thousand doesn't sound like an error. It sounds like theft. Embezzling is almost always the accountant."

"I trust her," Maddie said. "She isn't stealing from us. But to your point, I was thinking of having someone else look at our books."

"How many times has this happened?" Hawke asked.

"Four times in the past six months," she said. "Five if you count today."

"How much was missing the other times?" Hawke asked.

"It varied," Maddie said. "Usually between one and three thousand."

"Less than the twenty-five grand," Hawke said. "But not pocket change."

"It's adding up to quite a sum," Maddie agreed.

"You want," he said. "I can look into this. Probably have an answer in two or three days."

"Thanks," she said. "For now I prefer having you protect me. Maybe when we get to the bottom of who's trying to kill me, then you can get to the bottom of who's stealing from me."

"I can do both," Hawke said.

"I'm sure you can," she said, her smile unconvincing. "But for now I would feel safer if you were focused on keeping me alive."

"I understand," he said. "But I may still ask a question here or there when the opportunity arises."

"If the opportunity arises," Maddie said, "I suppose it would only make sense."

39

Maddie finished up while Hawke watched. It didn't take too long. After she met with Becky she was in anger mode. She moved in quick forceful motions. Over the next half hour, she became relaxed in the familiarity of her surroundings. By the time the day was done she was fully herself again.

"Let me take you to dinner," she said as she packed her briefcase.

"Excuse me?" Hawke said from the chair he had chosen to keep watch from.

"Dinner," she said. "You know. That meal people eat at the end of the day."

"I know what it is," Hawke said. "It's not necessary."

"Dinner isn't necessary?" Maddie said. "You have to eat."

"You bought me the truck and you're paying me for my time," Hawke said. "It isn't necessary that you take me to dinner."

"I know it isn't," she said. "But I want to. So, we're going."

"I don't eat salad," he said.

"I won't make you eat salad," she said. "But we are going."

Hawke grunted but didn't argue further.

Maddie said her goodbyes and the two of them made their way down the stairs and out of the building. Buckled into the truck, Hawke drove out of the parking lot onto the street.

"Where to?" he asked.

"Hang a left up ahead," she said. "It isn't too far."

Hawke followed Maddie's directions until she told him to turn into a restaurant he was familiar with. Not one he had eaten in, but rather one he had followed her to. It was La Cruste, the restaurant where she had lunch with her tennis partner.

He found a parking space and the two of them walked inside together. The hostess lit up when she saw Maddie, greeting her by name and only giving Hawke a side glance. She gathered two menus and led her customers to a small table in the center of the dining room. Hawke insisted on sitting where he was facing the entrance.

He looked through the menu and cringed at the prices listed next to the entrees. Maddie never opened her menu, simply sitting and watching Hawke. He finally laid his down. "Aren't you eating?"

"Yes," she said. "But I know what I want."

"This place is too expensive," he said.

"Relax. It's only money and I have plenty," Maddie said. "Besides, if someone kills me, I won't get to spend it."

The guests at the next table turned to them. Hawke nodded to them followed by a gesture aimed at turning them away. It worked.

"So, I may as well spend it now," Maddie continued. "What are you having?"

"I don't know," he said. "It all costs so much."

"Jesus, Hawke," she said. "What would you have if this was just an old run-down place?"

"This isn't an old run-down place," he said. "This is a nice place. An upscale, expensive place."

A waitress appeared and filled their water glasses. "Hello, Ms. Rochester. Good to see you this evening."

"Remy," Maddie smiled. "How's the little one?"

"Still cute," the waitress said. "Which is good for him. He hasn't been letting me sleep much."

"That must be hard," Maddie said. "With you working and going to school."

"You do what you have to, right?" Remy said. "Do you know what you're having?"

"We do," Maddie said. "I'll have my usual. Mr. Hawke here will have the ribeye, cooked . . ."

Maddie looked at Hawke. "Medium rare."

"Medium rare," Maddie repeated. "And the works."

"Right away, ma'am," Remy said.

The waitress made her way through the dining room to place their order. Hawke looked at Maddie. "The works?"

"Loaded baked potato and vegetable of the day," she said. "Don't worry. Salads are ordered separately."

"That's a relief," Hawke said. "I would hate to think your word was no good."

For the next several minutes they sipped from their water, nibbled on bread the waitress dropped off at their table and chatted about nothing important.

"When was the first time you noticed money missing from the business?" Hawke finally asked.

"Opportunity?"

"Exactly."

"About six months ago we noticed a nearly two-thousand-dollar discrepancy," she said.

"But that wasn't the first time," Hawke said. "You noticed smaller amounts before that."

"How did you know that?" Maddie said.

"How much and for how long?"

"It started about two years ago," she said. "A hundred or so here, a couple hundred there."

"And the amounts slowly climbed?" he said.

"Yes."

"If you look into this," Maddie said. "Do you really think you can find out who is responsible?"

"I can," Hawke said. "Are you sure you want to know? Maybe it would be better to find a way for them to quietly fix the problem."

"Listen to you," she smiled. "Mr. Detective showing compassion. I figured you would want to lock them up."

"Oh, I do," Hawke said. "But I didn't think you would want to."

"Let me think about it," she said. "I'm going to the restroom before the food arrives."

She stood and walked back to the ladies' room. Hawke turned in his seat and watched her until she was safely through the door. When he turned back he found himself face to face with the lawyer sitting in Maddie's seat.

"Good evening, Mr. Hawke," he said. "I hear you've been looking for me."

"That would make you Victor Osterman," Hawke said. There was a small twitch in the man's left eye.

"Very good, Mr. Hawke," Victor said. "But I doubt you want to make a scene in this nice restaurant. Good choice by the way. So, I'll get right to the point. I hired you for a job that you have yet to fulfill."

"She wasn't cheating on her husband," Hawke said. "And her husband didn't hire you."

"Right," Victor said. "Yet you received payment. You need to fulfill the contract you agreed to so you don't have to pay me back."

"I never signed a contract," Hawke said. "Did you sign a contract? I'd like to see it."

"So you don't owe me anything," Victor continued. "This is what you're going to do. You are going to stop protecting Mrs. Rochester. You're going to go back to your park bench or wherever it is you go and stay out of the way. Otherwise, she won't be the only target on the list. Understood?"

"Back off so you can have her killed?" Hawke said. "Is that right?"

"Stay out of the way, Mr. Hawke," Victor said. "And enjoy your dinner. This place is marvelous."

The man raised himself to his feet, gave Hawke a sneer and turned to leave. Before he could take his second step, Hawke was on his feet and clocked the man in the side of the head with his pistol. The fixer buckled and fell face-first to the floor. It was at that moment Maddie returned to the table and the waitress arrived with their plates. He looked from one to the other. "We'll need those to go."

40

It took some convincing to keep the staff and patrons from calling the police. It helped that everyone seemed to know and trust Maddie. It also took quite an effort to get the large unconscious man out of the restaurant and into the back of the truck. Once everyone was satisfied he would receive proper medical attention, they funneled back into the restaurant.

While Maddie sat in the front of the truck with two to-go containers in her lap, Hawke used zip-ties to secure his prisoner. He climbed into the driver's seat and turned to Maddie. "Sorry about dinner."

"How were you to know a psychopathic killer was going to visit?" she said.

"I shouldn't have let him get that close," he said. "I shouldn't have let myself be distracted."

"It's okay," she said.

"No. It isn't," Hawke said. "What if he had gone after you instead? What if my being distracted had let him get to you?"

"It didn't," she said. "He didn't. What exactly is the plan with him anyway?"

"I need to take him somewhere we can question him," Hawke said. "Somewhere secluded."

"So no one will see us carrying him in?"

"So no one will hear him scream," Hawke said, starting the truck. He knew just the place.

As a homicide detective, he and Roger had closed dozens of cases together. One of the last they had worked was the murder of a small-time drug dealer. Over the course of the investigation they uncovered evidence that proved he had been killed by members of a drug cartel that didn't want to share territory. The drug task force became involved and together they raided and took down an entire drug operation, netting three local leaders in the cartel and a couple dozen lower-ranking enforcers. Not to mention about three million in heroin. What Hawke was interested in was the building. The operation had been housed in an old office building that was confiscated from the landlord when it was learned that he was staying quiet in exchange for a little extra rent.

Hawke pulled up to the dark four-story building and watched for a short time before pulling around to the loading dock behind the deserted structure. He backed in and shut off the lights.

"We should eat these while they're hot," Maddie said.

"Good idea," Hawke said. "I'll get him inside. Then we can eat. Unless they cleared everything out, there are plenty of desks and chairs."

Hawke exited the cab and jumped into the truck bed. He checked Victor's vitals and pulled him up so he could get a grip around the man's massive chest. He pulled his prisoner out of the truck, onto the dock and to the closest door. It was locked.

He lay Victor on the concrete and returned to the truck where he dug out a crowbar he kept for just this kind of occasion. Maddie looked on as Hawke slammed the tool into the small gap between the door and frame. With a gut-wrenching heave, he pulled the door away from the frame until the latch gave way. Once open, he propped the door so it wouldn't close and dragged Victor inside. Maddie followed at a comfortable distance.

"Are you sure he's okay?" she asked. "He's been out a long time."

"He's not dead, if that's what you're asking," Hawke said. "And he's probably faking at this point. He knows if he starts talking before I'm ready, I'll just knock him out again."

He dragged the man through several sets of doors until he found an office with an outer office. He put Victor in the corner of the interior office and pulled the door closed, leaving him in complete darkness. In the outer office, he moved the desk against the door of the other and set up two chairs for the two of them to sit and eat. He produced a flashlight for more light than the distant exterior windows were providing at such a late hour.

Hawke had to admit, the meal was delicious. There was a reason upscale restaurants could charge so much. Maddie sat next to him barely touching her food.

"You should eat," he said.

"Not hungry," she said.

"I know that isn't true," Hawke said. "You're hungry. You're just letting concern take over."

"I'm not concerned," she lied.

"You're worried about what I'm going to do to him," Hawke pointed his knife at the door.

"Okay," she said. "I'm concerned. After what you did to the guy in my house. I just. . . I don't want you to kill him."

"I'm not going to kill him," Hawke said. "I may give him the impression that I will. But deep down, I'm a cop. I'll hurt him to get what we need, but I won't kill him."

"You promise?" She asked. "I couldn't live with it if you did."

"I promise," he assured her. "He can't talk if he's dead and I need him to talk."

"Okay."

"Now eat."

Maddie pushed her food around with her fork, taking an occasional bite. She still didn't eat much, but at least she ate some. When it was clear she was finished, Hawke had her help him move the table away from the door again. It was time. As if on cue, Hawke's phone rang. He looked at the screen and pressed the answer button.

"Hey, Rog," he said. "What's up?"

"You tell me," Roger said. "I'm down here at La Cruste, a joint I couldn't afford to walk into."

"What brings you there?" Hawke said. Someone had called the cops after all.

"Seems a man matching your description was here with a known patron, Maddie Rochester," Roger said. "He beat another man unconscious and dragged him out."

"Beat him unconscious sounds so brutal," Hawke said. "I only had to hit him once."

"You think this is funny?" Roger said. "You broke his nose, Hawke."

"I didn't touch his nose," Hawke said. "How would you know that anyway?"

"I'm talking about the Chief," Roger said. "When you punched him and got fired, you broke his nose."

"Why didn't you tell me before?" Hawke asked. "And why are you telling me now?"

"He hates you," Roger said. "Before, the union couldn't save your job, but they did keep you out of jail. He would love an excuse to put you behind bars and kidnapping is a pretty good reason."

"I didn't kidnap anybody," Hawke said.

"I have witnesses, Hawke," Roger said. "A restaurant full of credible witnesses."

"But you don't have a victim," Hawke said.

"What have you done?" Roger said.

"Christ," Hawke said. "Why does everyone think I'm capable of murder?"

"Why won't we have a victim?" Roger asked.

"This guy is not going to go to the police claiming to have been kidnapped," Hawke said. "I guarantee when I'm done with him, he's going to go crawl under a rock and wait until it's safe to come out again."

"Who is he?" Roger asked.

"He's the lawyer who hired me to follow Maddie," Hawke said. "Only he's no lawyer, he's a fixer. He was hired to have Maddie killed. I intend to find out who hired him and why."

Roger was silent on the other end of the call. For a minute Hawke thought they had lost connection.

"You better be right," Roger said.

"I am," Hawke said.

He put the phone away.

"You should go find a window to sit by," Hawke said to Maddie. "I'm going to need the light with me."

She nodded and left the room. Hawke took a deep breath, pulled his weapon and opened the door to the interior office. Victor was sitting up against the wall opposite the door.

"You made a bad decision, Mr. Hawke," Victor said. "You had a simple job. A lucrative job. And now, now you have a target on your back."

"You think you're the first person to try to kill me?" Hawke said. He stepped into the office and let the door close behind him. He pulled a chair up so he could sit in front of the fixer. "You're not even the third."

"Joke if you want," Victor said. "My men don't miss."

"First of all," Hawke said. "I'm not joking. If you had done your homework on me, you would have found out I was a detective. Before that I was military. I had a lot of enemies. They all wanted me dead. Some even acted on it. But I'm still here and they aren't."

"Is that supposed to impress me?"

"Second," Hawke said. "If your men don't miss, why is Maddie still alive? Why are so many of your so-called men dead?"

"That one's simple," Victor said. "I haven't used my men yet."

Hawke stared at him.

"What's wrong, Mr. Hawke?" Victor said. "Got nothing to say now? My men are coming and you won't be able to stop them. The entire police force won't be able to stop them."

"I know a bluff when I hear one," Hawke said. "Now, it's time for you to answer some questions."

41

Victor Osterman sat zip-tied to a chair, his swollen face covered with streaks of blood and sweat. Hawke stood over him, his own body wet from the exertion of their discussion. He swung and caught Victor just above the eye.

"Who hired you?" Hawke repeated the question he had asked dozens of times already.

Victor's head was thrown back and to the side. He slowly moved it back until he was facing forward once more. A fresh cut dribbled a thin line of blood that collected on the man's eyebrow. He blinked a couple times, then stared blankly at the wall as he had done since the interrogation had begun.

Hawke's hand was throbbing. But he worried that if he used his gun or some other object he might find lying around the building, he might cause too much damage or possibly even kill the man before getting the answers he needed. He studied Victor's eyes and the lines in his face, deciding it was time for a break. He stood straight, snatched the flashlight off the desk and walked out of the office. He pulled the door closed behind him, returning Victor to complete darkness.

Hawke worked his hand in and out of a fist to stretch the sore muscles and tendons. The knuckles were cracked and bleeding. It was obvious to him that Victor, despite his appearance, was militarily trained. If he wanted the man to talk, Hawke was going to have to change his tactics.

He found Maddie sitting in a corner office staring out at the night. He knocked on the open door as he entered, causing her to jump and spin defensively.

"Sorry," he said. "Actually knocked to keep from scaring you."

"I guess I'm a bit on edge," she said. "Did you get what you needed?"

"No," Hawke sat on the edge of the dust-covered desk. "He's hard to crack."

"It sounded like you were trying pretty hard," she said.

Knowing the man had hardly made a whimper, Hawke assumed she had come back to the office where they had eaten and heard the smacks of his fist on the man's face. Subconsciously, he slid his injured hand into his jacket.

"About that," he said. "I may have to up the pain level. You know. To get him to talk."

She looked at him with a blank expression that reminded him of Victor's.

"Why are you telling me?" she asked.

"The kind of pain I'm talking about," Hawke said. "It could kill him."

Her eyes closed. She stayed that way for a long moment. "Is it worth it? All that pain. What he still doesn't talk? What if he dies and never tells you what you want? Can you live with that?"

"I don't know," Hawke admitted. "But I do know that if I don't try to get him to talk and something happens to you, I won't be able to live with myself knowing I didn't try everything I could have."

"I don't know that I want that on me," she said.

"Well if it makes you feel better, he said I will be killed along with you," Hawke said. "So now it's on me. I don't intend to roll over and let them put me down."

"I'm sorry," she said.

"For what?"

"I asked you to look into my husband," she said. "You didn't have to be in the middle of this."

"First of all, you hired me to do a job," Hawke said. "That's how I make a living. Second, you didn't bring me into this. That asshole in the other room brought me into it when he hired me to be an unsuspecting witness to your kidnapping."

There was a deep sadness in her eyes when she looked at him. "I guess you could say he brought this on himself then."

"You could," Hawke said. "You good?"

"I suppose I have to be," she said.

Hawke nodded. He stood and left her alone. Even before he was out the door she had spun the chair so she could look out at the moon.

Hawke walked with purpose, returning to the room where Victor was strapped to the chair. As he entered the room, Victor looked up at him with defiance. Hawke pulled his pistol, slid a shell into the chamber, pushed the barrel up to Victor's shoulder and squeezed the trigger. The shot reverberated through the building. In the corner office, Maddie closed her eyes again.

"What the hell?" Victor cried out. "What happened to 'I used to be a cop'?"

"Used to be," Hawke said. "Now I'm just a guy with a gun."

He checked the chamber again and pressed the barrel to Victor's other shoulder.

"Wait!" Victor shouted. "Just wait!"

Hawke pulled the gun away. "Are you going to tell me who hired you?"

Victor said nothing. Hawke pushed the gun back into the man's shoulder. "Yes! I'll talk. Just don't shoot me again."

"Who hired you?"

Twenty minutes later Hawke left the room and informed Maddie it was time to go. He led her through the building to the dock where the truck waited for them. He helped her in and climbed into the driver's seat. He pulled his phone out, scrolled to Roger's name and pressed call. It rang twice.

"Hawke?" Roger said. "Where are you?"

"Remember that office building where we busted that drug ring?"

"You're there?"

"I left a gift for you in one of the ground floor offices," Hawke said. "And you should probably bring an ambulance."

"Hawke?"

"I'll call you again when I can," Hawke said.

"Talk to me, damn it," Roger said.

Hawke disconnected the call and started the truck.

"Did you learn what you needed?" Maddie said. "Is it over now?"

"He talked," Hawke said. "But it's nowhere near being over."

"What does that mean?"

"It means our friend Victor in there had been using local boys to come after you," Hawke said. "Earlier today he called in some professionals. Two guns for hire who have probably already landed."

"Two?" Maddie said.

"With a bonus if they complete the job tonight," Hawke said.

"Then we should go to the police," Maddie said.

"All that will do is put a big red flag up saying this is where you can find us," Hawke said. "The police can't stop them. Not unless they do something, and by then it will be too late. We're better off if we stay on our own and keep moving."

"You captured Victor and are turning him in to the police," Maddie said from the passenger seat. "Won't they just go away?"

"Normally, I would say, yes," Hawke said. He drove well above the speed limit, in and out of lanes of traffic. "But Victor made it clear he intended to see us dead. It's not about the money anymore. He won't call them off."

"So after all this," Maddie said, "I'm still going to die."

"No, you're not," Hawke said.

"You just said they won't stop," Maddie said.

"They won't stop," Hawke agreed. "But I will stop them."

"Two to one?"

"Two to one," Hawke said. "But these guys seldom work as a team. It will most likely be one to one."

"Twice," Maddie said.

"What happened to all that optimism you usually have?"

"You could say I lost it when I found out my husband was sleeping with my best friend and that two professional killers are coming for me," Maddie said.

"That does make it hard to stay positive," Hawke said.

"Do you at least have a plan?" Maddie asked.

"I do," Hawke said. "I just need to pick up some supplies. You may want to get some rest. This will take a while."

42

Hawke parked in front of Joe's Pawn Shop. Maddie had fallen asleep while they were on the highway and her head was resting on his shoulder. He hated to wake her, but had no choice.

"Maddie," he shook her gently. "We're here."

She opened her eyes and stretched, trying to force the sleep away. "Where are we?"

"I'm going in for supplies," Hawke said. "I need you to stay in the truck. No matter what happens, stay in the truck."

"What happens?" she repeated. "What's going to happen?"

"These guys aren't really fans of mine," he said.

"Is anyone?"

"That's hurtful," Hawke said.

"Besides me," Maddie said. "I haven't seen a single person that seems to like you."

"There's Mrs. Mancini," Hawke said.

"Oh, yeah, your neighbor," Maddie smiled. "I stand corrected."

"Now, stay in the truck," Hawke said, letting himself out and shutting the door.

Maddie watched him as he entered the pawnshop. Just as the door started to close, she saw his hand shift to where he kept his weapon. All the relaxing benefit of her nap washed away and she stiffened with renewed fear.

The door chimed as Hawke stepped inside. He expected the little person behind the counter to pull a weapon on him as soon as they made eye contact. It quickly became apparent that the man wasn't there. Instead, a young woman with a cobra tattooed on her neck stood behind the display cases. Her eyes were half-closed when she saw Hawke, and she did not open them any farther when she stood a little straighter.

In a soft voice, without inflection, she said, "May I help you?"

Hawke looked to his left at the reason he had come. The wall was lined with an assortment of shotguns, rifles and assault rifles. The cases below were filled with revolvers, pistols, military knives, scopes, and more. Hawke gestured in their direction, "Need help with these."

The woman rounded the corner of the cases until she was standing between the PI and what he was wanting. "I'm required to ask if you have a permit. Are you a felon? Do you have a history of mental health? And something else."

"Do I plan to cause myself or others bodily harm?"

"That's it." Her narrow eyes narrowed even more. "You've done this before."

"You could say that," Hawke said. "My answers are: yes, no, no, and probably. Others. Not me."

The woman made eye contact with him for the first time since he had entered. "I don't think I can sell to you."

"You can," Hawke said. "And you will."

"But . . ."

"Have Mr. Morgan clear it if you need to," he said. "I'll wait."

For a moment she looked as if she wasn't going to move. With a sudden spin she crossed the room and opened the door to the back. Standing in the doorway she spoke in a hushed voice to whoever was there. Hawke assumed it was Trey Morgan. Unexpectedly, she stepped fully into the back and disappeared from view. Hawke rested his hand on his pistol.

A second door opened and Trey walked into the room casually. "I thought I told you not to come back here."

"Is that what you said? I thought you meant for me to not go back there," Hawke pointed at the door the young woman had passed through.

"I doubt that," Trey said. "Why are you here?"

"I'm here as a customer," Hawke said.

"A customer?" Trey said. "What kind of customer?"

"Oh, not that kind," Hawke held his left hand up in a symbolic stop. "I don't need your services. I need weapons."

"Really?" the man grinned. "Just fill out the proper paperwork. We'll call you when it is approved."

"Yeah, that isn't going to work for me," Hawke said.

"That's what the law states," Trey said.

"You know as well as I do that following the law isn't exactly one of your strengths," Hawke said.

"Let's say I am who you think I am," Trey said. "What you think I am. Why would I help you?"

"Territory," Hawke said.

"I don't understand."

"The fixer I was looking for," Hawke said. "I found him. I propose that if you help me, I will eliminate him as competition. You can have his territory."

"We don't exactly work territories," the man said. "But I am intrigued. Who is this fixer?"

"Victor Osterman," Hawke said.

"Victor? Really?" Trey said. "You think you can shut him down?"

"I can," Hawke said. "But he has dispatched two pros that intend to stop me. That's why I need a little more firepower."

"As a businessman," Trey said, "wouldn't it make more sense for me to let them kill you and let everything else go back to normal?"

"I think a businessman would want to sell product," Hawke said.

"You make a good point," Trey said. "You want a nine mil. or a thirty-eight?"

"No thirty-eight," Hawke said. "I need two nine-millimeter semi-autos, two pump shotguns, one sniper and an assault rifle."

"Is that all?" Trey said. "Maybe you'd like a rocket launcher or a heavy machinegun?"

"Just what I listed," Hawke said. "And extra clips and ammo."

"That's a tall order," Trey said. "And I know you're aware the law won't allow me to sell you that much firepower in one transaction."

"Then sell me your backroom product," Hawke said. "You know. The ones you don't report."

Trey shook his head. "If I do this, if I give you what you want? Will you leave and never come back?"

"You have my word," Hawke said.

"Your word isn't worth much to me," Trey said.

"It's all I've got."

"Alice!" he called out.

One of the back doors opened and the young woman Hawke assumed to be Alice looked in. "Yes, boss?"

"You were listening?"

"Yes."

"Get our friend here the items he asked for," Trey said.

"Boss?" Alice said. "You sure about that?"

"What did I say?"

Alice's eyes enlarged. "Right away," she said just before vanishing to the back again.

"Now let's discuss price," Trey said. "I'm thinking ten should cover it."

"Ten grand?" Hawke said. "I could get them for half the price somewhere else."

"I don't think you can," Trey said. "If you could have, you would have. No. I think you're desperate. That's why you came to me. Ten is the price."

"Okay," Hawke said. "Just a minute."

He walked to the entrance and opened the door just enough to see the truck. When he made eye contact with Maddie, he motioned for her to come in. She slid out of the truck and came to him. Blocking the door, he whispered, "I need to borrow ten thousand dollars."

"Ten thousand?" Maddie whispered in surprise.

"That's the price for what I need to stop these guys," he said. "I would pay it, but I wasn't expecting it to be that much. So if you could, you know. That is, if you have it."

"I have it," she said. She pushed on the door and Hawke let her enter. She saw Trey and walked up to him. "I suppose you are who I pay."

"My, my," Trey said. "Aren't you a pretty one? And coming in here to pay for your boy's toys."

"He's not my boy," Maddie said. "He's my bodyguard."

"Oh, she's the one?" Trey said to Hawke. Then to Maddie, "You're the target."

"That's what they tell me," she said. "Can we get this done, please?"

"I like her," Trey looked at Hawke and then back. "I like you. You've got . . . what do I want to say? Spunk? I like spunk."

Maddie dug in her bag and pulled out a credit card. She held it out for the man. "Will this work?"

He looked at the card with skepticism. "Hard to keep a transaction off the books with a paper trail a credit card leaves."

"Well I don't have that much cash," Maddie said.

"Then I guess we're wasting our time here," Trey said. "Shut the door when you leave."

"Wait," Maddie said. She grabbed her wedding ring and worked it off her finger. "How about this?"

"I doubt that'll be enough," Trey said, as he took the jewelry.

"We paid nearly fifty grand for it," she said.

"For a wedding ring?" Hawke said.

"I was young," she said. "And rich."

"Really?" Trey pulled out a jeweler's loop and studied the stones in the ring. He nodded. "Yeah. Okay. This will cover it. You sure your husband won't mind?"

"Not at all," Maddie said.

The door to the back opened. Alice walked in carrying a box. She set it on the counter hard. "There it is."

Hawke inventoried the contents. "That's not a sniper. It's a hunting rifle with a scope."

"It's what we have," Alice said.

"Okay, fine," Hawke said. "How about a duffle bag?"

"That'll be forty bucks," Trey said.

"Really?"

"Just kidding," Trey smiled. He reached below the counter and came up with a bag large enough for the weapons and dropped it into the box.

"All right," Hawke said. He lifted the box and started for the door.

"And don't forget," Trey said. Hawke turned back to him. "This time you don't come back, or I'll shoot you. You, ma'am, are welcome anytime."

Hawke grunted and passed through the door after Maddie opened it for him. He loaded the box into the truck and the two of them piled in and headed back to the city.

43

The drive back was a quiet one. Hawke concentrated on the road ahead as he formulated his plan to keep them both alive. Maddie sat in silence, staring down at her empty ring finger.

"Why don't we just leave town?" Maddie said after about a half-hour. "We could just hide out until they gave up."

"If they were local goons, I'd say sure," Hawke said. "But he called in professionals. Professionals don't give up. They would track us down. Or wait for us to let our guard down when we returned. Our only option is for Victor to call off the contract, which he isn't going to do, so we need to prepare to defend ourselves. And we put a stop to this."

"When you say 'defend ourselves'," Maddie said. "You mean for you to defend us. Right?"

"I got two pistols and two shotguns," Hawke said. "If they get through me, you need to be ready."

"You mean if they kill you," she said.

"I do," he said. "That's the only way they'll get to you."

"I'm so sorry I brought you into this," Maddie said.

"You didn't bring me into this," Hawke said. "Victor brought me into this. You just made it more interesting."

"And what happens if we survive?" Maddie said. "Is it over then? Or will others follow?"

"He hired two pros," Hawke said. "He wants us dead. He didn't hire his mid-level men. He would have hired his best. If we survive, I doubt his second-best would pose much of a threat."

"Unless he thought two mid-level men would be sufficient," Maddie said.

"Let's get through this before you start blowing holes in my theories," Hawke said.

As they approached the city, Hawke slowed. He was sure Victor would have given a description of his truck to the men hired to kill him. Driving slowly would force anyone trying to follow them to slow down as well, allowing Hawke to spot them. It would work great as long as no one decided to risk exposure by pulling up alongside them and opening fire. But pros became pros by not doing things that got them caught.

"You said earlier that you were thinking about moving," Hawke said. "Is that still true?"

"I think so," she said. "Why?"

"I need somewhere to draw them to," Hawke said. "Somewhere that we would normally be, where they might not expect us to be ready for them. Somewhere not public. My apartment won't work because of the other tenants. My office is in a business district. Which leaves us with your home or your office."

"You want to use my house as a shooting gallery?" Maddie said. "The neighbors will love that."

"As a base of defense," he said. "And yes, there will most likely be shooting. Possibly a lot of it."

"That house is filled with memories," Maddie said.

"If you'd rather not," Hawke said.

"Let me finish," she said. "It's filled with memories of a husband who cheated on me. Not to mention all the years he spent on that hideous art. If I don't survive this and he gets the house, it wouldn't be bad that the house was, you know, damaged."

"The house it is," Hawke said.

Just outside the city limits Hawke steered into the parking lot of an abandoned department store. There he loaded the weapons he had purchased and transferred them from the box to the duffle. He gave one of the nine-millimeter pistols to Maddie, showing her where the safety was before telling her to tuck it into her waist.

Fifteen minutes later they were on the street that would lead them to her house. There was no tail and Hawke began to wonder if Victor had been bluffing. But that was exactly the kind of thinking that would get him killed. He pulled into her driveway and up to the garage. She gave him the code to open the door so they could pull inside. It was time to earn his money as her bodyguard.

He unplugged the garage door opener so no one could hack the code. Moving into the house, they first entered the mudroom. He locked the knob and the deadbolt, shoving the only piece of furniture against the door. The bench had shelves for shoes below and gloves and hats above and hooks for coats between. It was made of solid wood and weighed much more than it looked, making it the perfect barrier.

Hawke told Maddie to set the security alarm. He knew it would do little more than slow a true professional down, and then for only a few minutes. But he knew it would offer the woman some comfort to think they would hear them coming.

The front door received the same treatment, using a credenza from the dining room. The open concept home had advantages and disadvantages. The main advantage was having line of sight throughout the kitchen, dining room and living room, broken only by the staircase leading to the second floor. The high ceilings allowed anyone at the top of the stairs to see everything in the rooms below.

The disadvantages were the blind spots and the sheer number of windows throughout the house. The right half of the house had two levels, an office/library and two bedrooms downstairs and three bedrooms upstairs, one of which had served as Ricky's art studio. The hallway leading to the rooms below was the most notable blind spot. Entry into any of the rooms through the windows would all lead to that opening below the stairs. The garage could allow entry, though Hawke felt that had been neutralized. It was unlikely anyone could gain entry through the second-floor windows, but that hallway would have to be watched.

The floor to ceiling windows in the back of the house and the French doors leading to the backyard were easy access for anyone willing to break glass. They also left the entire floor plan exposed to a shooter from outside, including the strategic second-floor landing.

Hawke and Maddie shoved several pieces of furniture into the downstairs hallway and piled pots and pans and dishes on top to serve as a warning system of a breach from that area. Hawke grabbed the bag of weapons and led the way to the landing, setting up his defensive station just inside the hallway there. He leaned the rifles against one wall and lined the ammo along the other. He gave Maddie a quick tutorial on how to use the pistol he had given her earlier. Next he showed her how to use one of the shotguns.

"You only shoot as a last resort," he said when he was finished. "If they are coming for you and are close use the shotgun first. It has a wide shot pattern, harder to miss."

They sat across from one another at the end of the hall, Maddie facing the barricaded front door with the shotgun laying across her legs and Hawke facing the back of the house, the hunting rifle next to him.

"This is so surreal," Maddie said. "If someone had told me a week ago that I would be holed up in my own home getting ready to fight off trained killers, I would have laughed them out of the room."

"It may surprise you," Hawke said. "But this wasn't on my calendar either."

Maddie smiled. "What would you be doing tonight if you hadn't met me?"

"I would probably be home eating take out," Hawke said. "Watching a game. How about you? What does Maddie do for fun?"

"I don't know," Maddie said. "Seriously. I usually leave work, go home and set up in my office here and start working again."

"You don't do anything to relax?" Hawke said. "That isn't healthy."

"Why do you think I was in therapy?" Maddie said. "It was suggested that I was a workaholic, too obsessed to step away from it. When I couldn't break the habit on my own, it was suggested I try therapy."

"Because you work hard?"

"Well, yes."

"Whose suggestion was that?"

"Penelope," Maddie said. "The bitch was probably sleeping with Ricky while I was in my sessions."

"Probably," Hawke said.

"God," Maddie said. "Why am I telling you all this?"

"Because I'm so easy to talk to," Hawke said.

"You really are," she laughed. She looked at him with the fondness of a close friend. Motion caught her eye. Not on the floor below, but on the wall above. A bright red dot was above Hawke's head. It started to lower. She shouted, "Down!"

Hawke's military training kicked in and he dropped and rolled just as the drywall where his head had been burst and sprayed them with fine white dust. Maddie screamed and fell flat on the floor. He snatched up the hunting rifle and scrambled away from the landing, beckoning her to follow.

"Lay here facing the stairs," he ordered. "If you see anyone come up to the landing you shoot them with the shotgun, just like I showed you. Got it?"

Maddie shook, her eyes wide. She nodded her head and he moved further down the hall. There were two bedrooms on the front of the house, only the master suite on the back. He crawled through Maddie's bedroom to the bathroom until he was sitting below the small window next to the sink. He sat with his back to the wall and used his legs to push himself up until he could peer out just over the windowsill.

The window shattered, showering him with glass. As close as it had been, Hawke had been fortunate. He had seen the muzzle flash and knew he should be dead. The shot had hit the frame and ricocheted into the mirror above the sink. The flash gave him an idea as to where the shooter was.

Staying low, he moved back into the master bedroom. He stopped in the middle of the room and rose to his knee. He shouldered the rifle and fired three times in succession in the direction the shooter had been. Without waiting to see if he had hit anything, Hawke dropped down again and returned to the hall. Even as he was doing so, shots burst through the windows and peppered the walls.

Hawke leaned the hunting rifle against the wall and picked up the assault rifle. He checked the safety and moved down the hall to kneel next to Maddie.

"You okay?" he asked, never taking his eyes off the stairs.

"Scared," she said.

"Me too." He made his way toward the landing, staying close to the wall. He peered down into the living room. No movement. He looked at the kitchen and the dining room. Nothing there.

"We wait for them to come to us," Hawke whispered. Maddie nodded.

They waited in silence for nearly half an hour. The sun had completely set and they wondered if their attacker had left or was waiting them out, just as they were doing. Hawke found it curious that no one in the neighborhood had reported shots fired. The man shooting at them was using a silencer, but the hunting rifle Hawke had fired three times did not have one. The sound would have been muffled by being fired from inside the house, but close neighbors should have heard something.

"I could use a cigarette," Hawke said.

"You should quit," Maddie said. "They'll kill you."

"Really?" he said. "Two trained killers coming after us and you're worried about lung disease."

"I'm not," Maddie said. "But you should be."

A slight scraping sound from somewhere in the house perked Hawke's ears. He shifted slightly to get a better view of the floor below. Nothing moved. There was nothing out of place. He held his awkward position and waited for something to move, something to explain what he had heard.

44

His patience paid off in the form of a shadow. It was just that at first glance. A partial shadow of a decorative pillow or a dish next to an armchair cast on the floor by the moon. Watching the room with intense scrutiny he noticed the shadow's size change. The object casting the shadow had moved and there was only one way that could happen.

Hawke stepped out with the assault rifle aimed at the chair. He fired several bursts into the cushioned back. The man hiding there lurched back against the wall and fell into a growing puddle of his own blood. The PI retreated to the safety of the hallway and changed the clip in his weapon.

"One down," he whispered.

"That wasn't so bad," Maddie said. "I thought they would be harder to, you know, kill."

"Don't get overconfident," Hawke said. "There's more to come."

As if on cue a gun discharged, followed by the floorboards splintering inches from Maddie's foot. She screamed and Hawke grabbed her arm and pulled her up. "Run!"

They sprinted down the hall, Hawke firing into the floor as they went. Each step they took was followed by a gunshot and splintered wood thrown up at them. As they passed the first doorways, the PI shoved Maddie into the room across from the master. She rolled onto the carpeted flooring and Hawke continued down the hall followed by gunfire.

Hawke slammed into the door to Ricky's art studio, busting the latch, turning into the room away from the hall below. He collided with a table full of paints and brushes along with a half dozen butane tanks Ricky used for his torch. Everything scattered across the floor in a chorus of clangs and thuds, followed by shots from below. Hawke sidestepped to move away from the objects, and shot after shot traced his path. He aimed the assault rifle down at the floor and let a barrage of bullets rain down into the room below. The return fire was intense and well placed. Unlike the first would-be assassin, this man was not going down without a fight.

In the next bedroom, Maddie sat in a corner cradling the shotgun. With each shot she flinched and wondered if Hawke was hit or dead. At the same time, each shot reassured her that he was still alive. She considered briefly if she should try to help the PI, but could not find it in her to move.

Hawke stopped moving and the shots stopped as well. He took a moment to think and listen. The shooter below had to have excellent hearing, being able to track Hawke by his steps. He was fairly accurate using sound as his guide. Hawke wondered how much better the man would be with a visible target. He was sure he did not want to find out.

Not being able to hear or see the man trying to shoot him was a disadvantage, as was not being able to move without being shot at. But he could not remain motionless forever. Eventually the man would seek out another way to get to him and Maddie. Hawke would have to come up with a plan and soon.

Hawke took inventory of his advantages; the assassin could not see him, did not know where Maddie was and could not quickly access the second floor. He scanned the room for the safest possible route out and his gaze landed on the blow torch and the spare butane tanks. His plan formed, he slung the assault rifle over his shoulder and jumped into motion.

Running in an arc, drawing fire with each step, Hawke scooped up the blow torch with one hand and, cradling it like a football, dashed out of the room. In the hall, he shouted for Maddie to run as well. She hesitated only a moment before springing to her feet and racing to the hallway. As he ran past, Hawke reached out and grabbed her about the waist and ushered her along with him. The shots ripping through the floor were getting closer and closer, until they stopped altogether.

"Why did he stop?" Maddie struggled to stay up with her protector.

"Reloading," Hawke said. "Get ready."

"Ready for what?"

"When I stop," Hawke said. "Go to the garage."

"Stop?" she said. "Why would you stop?"

They reached the stairway and Hawke pushed her ahead of him. He turned on the blow torch. Its blue flame burned bright in the dim room and the gunfire returned. There was a crash of the pots and pans they had piled on the furniture below. Hawke did not hesitate. He dropped the blow torch onto the nearest cushioned chair as he ran. The flame rested against the cloth covering before it erupted into a blaze. Hawke pulled his pistol as he ran and when he reached the ground floor he spun and fired a single shot into the tank of compressed flammable gas. The explosion was small, but the flames sprayed over the furniture and spread hungrily across the hallway opening.

The man on the other side of the wall of fire took two more random shots before retreating. Hawke ran after Maddie and found her fighting with the bench he had used to block the door. He took hold of it and together they shoved it out of the way.

"Sorry about this," he said. "The fire, I mean."

"Not what I'm worried about," Maddie said, desperately pulling the door open.

They entered the garage and Maddie climbed into the truck. Hawke wasn't sure he could get enough speed to break through the garage door, so he jumped into the truck bed and plugged the opener back into the outlet. He jumped down, pressed the opener on the wall and ran to the driver's side of the truck. As the door pulled up and out of the way, Hawke started the engine and put the truck in reverse.

"Hawke." There was stress in Maddie's voice.

She was staring at the side-view mirror. Hawke looked up at the rearview and saw the form of a man standing in the driveway. Hawke slammed his foot on the accelerator and the truck's tires spun in protest until they gained traction, thrusting them out of the garage. Hawke grabbed the shotgun that lay across Maddie's lap.

"Get down!" he ordered. She lowered herself in the seat, becoming as small as possible.

The man in the driveway raised his weapon and fired into the rear window of the truck, shattering the glass. Hawke spun the wheel so that the man was framed in the passenger window, raised the shotgun and fired a single shot before dropping the weapon to the floorboard so he could shift.

Pellets and glass nuggets peppered the man as he spun to protect himself. He fell to the ground, rolled and came up on one knee, gun in hand. Hawke accelerated through Maddie's front yard and freed his pistol. He slung his arm through the broken rear window and the two men opened fire. The truck bounced through the yard making it impossible to aim. Three times bullets struck the cab of the truck. Once Hawke found his mark and the man went down. He did not slow to check if the man survived. He steered into the street, glancing back at the flames growing throughout the house. The police would definitely be called now.

45

"It's clear," Hawke said.

Maddie raised her head tentatively. She looked out the back window, anticipating a car chasing them. There was nothing there. With a sigh she turned back to the front.

"Sorry about the house," Hawke said. "It was the only thing I could think to do."

"It's just a house," she said, her voice flat.

"All the same," Hawke said. "I thought it might get shot up a bit, but that fire is going to cause some major damage."

She did not respond. Staring out the windshield, she watched anxiously as oncoming cars passed by. "What do we do now?"

"Now we find a place to lie low," Hawke said. "I don't know if that guy is dead or alive, but he's too good a shot to let him find you."

"You said they wouldn't give up," Maddie said. "Will hiding really help us?"

"Not in the long run," Hawke said. "But it will give us some time to regroup, maybe come up with a plan."

"I would prefer one where we survive," Maddie said.

"First we find a place to hide," Hawke said. "Then we can figure out how to do that."

"Like a hotel or something?"

"If they run our cards, they'll find us," Hawke said. "We would have to go to a less reputable motel that doesn't keep electronic records and pay cash."

"That doesn't sound good," Maddie said.

"Not the best place in the world," he said. "But safe."

"We have a place for visiting clients," Maddie said. "It's owned by Rochester-Kinsley. Not known publicly."

"That might work," Hawke said. "Where is it located?"

"Out by the airport," Maddie said. "But we would have to go by the office to get the keys."

"Okay," Hawke said. "But let's make it fast. In and out."

He turned the truck toward the Rochester-Kinsley. The two of them talked while they drove through town, more to keep their minds occupied than anything. Hawke kept his eyes on both the road and the mirrors, trying to identify anyone that may be following them. A couple of times he thought he had singled out a tail only to watch it turn off on a side street.

When they arrived at the offices of Rochester-Kinsley, Inc. Hawke slowed and coasted into the parking lot. He immediately spotted the single car in the lot; a Mercedes he was sure he had seen the last time he was there.

"Whose car is that?" he said.

"It's Jevon's," she said. "What would he be doing here at this hour? I don't think we had any roll-outs scheduled and even if we did, there would be more techs here."

"A quick in and out," Hawke reminded her. "We don't have a lot of time for chit-chat."

"Chit-chat?" Maddie said. "Do people still say that?"

"Whatever." Hawke parked in Maddie's space. "You can ask him why he was here next time you see him."

They left the truck and walked to the building. Maddie led him to a side door to the right of the main entrance. There was a keypad next to the door and she quickly punched in a code. She hit enter and grabbed the handle, pulling it open. They entered and secured the door behind them.

They were in the stairwell and Maddie automatically started to climb. Hawke sighed heavily then started after her. They arrived at the executive floor and made their way to Maddie's office. She stepped behind the desk and searched for the keys. Her frustration grew with each drawer she opened.

"They aren't here," she said.

"Maybe someone is staying there," Hawke offered.

"Not that anyone told me about," she said. "Maybe Jevon knows where they are."

"You're just determined to find out why he's here this late, aren't you?" Hawke said.

"Well, since I'm going to be there," she said. "I may as well ask."

"In and out," Hawke said, again.

Maddie left her office with Hawke close behind. She walked at a fast pace, apparently taking Hawke at his word. She rounded the first corner just as Hawke was catching up to her. He was constantly scanning the main room and the offices that lined the outside wall, looking for anyone who shouldn't be there.

A line of light stretched from Jevon's cracked door halfway down the hallway. Maddie slowed, suddenly having a vision of Ricky and Penelope. Did she really want to rush into that office at this hour? Did she want to know if Jevon was entertaining someone other than Mrs. Kinsley?

"What's the holdup?" Hawke said beside her.

"Last time I barged into a room it didn't go so well," she said.

"Oh, yeah," Hawke said. "Ricky. You don't think this will be the same thing?"

"I don't know what to think anymore," she said. "Let's get this over with."

With renewed confidence, she marched forward to the office door. She hesitated for just a second before pushing her way in with a single knock as she entered.

"Jevon," she said. "What are you doing here at this hour?"

Jevon jumped to his feet and hit at the keyboard of his computer. "You scared the hell out of me. What are you doing here?"

"I asked first," Maddie said, stepping to her side to get a look at the screen.

"You know," Jevon said. His eyes shifted to Hawke as the PI entered the office. "Just going through the financials. Trying to find where that missing money went. Who is this?"

"That's right," Maddie said. "You haven't met. Hawke this is Jevon, my partner. Jevon, this is Hawke, my bodyguard."

Hawke held out his hand and the other took it in a firm handshake. Jevon was taller but lean. His angular facial features were partially obscured by his full beard. Hawke studied the man's face, realizing he had seen the man before. He was the man from the restaurant meeting, which seemed ages ago. He had been the man who made the phone call in the men's room.

"Any luck?" Maddie asked, looking at the computer.

"Not yet," Jevon said. "But I'm sure I'll find it."

Hawke stepped toward the door to wait. There was a distinct difference between Jevon's office and Maddie's. Where hers was plain, professional and tastefully decorated, his was ornate, borderline tacky. The walls were covered with pictures and souvenirs. One picture, a jockey standing next to his horse, was the centerpiece. Hawke guessed it was the winning horse that gave Jevon his stake in the company. Other pictures were of Jevon and a woman, his wife maybe, in various settings; Chicago, Mount Rushmore, Las Vegas, The Grand Canyon, New York, Atlantic City, Hollywood. They liked to travel.

"I hope you do," Maddie said. "We can't afford to keep losing money like that."

"Believe me, I know," Jevon said. "Why do you think I'm here in the middle of the night trying to find it? What brings you here at this hour?"

"I was looking for the keys to the guest property on Riverdale," she said. "Have you seen them?"

"I think so." Jevon opened the top drawer of his desk and rummaged through the contents, ultimately producing a ring of keys. He held them out to her. "Here you go."

Maddie took the keys. "Thanks, Jevon, you're the best."

Jevon looked at Hawke. "Hope he can keep you safe. This company isn't much without you."

"Thanks," she smiled. "That means a lot."

Maddie and Hawke left Jevon alone in the office and took the stairs back to the ground level. Hawke insisted on checking the area before letting her leave the building. There was no one there. A few minutes later they were on the road again, driving in the direction of the airport.

46

The guest house was a one-bedroom townhouse sandwiched between identical townhomes in a small complex about two miles east of the airport. The generic buildings were so similar and void of distinguishing characteristics that Hawke and Maddie had to watch closely for the house number in order to locate the correct unit.

Hawke parked in the short driveway and the two of them stepped out and stretched their legs. Each townhome was three stories with nothing more than a door and a garage on the ground level. Maddie worked the key into the lock and opened the door, exposing a stairway that led up to the second floor. A garage door opener was mounted next to the entrance and Hawke activated it.

"I'll put the truck inside," he said. "No point making it easy for them to find us."

The truck secure, Hawke joined Maddie at the entryway and closed the garage. Together they climbed the stairs which spilled out into a combination living room and kitchen. Another set of stairs continued up to the bedroom and bath housed in the peak of the roof. The furnishings were as bland as the structure and Maddie sat on the small sofa in disgust.

"Why we bought this place is beyond me," she said. "I know we wanted a place for clients to stay, but this is very unimpressive."

"Haven't you been here before?"

"No," she said. "I let Jevon take care of it. He found the place. He picked up the clients. God, what they must have thought of being dumped in this place."

"It's not so bad," Hawke said. He sat in the chair and let his legs stretch out in front of him, the shotgun lying across his thighs.

"I've seen your place," Maddie said. "Even it's better than this."

"What do you mean 'even'," Hawke said. "I like my place."

"Your place is fine," Maddie said. "But when this is all over, we're selling this place. I would rather put clients in a nice hotel rather than here."

"A nice hotel would be good right about now," Hawke said.

"So you agree this place is awful?" she said.

"No," he said. "But a nice hotel would be better."

"With a jacuzzi tub," Maddie said. "I would kill for a hot bath right now."

"You could go upstairs and take one," Hawke said. "It's not like we have anything else to do around here."

"Are you sure?"

"You go ahead," Hawke said. "I need to call Roger to find out about the guy we shot in the driveway."

Maddie climbed to the third floor and Hawke took out his phone. He saw that he had two missed calls from Roger and hit the call button.

"Hawke?" Roger said. "Are you all right? I've been trying to reach you."

"I'm fine," Hawke said.

"I'm at that woman's house," Roger said. "Rochester. It's going up in flames. You know anything about that?"

"I might," Hawke said.

"I take it she's not inside?"

"No," Hawke said. "But you will find one body near the back door."

"The blood in the driveway?" Roger said. "Is it yours?"

"Nobody there, huh?" Hawke said.

"So not yours," Roger said. "Can you tell me whose it is?"

"Don't know his name," Hawke said. "But he has quite the itchy trigger finger."

"Is he still a threat?"

"Hope not."

"Where are you?"

"Some place he won't find us," Hawke said.

"By he, you mean . . .?"

"The bleeder," Hawke said. "Courtesy of Victor Osterman. Is he talking?"

"About that," Roger said. "We had to cut him loose."

"You what? Why?"

"We didn't have anything to hold him on, Hawke," Roger said. "As soon as his lawyer showed up we had to let him go."

"Crap," Hawke said. "You couldn't even hold him for twenty-four hours?"

"Sure," Roger said. "Maybe if he didn't have a lawyer and a bullet hole in his shoulder. But . . ."

"I know," Hawke said. "At least he doesn't know where we are."

"You sure you don't want to let me know where you are?" Roger said. "I could help."

"Better not," Hawke said. "This guy is a pro. If he did his homework he'll know of my connection to you. They might expect me to reach out to you for help."

"Okay, I offered," Roger said. "Kind of busy here anyway."

"I bet," Hawke said. "I should let you go. I'll catch up with you later."

Hawke lay his phone on the small end table and sat back. He pulled his pistol out and checked the magazine. He reloaded it and the assault rifle. Only one shell was spent from the shotgun. He inventoried the ammo in his pockets; three magazines for the two pistols, one clip for the assault rifle and nothing for the shotgun. He wished there had been time to pick up the boxes of shells he had set on the floor at Maddie's house.

He heard a dog bark outside somewhere and wondered if that was the norm for the neighborhood. He turned off the lights nearest him and stepped up to a window, moving the blinds just enough for him to peer out. There was nothing there that he could see. The barking eventually stopped and Hawke let the blinds fall back into place.

"You hiding in the dark?" Maddie said, descending the stairs.

Hawke turned to her. She stepped into the dim lighting dressed as she had been before with the exception of the towel wrapped around her head.

"Just looking outside," he said. "That was a quick bath."

"Decided a shower would be more appropriate," She stepped up next to Hawke. "Is there something out there to worry about?"

"No," Hawke said. "Just being cautious."

"Did I hear you talking to someone?" Maddie crossed to the kitchenette where she searched the cabinets for a cup. She found one and examined it for cleanliness before filling it with water from the faucet.

"I called Roger," Hawke said. "He was at your place."

"Do I want to know how bad it is?" she said.

"No," he replied.

"Was he still in the driveway?" she said.

"No," Hawke answered again. "Left some blood, but that was all."

"Not that I would ever wish anyone dead," Maddie said. "But that's too bad."

"Roger had to release Osterman," Hawke said.

"Why?"

"Evidently my word of what he did wasn't enough to hold him," Hawke said. "Lawyer got him released."

"What do we do?"

"Nothing," Hawke said. "As long as he doesn't know where we are, we're safe. We'll come up with a plan. Then we can deal with him."

"That's great," Maddie said. "But we can't stay here indefinitely. There's no food."

"Then I guess we'll need to come up with a plan before breakfast," Hawke said.

The two of them sat and discussed their options for surviving long term. They would need to defeat, or at least outlast, the man trying to kill them. They would then need to find the proof to put Osterman behind bars for good. And, of course, ultimately they would have to find who was behind it all, to prevent them from hiring someone else.

Maddie sat curled up on one end of the sofa with her head resting on the arm. Hawke was in the chair with his legs stretched out before him. He looked at Maddie for a long moment then turned his attention to the stairway leading to the ground floor. He should have done something to barricade the door, but there was little in the way of furniture in the apartment. That, and the fact that there was no way for the wounded assassin to find them made it unnecessary.

He sat in the dark and felt his eyes grow heavy. Outside, the dog barked again. He thought about checking it out, but decided it would be exhausting to check every time it barked. He decided to close his eyes and let them rest for just a minute.

He was awakened an hour later by a creak.

47

Hawke became instantly alert and searched the darkness for a threat. He held his pistol in front of him and scanned the room. There was no one there. Maddie was asleep on the sofa. He could have dreamed the noise, but didn't think so. He slowly rose to his feet to avoid waking Maddie and stepped to the middle of the room trying to get a look down the stairs.

The cold hard barrel of a gun pressing into the back of his neck made him stop.

"God, this was way easier than I thought it would be," the man said. "Gun."

Hawke spread his arms and handed his pistol back to the man. The gun at his neck moved away and Hawke turned toward the man who had gotten the drop on him. He was smaller than Hawke. Maybe five-six, and a buck-fifty soaking wet.

"I can see in your face I'm not what you expected," the man said. "I get that a lot."

"Not very intimidating," Hawke agreed.

"I don't need intimidation," the man said, waving his gun.

"Guess not," Hawke said. "Must make it easier to get into tight places."

"It does. I've been standing in the corner over there for half an hour," the man said. "Just waiting for you to wake up and let me know where you kept your weapon. Thought you might shoot me again if I startled you."

"Didn't hurt too much, I hope," Hawke grinned.

"Just a bit," the man said. "Now the shotgun blast stung."

"Would have killed you had it not gone through the window first," Hawke said.

"Perhaps," he said. "I guess we'll never know."

"You're awfully talkative for a killer," Hawke said. "Why haven't you killed us already?"

"Normally I would have," the man said. "Can't ask for more than two sleeping targets. But unfortunately there's someone that wants to see you."

"See me?" Hawke said. "What the hell for?"

"Because you hurt me, Mr. Hawke."

Hawke turned to the voice to where Victor Osterman stood at the top of the stairs, his arm in a sling. He moved forward slowly. The gunman circled Hawke to stand near his employer.

"I wanted to see you hurt," Victor said, stepping up to Hawke. "I wanted to watch as my associate put the first bullet in you. Nothing fatal, mind you. Just something painful."

On the sofa, Maddie stirred. She blinked her eyes open and looked in the direction of the voices. She sprang to a sitting position when she saw the two men facing off with Hawke.

"Look who has joined us," Victor turned to her. "The woman of the hour. Our guest of honor."

"Maddie, stay calm," Hawke said. "Everything's going to be okay."

"Really?" Victor turned back to Hawke. "You really want your last words to the woman to be a lie?"

"It's no lie," Hawke said.

"Mr. Green," Victor said.

Mr. Green, standing a step behind Victor and toward the stairs, pulled his gun away from Hawke and swung it in Maddie's direction. Hawke stepped forward, raising his hand to Victor's chest and shoved him backward into the assassin. The two men stumbled and the weapon discharged, shattering the lamp on the corner table. Maddie screamed and rolled off the sofa onto the floor.

Victor tried to keep his footing but failed, while Mr. Green recovered with relative ease. Hawke continued his forward momentum and body-slammed the gunman. The heavyset detective hit the slender Mr. Green like a sledgehammer and threw him into the wall. To his credit, the man did not drop his weapon and twisted his arm to bring it to bear on Hawke. The PI grabbed his wrist and pounded it repeatedly into the wall.

Next to them, Victor was pulling himself to his feet again. Beyond him, Maddie was crawling to put more distance between her and the violence. Standing again, Victor reached inside his jacket for the gun he kept there. Hawke stopped trying to free the weapon from Mr. Green and pulled it away from the wall and squeezed the man's trigger finger. The shot tore through Victor's chest and threw him back to the ground. This time he did not try to get back up.

Taking advantage of Hawke's maneuver to neutralize Victor, Mr. Green spun free of the PI's hold and yanked his gun hand free. There was nothing Hawke could do but watch as the barrel arched toward him. The blast that followed was fierce. Blood splatter covered Hawke's clothes. He didn't feel anything.

Mr. Green dropped to his knees, then collapsed to the floor. Behind him, Maddie sat with her back against the chair, the shotgun pressed firmly to her shoulder. Hawke looked at her and relief flooded her face as she let the barrel of the gun fall to the ground. Tears followed.

Hawke secured all the weapons in the room, and checked the two men's vitals. Both of them were gone. He gave Roger a call to let him know what had happened and where they were. Then he helped Maddie off the floor and into the chair.

"Are they . . .?"

"Yes," Hawke said.

"But he never told us who hired him," Maddie said.

48

After the police arrived and took their statements, Hawke took Maddie to a motel and checked them in for the night. He sat in a chair next to her bed as she slept, assuring her that she was safe. As morning came, he caught a couple hours of shut-eye as well. When the alarm he had set went off, both jumped upright in search of danger. They might have laughed had it not been for the events of the night before.

"Let's get out of here," Hawke said. "Grab some coffee. Maybe a donut."

"No donut for me," Maddie smiled. "If I'm going to live, I have to watch my calories."

"A strong wind would blow you over," Hawke said. "What do you need to watch your calories for?"

"So I don't turn into an anchor weight," she said. "But I would kill for a cup of coffee."

"Is that what happened last night?" Hawke said.

The smile faded from Maddie's face.

"Sorry," Hawke said. "I shouldn't have said that."

"It's okay," Maddie said. "I've just never . . . you know."

"I know," Hawke said. "Let's go get that coffee."

They left the room and stepped out into the morning sun. Maddie raised her face to the warmth and stood motionless for a few minutes. Hawke took advantage of the daylight to give the truck a quick examination. The bullet holes would require some work to repair.

"Sorry about the truck," Maddie said.

"Better it than us," he said. "Besides, patch it up and replace the glass and she'll be as good as new."

"I'll pay for it," Maddie said.

"I'll take care of it," Hawke said. "You just lost everything in a fire. You've got enough expenses coming your way."

Hawke patted his pockets and pulled out his pack of cigarettes. He opened it and found it was empty. He smashed it in his hand and shoved it back into his pocket.

"I guess we'll be stopping for cigarettes first," Maddie said.

"No," Hawke said. "It's a good time to stop."

"Good for you," she said.

"Don't get too excited," he said. "I may change my mind by noon."

They climbed into the truck and Hawke drove them to a donut shop that he swore sold the best brewed coffee in town. As it turned out, Maddie thought it was pretty good, not the best, but good. Hawke happily used it to wash down the three donuts he had selected.

"I don't know where to begin today," Maddie said. "So much has happened. There are so many things I need to take care of. It all seems so daunting."

"You should take some time off," Hawke said. "Get yourself back to normal before you start dealing with anything else."

"What is normal?" Maddie said. "But you're right. It would be good to take a couple of days. I'll need to go by the office to let them know. Would you drive me?"

"It would be my pleasure," Hawke smiled.

49

Hawke pulled into the Kinsley-Rochester parking lot and parked in Maddie's reserved space. They entered through the main doors, greeting the guard on duty as they turned toward the elevators. Hawke let out a silent sigh that she hadn't chosen to take the stairs.

The doors opened and Maddie turned toward her office. A number of people stared as they walked. News of what had happened at her house had obviously reached them. As they approached the office, Maddie's assistant jumped to her feet.

"I wasn't expecting you today, Ms. Rochester," Delia said. "Are you okay?"

"I'm fine, Delia," Maddie said. "I am going to take a couple days. Just came to get a few things."

"I'll clear your calendar," Delia said. "Do you want me to reschedule what I can?"

"That would be great," Maddie said. "Thank you."

Hawke followed Maddie into her office where she gathered a few things and put them into her purse. When she was ready they stepped back out into the main room. She looked at the faces looking back at her and tried to smile.

"You ready?" Hawke asked.

"Just need to let Jevon know I'll be out," she said.

Dutifully, Hawke fell into step with the woman and they followed the hallway around the building to Jevon's office. His assistant stood.

"Is he in?" Maddie asked.

"Yes, ma'am," the young woman said.

Maddie, followed by Hawke, stepped through the door into Jevon's office. He sat at his desk as he had the night before. The man rose to his feet as they entered.

"Maddie," he said. "What a surprise."

"Surprise?"

"With all the news," Jevon said. "I didn't expect you would be in today. But since you're here, I have something to tell you."

"And I have something to tell you," Maddie said. "You go first."

Hawke stepped around Maddie and took a position against the wall where he could watch. His eyes were drawn to the photo of the winning horse that occupied a place of honor on Jevon's wall.

"It took half the night," Jevon said. "But I figured out who's been taking money from our accounts."

"You did?" she said. "Who?"

"You won't like it," he said.

"Who is it, Jevon?" she insisted.

"It was Becky," he said. "She kept reporting it to throw suspicion off of her."

"Becky?" Maddie said. "Are you sure? It's just so hard to believe."

"That's because it isn't true," Hawke said.

"What was that?" Jevon said.

"It isn't true," Hawke repeated. "Becky didn't have anything to do with the missing money."

"What makes you so sure?" Jevon said. "It was her. I found the proof."

"The amounts didn't make sense to me," Hawke said. "Small sums over a long period of time and then suddenly a large amount."

"She got away with it for so long she got emboldened," Jevon explained. "She just got too greedy for her own good."

"She's the bookkeeper," Hawke said.

"Exactly," Jevon said. "That's why it was so easy for her."

"First of all," Hawke said. "As the bookkeeper she would know it's a lot harder to hide twenty-five thousand dollars than the smaller amounts."

"That's true," Maddie said.

"And as the bookkeeper," Hawke said. "It would be a lot easier to cover up the thefts instead of reporting them. She could have just fixed the books to make them go away."

"True again," Maddie said.

"What do you know?" Jevon said. "You're no accountant."

"How long have you had a gambling problem?" Hawke asked.

"Problem?" Jevon said. "I don't have a gambling problem."

Maddie offered, "Sure he likes to gamble. But I've never known it to be a problem. How did you know about the gambling anyway?"

"He won the money to become your partner," Hawke said. "He has pictures of himself in Vegas and Atlantic City. I'm guessing he spends a lot of time at casinos. I'm also guessing that unlike the win that helped him finance the company, he hasn't been doing too well lately."

"Jevon?" Maddie said. "Is that true?"

"No. It's not true," Jevon said. "He's just making stuff up."

"The twenty-five thousand," Hawke said. "That didn't add up. Sure you could have lost big. Maybe you were behind on payments and they were threatening you. But the timing suggested otherwise."

"What timing?" Jevon said.

"Hawke?" Maddie said.

"Victor told me some of the details about the contract," Hawke said. "He told me the man gave him a down payment of twenty-five thousand dollars to get the job done."

"Who is Victor?" Jevon asked.

"The man you hired to kill Maddie," Hawke said.

"What?" Jevon said. His eyes darted back and forth between the two of them. "Are you insane? I would never do that."

"That's what the twenty-five thousand was for?" Maddie was looking at Hawke. "Are you sure?"

"That's what happened," Hawke said. "Isn't it, Jevon?"

Maddie turned to her partner, "Jevon?"

"Listen, Maddie," he said. "I didn't do this. I wouldn't."

"You did," Hawke said. "You kept gambling and kept losing. You've been taking extra money out of the company accounts to cover your losses but it wasn't enough. You owe someone real money. That's why you wanted to sell the company, but Maddie wasn't budging. That left you with one option. Getting rid of Maddie."

"Jevon?" Maddie said. "Is that true? You've been working to sell the company? Is that why we've been getting offers lately?"

"No." Jevon pointed at Hawke. "He's making this up. Trying to turn you against me."

"Why would I do that?" Hawke said. "What would I benefit?"

"It wasn't me," Jevon said. "Did this Victor guy say it was me?"

"He named you," Hawke said.

"No he didn't," Jevon said.

"He did," Hawke insisted.

"He couldn't have," Jevon said.

"He could and he did," Hawke said.

"No, he couldn't," Jevon whined.

"Why couldn't he?" Hawke shouted.

"Because he didn't know my name," Jevon yelled back. He froze. His shoulders dropped, followed by him collapsing into his chair with his face buried in his hands.

"And there it is," Hawke said.

"Oh, Jevon," Maddie said. "What have you done?"

There was a knock on the office door. Jevon's assistant said, "Mister Kinsley? Is everything okay?"

"It's fine," Jevon's voice cracked. "We're almost finished here."

"I would have loaned you some money," Maddie said. "Or bought you out, if that was what you wanted."

The man sat with his hands over his face. "I didn't mean for it to go so far."

"I know, Jevon," Maddie said. "I know you didn't."

"That's bullshit," Hawke said.

"Hawke," Maddie said. "I believe him."

"It's true," Jevon said.

"You chose to gamble," Hawke said. "Even after you started losing, you continued. Then you chose to steal from the company, from Maddie, to cover your increasing debts. Even after they started noticing the missing money, you continued."

"I just . . ."

"Then you put the word out to potential buyers, hoping to convince Maddie to sell the company," Hawke said. "And when that didn't work, you decided to get rid of her. You can't say you didn't intend for it to go so far. The man you hired to take care of it isn't someone you casually meet at a diner. You sought him out. You set up meetings and stole money to pay for his services. At any stage of the process you could have come to your senses and called it off. But you didn't do that, did you?"

Jevon sat silently.

"Did you!?" Hawke shouted at the man, causing him to push his chair back into the wall.

"No!" Jevon said.

"You say you didn't mean for it to go so far," Hawke said. "But you could have stopped it any time. You were the only reason it went as far as it did."

"Maddie," Jevon pleaded. "You have to believe me. I couldn't think of any other way. They're going to kill me."

"You were going to kill me," Maddie said. "To save your own life? Our friendship means that little to you?"

"Please, Maddie," Jevon said. "I didn't . . ."

"Save it," Maddie said. "Hawke, I need to get out of here."

Hawke lingered a moment, hovering over Jevon, fists clenched as tight as his jaw. He let himself relax and backed away. "Let's go."

Hawke was on the phone when Maddie pulled the door closed on the longest relationship she had ever had. She stopped next to the PI looking like a lost pup waiting to be told what to do. He put his hand on the small of her back and walked her toward her office.

"That's right," Hawke said. "Kinsley-Rochester Inc. His name is Jevon Kinsley. Murder for hire. He's probably a flight risk, he has means and very little left to lose."

"Is this Kinsley guy in as bad a shape as the other two?" Roger said.

"No," Hawke said. "He rolled over like a well-trained dog. Apparently owes a lot of money to some scary people. He may roll over on them too, if you ask nicely."

They entered Maddie's office and she sat behind her desk staring at nothing. Hawke ended his call with Roger and sat across from her. Everything in her life had come apart in a matter of days. She was hurting and Hawke didn't know what to do to comfort her. So he sat with her in silence.

THE END

Thank you for reading!

Dear Reader,

I hope you enjoyed reading **Murder Revisited** as much as I enjoyed writing it. At this time, I would like to request, if you're so inclined, please consider leaving a review of **Murder Revisited**. I would love to hear your feedback.

Amazon: https://www.amazon.com/dp/B084DGQDS6

Goodreads: https://www.goodreads.com/author/show/18986676.William_Coleman

Website: https://www.williamcoleman.net

Facebook: https://www.facebook.com/williamcolemanauthor/

Many Thanks,

William Coleman

Other novels by William Coleman:

THE WIDOW'S HUSBAND

PAYBACK

NICK OF TIME

MURDER REVISITED